inference

stephanie mcdonald

To,

Sandy,

Best wishes,

Stephane

xxx

RINGWOOD PUBLISHING
GLASGOW

First published in Great Britain in 2019

By
Ringwood Publishing
www.ringwoodpublishing.com
mail@ringwoodpublishing.com

ISBN 978-1-901514-68-1

British Library Cataloguing in Publication Data
A catalogue record for this book is available from the British Library

Typeset in Times New Roman 11

Printed and bound in the UK by
Lonsdale Direct Solutions

inference

part one

1

I wake up naturally, to the sound of birdsong. That can't be right. What happened to my alarm?

I open my eyes, but it's not a wise move and I immediately snap them shut again. Bright light assaults my senses, and I feel like I've been slammed face-first into a wall of pain. The sun is already fully awake, far more so than I am, and that is not good!

I pull the duvet over my head; I need a few seconds to come to, my head reeling even though I haven't managed to lift it from the pillow yet.

I know I have overslept, but just how badly? The clocks were turned back more than two weeks ago, signalling the end of daylight-saving time and the official dawning of winter. Which means that, since the murky grey sky that I would usually expect to see when I wake up has given way to daylight, then at the very least it must be around seven-thirty; and I've got little to no chance of making it to work on time. Add to the mix the fact that I will definitely be dealing with a food *and* drink hangover from the date I went on last night … My prospects for a productive day at work are not looking good at all.

I definitely set my alarm last night – I remember wincing with dread when I did it. I partook of a few alcoholic beverages, I concede, but I wasn't so out of it that I forgot to carry out my pre-bedtime ritual. The front and back doors to the house were securely locked. The central heating was stood down in order to prevent its rumblings from disturbing my sleep. My face was scrubbed of any remaining make-up that had survived the evening. My teeth were vigorously

3

brushed (the consequences of not doing that after the evening I'd had didn't even bear thinking about. Besides, I have a deep-rooted obsession vis-à-vis teeth-brushing before and after bed, so there's no question at all in my mind that I did it). My alarm was grudgingly set, I remember letting out a little groan when I spun the dial round to six, and my phone plugged in to recharge.

So why didn't the heavy beat of my chosen alarm track rouse me?

I stretch my right arm out from under the protection of the covers and fumble around for my phone, which takes its nightly rest on my bedside table when I'm out for the count. I flounder around for a few seconds, bewildered by its absence, wondering where it could be.

Wondering doesn't aid me in finding it, so I make the bold move of opening one eye. This second, equally potent attack from the sun, along with the view that I am met with, causes me to leap suddenly into a sitting position, jerking my head and neck violently, and bringing forth a wave of nausea as I do.

'What the ...?'

I'm utterly confused by what I see. I look to my left, to where my phone should be, and appear to have solved the mystery of why my alarm didn't wake me. Because my phone is not there. Neither is the bedside table that it ritually lives on during the hours of darkness.

I scan the room, and little pockets of pain burst open all around my head, as my hangover conspires with my panic to make my skull feel like it's about to explode. I am panicking because nothing in this room is familiar to me.

This room is small, a perfect square, whereas my bedroom is large, and wider than it is long.

The furniture in here is sparse, and entirely white – my room is kitted out (arguably too fully) with furniture made from naked, unpainted wood.

The ceiling above my head is unusually low; the ceilings in my house are so tall that, frustratingly, I can't reach the smoke alarm even with the aid of a three-tier step ladder, a fact that sets changing the batteries in the critical device on a par with a military operation.

Where the hell am I?

I look down, my nausea building, and see that I am dressed in pyjamas that I neither own, nor recognise. A tiny tingle of relief soars through me at the realisation that at least I am not waking up naked in a strange bedroom, but the feeling is short-lived, and the panic returns with a vengeance.

I jump out of the bed – again, it's different from mine: this one is made out of metal, and creaks in complaint when I move; my bed is made out of sturdy wood which matches the other furniture and is always respectfully silent.

I rifle through the drawers that I find on the right side of the room, desperate to get myself dressed and out of here – wherever here is! I find a pair of blue jeans and a hoodie, and pull them on, looking around for shoes as I do. I don't see any, but what I do see when my eyes are drawn to the window sends an icy shiver down my spine.

I live in the city. Well, approximately five miles away from the city centre, but close enough. Close enough that if I listen intently, I can hear the low hum of traffic from my living room window at any time of the day or night. Close enough that my house is situated in the midst of lots of other houses, and cars, and a well-used railway line. There are signs of life on all sides. With ease and regularity, I can jump on a bus, or a train, and be in the centre of town, a stone's throw from the office, in twenty minutes. Why, then, am I looking out of the window and seeing what appears to be the face of a mountain?

I let out a little chuckle of relief, as I figure out the explanation for all this madness. I'm dreaming. I must be. I had a few drinks too many last night, and I'm having a funky

5

dream. Any minute now I'm going to wake up, whisper a curse at my untrustworthy alarm, jump in the shower, and get myself ready for work just like always. Later, I'll laugh when I tell my colleagues about it, about how frighteningly real it was. I pinch myself on the arm to try and speed the process along, but nothing happens. Without thinking too much about it, I aim a punch at the wall, and the resulting pain that reverberates through my hand feels all too real. *Am I dreaming?*

'Morning, babe,' I hear a voice say, and I feel the hairs stand to attention on the back of my neck. Horrified, I resign myself to the fact that this is not a dream at all. I slowly turn to see where the voice came from.

'Come here,' are the next words to come out of the man's mouth, and he pulls me into a hug. 'Did you get a good sleep?'

I don't answer. I can't. I'm rooted to the spot where I stand, where my view of the mountain outside is now partially obscured by the body of the man holding onto me. He cuddles me for a few seconds, receiving no response, then pulls back, looking puzzled.

'Babe, are you okay?' he asks, searching my face for answers.

All I can do is stare at him, my mind working hard and fast to try and work out who he is, why he is calling me 'babe', and why he thinks it's perfectly acceptable to cuddle me. There is not even the faintest flicker of recognition in my brain as I study his face. He is about thirty, I would guess, with a long, narrow face that is half-covered by a blonde beard. He has blue eyes, magnified by the heavy-rimmed glasses he is wearing, and long eyelashes which give him an almost feminine look. That hint of femininity is offset by the fact that his hair is cropped very close to his head, like the kind of buzz cut a marine would be duty-bound to acquire, and although his shoulders are wider than mine, his build is slender.

His face, like his manner, do not appear to be threatening, but both are unfamiliar to me – I have never seen this man before.

2

I decide that there is no time to waste asking myself questions about who he could be and why he's acting the way he's acting. Since the man has relinquished his physical hold on me, I squeeze past him and head for the door.

'Babe, where are you going?' he asks, and I can sense him coming after me.

My feet are bare, and when they make contact with the freezing cold stone floor in the hallway, a shock is transmitted through my whole body. I accept it with a loud gasp and move on, now on a mission to get out of this house, and away from this strange man.

I can see a door to my left, at the end of the hallway, so I make a dash for it. There is a pair of shoes next to the mat which look like they could be my size, so I grab them and shove them on, not keen to brave the outdoors without any protection for my feet.

'Jen, what's going on, babe, where are you going?'

The man has arrived at the door with me, and now uses his body to form a barrier between me and whatever lies beyond there.

'I need to go,' I tell him, making a grab for the jacket that hangs from a hook on the wall.

'Jen,' he says, more sternly this time, 'do you want to tell me what's going on right now?'

Jen? Who the hell is Jen?

My mind retraces a few steps, and I realise that he has addressed me as 'Jen' twice now.

'Who's Jen?' I blurt out. I can hear my pulse racing around my head as I stand here, feeling like a caged animal, desperate to get beyond that door and get back to my life.

The man looks at me as though I've asked him to perform the most complex maths query in the world without so much as a pen and some notepaper to help him out. He gives an uncertain smile. 'What are you talking about, babe?'

I decide that I don't care anymore why he is calling me by the wrong name, and that I am not going to hang around and wait for an explanation.

I make a lunge for the door handle and manage to ease the door open a few inches before the man can react. But when he does react, he takes control of the door and closes it, and I'm back to square one.

'Jen, seriously, what has gotten into you?' he demands, his voice louder than it was a moment ago, and loaded with concern. 'Where do you think you're going?'

I size him up, along with my chances of getting the upper hand on him. He is far taller than me, perhaps by a whole foot, and although he is slim, he looks wiry and strong. He probably carries twenty-five to thirty pounds more than me, even on that slim frame of his, and from what I've witnessed so far it seems like his reflexes are decent. To sum up, I conclude that my chances of overpowering him and making my escape are slim to none. Unless ...

I wonder if there is another way out of the building, perhaps a back door. I step away from him wordlessly, leaving his question hanging in the air.

I check the options in all the rooms I find: a bathroom, a living room, a kitchen, and of course the bedroom that I've already stormed out of. My best hope of a back door was probably in the kitchen, but unfortunately my hopes are dashed.

I consider making my exit through a window, but the man has halted me from leaving through the door already; trying to squeeze myself out of a smaller space will surely not fox his attempts to keep me indoors.

'Why am I here?' I demand, my voice close to breaking with tears of frustration and fear. 'You need to let me go; I'm supposed to be at work right now!'

He frowns in bewilderment once more, and lets out a long, laboured sigh. 'Jen, you're not, babe. It's Saturday. Since when do you work on Saturdays?'

Okay, so now he's not just mistaken – now he's blatantly lying to me. I know what day it is. I know that I went out, on a date, with Kevin last night. That was Thursday night, and after we parted company I went home and went to bed. My bed. I know that I set my alarm reluctantly for six o'clock because I had to, because today is Friday, and I'm supposed to be in the office, at my desk right now.

'What the hell are you talking about?' I yell at him, frustration now overtaking my fear. 'Who the hell are you, why am I here, and why are you telling me it's Saturday when I know fine well that today is Friday?'

I see his Adam's apple bob up and down in his throat as he swallows, looking decidedly uncomfortable. 'I think you should sit down, babe,' he tells me, taking hold of my elbow. 'I think we need to talk.'

I allow myself to be led onto one of the dining chairs, accepting defeat for the moment. Is there any point in trying to edge past this man again, and make another break for freedom? If he won't let me out, then maybe the best course of action will be to gather my thoughts and figure out a way to force my way out, and away from him, without him being able to stop me.

He fills the kettle with water and flicks the switch on. As he makes himself busy preparing two mugs and teabags, I think of potential weapons that I may be able to lay my hands on, that I might be able to use against him. I just need to incapacitate him long enough to allow me to get out of the house. There are bound to be knives in the cutlery drawer, and even though I don't see the contents from where I'm

10

sitting, when the man opens and closes it, the clanging of multiple implements is reassuring.

I won't actually stab him, of course, but if I were able to get hold of a knife, I could use it as a threat, and hope that he believes I do have the nerve to attack him with it. Once I get outside that door, I can make a run for it, and yell and scream for someone to help me. Whoever this man is, he is holding me here against my will, in a place that I must have been brought to against my will, and if I need to use the threat of physical violence to escape his clutches, then so be it.

'Here you go,' he says, laying down a mug of tea in front of me. 'Nothing in it, the way you like it.'

I accept the mug, playing along with his charade whilst trying to conjure up a way to distract him and find a way to get hold of a knife. 'Thanks,' I mutter, and the question of how he knows that I drink my tea with no milk and no sugar niggles momentarily at the back of my mind.

'So,' he says, taking a sip of his own tea, 'I guess it's happening again, babe.' He flashes me a look of pity, and for a fraction of a second, I wonder whether I have it in me to toss the mug of hot tea in his face and make a run for it. I don't. I couldn't possibly. The liquid is literally piping hot; it would scald him, perhaps even permanently damage his eyes, and in spite of what he has done in bringing me here, I would probably be the one who ended up going to prison.

'What is?' I ask, gripping my mug tight, seeking comfort from the warmth that comes from it.

'I feel like I'm patronising you, telling you this, but obviously you don't remember.' He looks away, and the nausea I felt earlier makes a reappearance. The man puffs out his cheeks and lets out a long stream of air. 'It must have been about two years ago,' he starts. 'At the time, the doctor put it down to the amount of stress you were under: working so hard, trying to fit in your studies, all the exams you were taking … '

11

Studies? Exams?

'It happens, sometimes, the doctor said. They don't really know what causes it, other than some kind of malfunction' – he holds his hands up apologetically – 'sorry, but that's the word they used – in the brain. Your mind can get overloaded, you know? And then it just snaps.'

'What are you saying?' I ask him, dreading his answer.

He looks directly at my face, and the pity is back. 'Last time, you … created your own version of reality. You flipped out, started saying that you didn't know who I was, who anybody was.' He makes a pained face. 'You even got confused about who you are, Jen.'

I stare at him for a few moments, dissecting what he has just said. Is he trying to imply that I'm in the throes of some kind of nervous breakdown? That my name, my home, even my date with Kevin last night, are all just figments of my imagination?

'Stop calling me that,' I tell him, my voice a little more forceful than before. 'My name is not Jen. It's Natalie.'

Another sigh. 'Yeah, that's the name you told us last time,' he says mournfully, as though this claim has cemented my status as a crazy person.

'Last time? There was no last time!' I yell, rising from my chair. 'I don't know what you're trying to pull here, but I am not schizophrenic, or psychotic, or whatever else you're trying to suggest I am. I haven't "created my own version of reality"! The reality is that my name is Natalie, today is Friday, and you have somehow managed to bring me here, from my home, and are now keeping me here unlawfully. The reality is, that you have to let me go. Now!'

I yell the last word so loudly that he winces, as though the sound has hurt his ears.

'Oh, I've had enough of this!' I add, and since I am already standing, and now wearing shoes, I have probably a good second's head start on him, and I make another dash

12

for the door, tossing my chair into his path to slow him down a little and enhance my chances of evading him.

'Jen, wait!'

He follows, of course, but this time I manage to open the door and actually make it outside, where I begin to run. The path is uneven, covered with gravel and stones, and I almost trip as I engage my leg muscles with a vengeance and push forward. I yell out 'Help!' as loudly as I can, which is not very loudly due to the demand on my lungs from the running, but even as I do I realise that it's a pointless exercise. Ahead of me there is nothing but grass, and mud, and the mountain that loomed so large from the window. If there is anyone else in this part of the world, then they are not in the immediate vicinity. They are not close enough to be of any help to me at all right now.

I look back to check whether I have simply made the wrong decision, chosen to run in the wrong direction, but beyond the house, and the man, who has now caught up with me, I can see only more of the same. Wilderness.

'What is this place?' I ask, my voice barely audible above the wind that howls above our heads. I have to stop running, for fear that my heart might explode, or that my legs will give way and I will fall onto the gravelly path.

'It's Carn,' he answers incredulously, as though he's stunned by the question. 'It's where we live.'

3

'Are you okay?' he asks softly, stroking my back. He has led me back indoors and escorted me back to the bedroom. I sit down on the edge of the bed, my body weak and trembling.

'Who are you?' I manage, the pain in my head surging from the effort of speaking.

'I'm Jamie,' he answers. 'Your boyfriend.' He says it with conviction; there are no signs in his face or his voice that he is deceiving me.

'But … I don't know you,' I insist. 'I've never met you before. Why are you doing this to me?' My voice sounds feeble.

He takes hold of my hand and gives me that look again – the one that conveys nothing but pity for me.

'I think we should get you to the doctor on Thursday,' he says, kissing my hand and holding onto it.

'Why Thursday? Why not now?'

'Dr Reagan only comes over every second Thursday,' he explains. 'Thankfully, it's this Thursday that she's due to come over. She'll be able to give you some of the same pills that helped you last time, I'm sure.'

My brain does now actually feel as though it's about to overload, and snap, like an elastic band stretched beyond its natural capacity.

'What do you mean, she comes over? Over from where?'

A shadow of something that looks like it could be annoyance flashes briefly across his eyes, but he switches back to nice guy mode straight away.

'Jen, this is Carn,' he begins, in a patronising tone. 'There are twenty people here at any one time, at the most, during

14

the season, and most of them only work here, four days a week. Even during the season, they would all be home for the weekend by now. There's no reason to have a doctor here full time – there's just no way to justify it.'

'Twenty people?'

Jamie gives a shrug. 'Right now? Probably about five, including you and me.'

'So, if this is Saturday, why aren't *we* "at home"? Why are *we* still here?'

I think, for a brief second, that I have caught him out in a lie, since his eyebrows crease into a frown.

'Because we live here, babe,' he says, and I reluctantly remember that he told me this already, outside.

'Look, let me run through a few things, see if any of it jogs your memory, okay?'

He shifts his weight and rests his body on the bed alongside me, and I flinch and edge away from him. He proceeds, regardless.

'We came here for me,' he starts, 'for my research. I wasn't sure about it at first, because I didn't want to leave you, and I didn't think for a moment you'd actually come with me, but you did.' His frown gives way to a smile. 'You said you wanted to be wherever I was, and if that meant living here, then that was what you would do. It meant so much to me.'

He traces his hand along my arm, smiling affectionately at me.

'Anyway, in the beginning, we went home most weekends. We kept it up for a few months, but it was just too much. It's almost two hours from here to Mallaig, then a good six hours down to Glasgow from there. Plus, the ferry stops running at the end of September, and we couldn't keep relying on Davie to take us back and forth every weekend on his own boat. We decided to stay here full-time for the duration of my contract – two years. We've been living here since June.'

There are a million questions racing around inside my head, but before I can send the words to my mouth, Jamie carries on.

'I do all my research work here for Scottish Natural Heritage, and working remotely is easy enough for you – all of your pieces are submitted online, so there's no real need for you to keep popping back home all the time. And you rent out your place, so we don't really have anywhere to stay when we go back.'

'My "pieces"?'

'Sorry,' he says, with a little laugh, 'I keep hoping that something will trigger your memory to come flooding back. When I say "pieces", I mean the translation work you do. You're a fiction translator. Spanish to English. And you're good.' He flashes a smile at me again, and gives me a little nudge on the arm, with an air of familiarity that is unacceptable.

I'm not interested in listening to the fictional narrative that this man has invented to describe 'my' life, I am only tuning in with the intention of garnering snippets of information that will help me – namely where on earth Carn is, how I can get off this island to safety away from this madman, and the soonest point in time that 'popping back home' is likely to be possible.

'Can't we ask ...' I search my mind for the relevant nugget, interrupting Jamie's untruths, '... Davie!' I exclaim, thrilled to have remembered this vital fact about the man who Jamie claims owns a boat. 'Can't we ask Davie to take me ho ... to the doctor? I mean, I can't really go on like this until Thursday, can I?'

He appears to ponder my suggestion, but soon his face contorts into an expression of regret and he replies grimly. 'Any other week we could, but I'm sure I remember Davie saying that he was going to be on the mainland all week.

16

He's got family in Inverness, you see. I'm pretty certain he's gone to spend some time with them.'

'Of course he has,' I mutter sarcastically. I don't believe a word of it, but what options do I have? From my vantage point outside the house I drew the conclusion that I am stranded in a large, rocky, open space. Aside from hiking around, yelling out 'Davie!', how will I ever find the man with the boat? If he and his boat even exist, I think to myself, and a now familiar shudder of dread makes its way through my body.

So, option number one has been considered and exhausted. What is option number two?

'So, you're saying that apart from the ferry and Davie's boat, there's no other way to get off this island? How on earth is that even possible?' I demand angrily. 'I mean, what if someone has a heart attack or something? How do they get to a hospital?'

Jamie regards me as though I am the dunce child in a classroom who has asked a pitifully stupid question. 'We'd call 999, and they'd be airlifted to the hospital in Inverness. We can't exactly demand they send a helicopter just because you're feeling a bit off, babe.'

His patronising tone kicks off the anger that has been lurking under my fear since I woke up this morning.

'I am not "feeling a bit off"!' I yell at him, causing him to recoil. 'I'm not ill, I'm not imagining things; I've been kidnapped, and you can't keep me here like this, like some kind of prisoner!' My fury brings forth tears that I now realise I've been bravely holding back, and I cover my face with my hands.

I feel Jamie's hand on my shoulder. 'Jen, please, I can't bear to see you like this,' he says, maintaining an air of calm in the face of my accusations and trying to sound soothing.

'Then why don't you let me go?' I fire back at him. 'If I'm really your girlfriend, and you care about me, why aren't

17

you trying to help me? If you really believe that I'm not well, why aren't you doing everything you can to get me a doctor?'

'Because there's nothing I can do,' he cries. 'Believe me, babe, if I had a boat, I'd be taking you to Inverness right now, myself!'

I let out a noise that is part exasperated sigh, part growl, and try once more to run through any options that I might have. I tell myself that I only have Jamie's word to go on about where I am, and since this is a man who has spent the last half hour trying to convince me that I am insane, I am not in a desperate hurry to accept his version of events at face value. He said there were probably five people here, including the two of us, didn't he? Which means that there could be at least three people close by who are not kidnapping psychopaths, who might be able to help me get away from this liar, and home to Glasgow.

Which means that the only realistic option available to me is to go in search of those people. In search of the truth. Assuming that Jamie has at least been truthful about this location, and the limited resources available for vacating it, more than likely what it will take for me to be rescued is for the police to come and find me, and to transport me off this rock.

I feel a little frisson of hope as I picture the scene: me being wrapped in a foil blanket – because that's what they do in these types of situations, in movies and television shows, at least – and being led into the police boat, or helicopter, depending on what they deem to be the most suitable means to get here, by a caring officer, whispering assurances to me that I'm safe now, that everything will be alright. It could work, I convince myself. It *has* to work.

But in order for me to execute my plan, I need to get away from Jamie, just long enough to be able to raise the alarm. He may be a psychopath, but he has to sleep at some point, doesn't he? It's only just gone nine o'clock in the morning, which means that it could conceivably be twelve hours or more before he feels compelled to nod off. I'm not sure that I can survive this madness for that long.

Could I knock him out? That would mean clocking him over the head, hard, with a suitably sturdy weapon, but what? I think about it, plotting an opportunity to catch him off guard. I've never hit anyone before, unless you count the petty playground fight I got embroiled in when I was about seven, when I took a swing at Ross Shields because he pulled my hair. I managed to get him good, I remember with a wince of guilt. I knocked him to the ground and he ended up out cold, and I was rewarded with the first and only visit to the headmistress's office of my entire school career. What if I don't know my own strength, I suddenly think to myself, and I hit him so hard that I actually kill him? I can hardly get the police involved when I've committed and fled from the scene of a possible murder, can I?

My mind is weary; it has never felt so exhausted as it does right now, and I close my eyes to try and reduce its workload, even just a tiny little bit.

Jamie is talking, but I can't bear to listen to any more of his fiction, so I zone out, opening my eyes and staring out of the window. The view is the same as that from the bedroom: of a huge mountain. From the manic tour of the property I went on earlier, I've deduced that the kitchen and the bedroom are on the left of the house as you enter through the front door, while the living room is to the right, and the bathroom at the end of hall, opposite the door. This information doesn't seem particularly useful to me but thinking about the layout distracts me from the lies that continue to pour out of Jamie's mouth.

I've been awake for about half an hour now, I estimate, but I feel as though I have been living this nightmare forever. Jamie continues to waffle on. He gesticulates a lot, and then

19

pauses, obviously looking for a response from me every now and again, which he doesn't get. Then he goes back to rambling, as though he believes that by repeating the fallacies over and over he will finally get me to concede that he is telling the truth.

The point where he started talking about how blessed he is that I was so supportive of his plans and ambitions was around the time I stopped listening. Since not a word of what he's told me so far has been remotely true, I couldn't muster up enough energy to query with him how I seem to have managed to miss out on a whole day of my life, only for him to make up some more nonsense to try and explain it away.

I feel numb now. I've been through a range of emotions in the last thirty minutes or so, from fear, to anger, to frustration, and now an odd sense of detachment seems to have washed over me. The weight of my weary head feels far too heavy for my poor neck to have to support, and my shoulders ache, probably due to the fact that I've been ferociously tensing all the muscles in there – firstly in response to the cold, and then in panic.

My head felt fuzzy when I woke up, but I originally put that down to the drinks I'd had over dinner with Kevin. I had been fully expecting (and somewhat prepared) to wake up with a pretty nasty hangover, after all. But now I can't shake the thought that maybe my wooziness was down to something more sinister than my indulgence on Thursday night. I mean, in order for me to get here, against my will, without me knowing a thing about it, I would have to have been pretty seriously out-for-the-count, wouldn't I? Considering I am now reportedly a few hundred miles away from my home, dressed in different clothes than I was when I went to bed on Thursday night, I would have had to have been completely unconscious for a considerable period not to notice any of the events that occurred between then and now! I shudder at the thought of what might have gone on in the hours that have passed since I was last awake; since the last time that I felt safe. Jamie notices the involuntary motion, and stops talking, mid-sentence. He reaches a hand out to touch my shoulder. 'Are you cold, hun?'

'I want to lie down,' I say. I can hear that my tone is robotic, expressionless.

'Of course, my darling,' he replies, putting his arm around me gently, like I'm a fragile trauma victim. 'Maybe a rest will do you good,' he says, trying to sound hopeful. 'Let me check you haven't got a fever.' He presses his hand lightly against my forehead, and it feels cold, which isn't exactly a surprise, given the general temperature in this place. 'Hmm, it doesn't seem so,' he says, sounding like he doesn't have the faintest idea what he's talking about.

He plumps up the pillows while I sit on the edge of the bed, looking out again at the vast, foreboding landscape that lies to the rear of the house.

'Thanks,' I murmur, when Jamie has finished organising the pillows.

'No problem, sweetie,' he says, smiling, and brushing his hand softly against my cheek. 'If you need anything, anything at all, just yell, okay?'

I nod, and he gives me a sympathetic smile, then leaves the room. *Darling? Sweetie? Seriously, who is this guy?*

I sit back against the pillows and draw my knees to my chest. I close my eyes and try to think clearly.

My initial gut feeling is that I don't think I'm in any immediate physical danger from Jamie, but then I've never been kidnapped before, so I don't really know what to expect. He hasn't given any indication that he's about to cause me any physical harm – conversely, he's shown signs of being quite caring and considerate so far, but I can't afford to be taken in by him. He has kidnapped me, and therefore is likely to be somewhat unhinged. And if so (or even if not), what does he intend to do with me?

21

I need a plan of action, obviously. I need to figure out all the key facts: how I got here; why I'm here; who this strange man is and how I can get away from him, and this island, and back to my own life. I think about my family; about how good it would feel to just hug them right now, and the tears that have been threatening to spill out since I woke up can't be suppressed any more.

4

I've eaten far too much. The temptation is always there, with buffet meals, but while some have the willpower to stop when their stomachs start to feel uncomfortably full, I have a dangerous tendency to carry on until I feel that I have got my money's worth out of the deal. Which usually, shamefully, means shovelling down enough food to account for several days' worth of calories.

A feat that I've achieved this very evening. To force down enough food to feed a rugby team in one sitting, most of which was 'bad' carbohydrates, is neither a sensible nor a healthy thing to do. To follow that folly with coffee is verging on insanity, yet that is precisely what I have done. At least, I have agreed to the coffee. Aside from the fact that adding caffeine to the mix of stimulants currently flowing around my body (alcohol and sugar) is utter foolishness and likely to lead to some major intestinal flux, there is the added consideration that drinking coffee right now will probably keep me uncomfortably awake for hours.

I only agreed to it because I didn't want this date to end just yet. I didn't think it all the way through, granted, but I am more than a little tipsy just now, and making wise decisions whilst under the influence is not a weapon I have stored in my armoury.

Kevin smiles at me from across the table, and I grin back girlishly, wondering just how drunk I appear to him. I wasn't even supposed to be drinking this evening. I recited an instruction to myself over and over in the hours before meeting him, to be ultra-sensible and stick to mineral water, but I buckled at the first suggestion of an aperitif with the *ease of a pencil tip snapping under pressure. Kevin has been drinking too, matching me glass-for-glass, but while I suspect that my eyes are red, my mouth is racing out of control, and my legs may not comply with my instructions when I urge them to transport me to the ladies' in a moment, frustratingly the man seated opposite me looks exactly the same as he did when we met at seven-thirty.*

He looks amazing, in fact – a point I noted prior to the commencement of the drinking. Tanned, with just enough beard to look rugged, staying far away from 'Santa Claus' territory. His hair is neatly trimmed, his eyes sparkling green, and his teeth flawlessly white. Another promise to myself, made and broken within mere moments of my resolve being tested: that I wouldn't fall for him again. Again, as in, second time around. Because this is not a first date that I am on. This is the second date of round two in the game that is mine and Kevin's 'relationship'.

I declare to him (more loudly than intended – that damned alcohol!) that I will be back in a moment and make my bid to get to the ladies' without falling over and baring more than the other restaurant-goers will have bargained for. I manage, with a couple of scary moments along the way, and head straight for the mirror, to check just how bad I look, now that Kevin and I are two and a half hours into our date.

Bad, is the answer. Without intending it, I have achieved a sort of quiff in my chestnut-brown hair, and it reminds me of Cameron Diaz's infamous look in the Ben Stiller movie, There's Something About Mary. *The mascara around my red-tinged eyes has become smudged, on account of all the laughing I've been doing, and has created tracks down my cheeks where it has mixed with my foundation.*

I shake my head as I glare at myself, disappointed with my conduct overall. What am I doing here? I should never have agreed to go on a second first date with Kevin, never mind a second-second date. But boy, that man is convincing. Against my better judgement he has managed to convince me that I do, in fact, like him. Again. And now here I am, in the restroom of a trendy restaurant, sporting deeply questionable make-up and, I've just noticed, a rather unsightly, curry-coloured stain on my dress.

I make a harried attempt at recovering the make-up situation, and bribe my hair to play along, to look borderline acceptable. When I return to the table, I find that my fatefully-ordered coffee has been duly delivered, and my stomach emits a growl of displeasure at the prospect.

'So, when can I see you again?' Kevin asks when I've replanted myself. He leans forward in his chair, affording me a direct blast of his delicious aftershave that goes straight to my head and makes it swim a little.

'You want to see me again?' I ask him, flabbergasted by the insinuation in light of what I witnessed in the mirror a few moments ago.

'Sure I do,' Kevin admits, with an amused grin. 'Why wouldn't I?'

I smile coyly, and revel in the feeling of being wanted, at least for a further instalment of dinner and drinks. I don't offer any answers to his question, keen to avoid pointing out all the potential reasons why he may have opted to run for the hills after this evening: the wanton over-eating, the inebriation, the mess I managed to make of myself while we ate ... Instead, I say, 'We'll work something out.' What is it they say again? Treat 'em mean; keep 'em keen? I've never tried this approach before, but as much as I'm attracted to Kevin, a part of me is still very reluctant to jump into anything too soon. He hurt me last time round, and what kind of mug would I be if I walked straight into the same trap all over again? I intend to go on another date with him and treat it as kind of a make-or-break scenario, but he doesn't need to know that. Not right this minute, anyway.

25

'Cool,' he says, quietly confident, and retreats, taking a sip of his coffee.

I take a sip of mine, forgetting that I was about to forego it on account of not wanting to be ill, or up all night. It burns on the way down, and I wish once more that I had stuck to my guns and drunk nothing but water all night. But then, would sober Natalie have secured a third date with cute Kevin? Indubitably, she would, my ego assures me, and the warmth of the coffee mingles with the warm glow of smugness that has begun to spread throughout my body.

5

I come to with a gasp, sucking in air as though it is in dangerously short supply. I survey the room with hungry eyes, praying that the urgent nature of my awakening is down to the fact that I've been released from the nightmare that I had come to believe was real life. But prayers, as I accepted a long time ago, are pointless. No-one is listening. At least, not to me.

I run over the memories of my date with Kevin again – for that's what they are, *memories* – and verify every part of our conversation, every bite of my meal, every light brush of his hand against mine. It wasn't a dream. It happened.

I didn't want to fall asleep again, for fear of where I might be, or what might have happened to me, by the time I woke up again. And now that I've awoken for the second time in this strange room, I have to agonisingly come to terms with the fact that what I am enduring right now is definitely not a dream, and that my only hope of getting out of this hell-on-earth predicament that I'm in is to figure out why I am here. And why this is happening to me. The only explanation I can produce is that I've been kidnapped. But how? And why? And why is this man trying to make me believe that I'm someone else entirely?

I burst into tears, shivering with cold and with the despair that slides through my veins like an icy ink. The room is darker now, with barely any light illuminating its contents. But only a glance to my left, to where the heavy curtains are drawn, is needed to confirm my fear: that I am not at home.

Jamie is not in the room, which is at least something to be thankful for. I don't even remember falling asleep, but

27

a glance at the clock, which I'm noticing for the first time because its hands are neon yellow, tells me that I have been *offline* for about three hours. The fact that not a single morsel of food has passed my lips since the sticky toffee pudding I had for dessert on my date with Kevin is brought to my attention by a loud, uncomfortable growl emanating from my stomach. Jamie offered to make me something earlier, but how could I possibly think about eating? I feel like I am literally living a nightmare, and the sensation does not support a healthy appetite.

Last night, I was a carefree, single woman of thirty-two, enjoying dinner and a few drinks with an old flame. The most pressing issues working on my mind when I laid my head on my pillow after returning home were whether it was truly wise to see Kevin again, and whether it would be obvious to my boss that I had been out drinking on a school night. Now, less than a day later (or two days, if Jamie's assertion that today is Saturday is to be believed), I'm trapped on an island that I apparently have no means of getting off of, with a man who claims that I have been in a relationship with him for over three years, and furthermore claims that my recollections of my past, my life, are nothing more than hallucinations created by a malfunctioning psyche. What am I supposed to do with that?

The only thing I can think of doing, in this instant, is reinforcing the truth in my mind.

My name is Natalie Elizabeth Byron. My first name was chosen at random, for no other reason than I 'looked like a Natalie' when I was born, but my middle name is an homage to my grandmother on my mother's side. My father is a railway worker of thirty years' experience, by the name of Iain Byron. My mother is a paralegal; her name is Gillian.

I was born in Glasgow's bespoke maternity hospital on the twenty-ninth of July nineteen eighty-three, which means that I am still closer to thirty-two than thirty-three by the skin of my teeth, and I'm going to cling to that status for as long as possible. I am the second eldest of four, with an older sister called Gemma, a younger one named Anna, and a younger brother called Max.

I live alone, and have done so for some years now, having flown the coop at the tender age of nineteen when I opted to live a little closer to the university that I attended for one year, then abandoned in favour of gainful employment. My home is a relatively small but cosy house that I was fortunate enough to procure for a decidedly knock-down price when the property market took a nose dive a few years ago.

I work full-time, for the Criminal Records Bureau in Glasgow, ritually performing mind-numbing tasks that I have been carrying out for so long that I could do them with my eyes closed. As jobs go, it's not the worst – it is far from difficult, and affords me a decent lifestyle. I have a nice home, a recently-purchased car (not brand new, but not an old banger either), and usually manage to enjoy two or three holidays per year.

I have a loving family a stone's throw from where I live, and a small but close circle of friends that I see often and would trust with my life.

My love life doesn't read like a list of triumphs, but my dates with Kevin were my attempt at 'dipping my toe in the water' as it were, in terms of returning to the dating 'scene' after a period of living a partner-free existence.

Feeling a little calmer now that I have managed to cement the memories that I know are real in my consciousness, I feel anger stir once again, as my thoughts return to the mental torture that this man, Jamie, is inflicting on me. He would have me believe that all the things I have remembered about my life are not real. He wants me to believe that I am Jen, his girlfriend, and the kind of woman who uproots her life and relocates to some place she's never even heard of because it's what her guy wants.

Sadly, for any potential boyfriends, that is not something I would do. Never say never, and all that, but my family, my friends, my home, and even my job are far too important to me for me to ever think of leaving them all behind. I've had two pretty serious relationships throughout my life – one a little more so than the other – and although I believed myself to be in love with those men at the time, it would have taken something utterly momentous for me to drop my life like a ton of hot bricks and follow them to the unknown so that they could fulfil their own professional ambitions.

I've been wracking my brains, trying to come up with a motive, a reason why Jamie would do this, but other than him being the one out of the two of us with serious mental health issues, I am at a loss. Something like this takes meticulous planning, surely, so there must be a part of him that lives in the real world. An organised, calculating part. He has managed to get me here, all the way from Glasgow, so he must have had a pretty detailed plan in order to pull that off. Perhaps he had help, I think to myself with a shudder of unease.

There must be something I'm missing. First of all, why have I been chosen? I have never so much as laid eyes on Jamie before, and I can categorically say that I had no idea that the Isle of Carn even existed before today. So, perhaps I was kidnapped at random. I don't know whether the randomness is a good thing or a bad thing, but I do know that being kidnapped is most certainly not good. Secondly, whilst it's probably safe to assume that the person doing the kidnapping is something of a crazy person, what does he have to gain by telling me that I'm crazy? *So that I am more likely to comply*, I quickly provide in response to my own question. If he can wear me down, and make me dance to his tune, then by definition his life will be a lot easier than if I were hell-bent on escaping from him and returning to my life.

A ripple of fear travels the length of my spine as I try to assess just how scared I should be of this man who has me here at his mercy. So far, he hasn't done anything to hurt me, physically. He hasn't been mean or nasty to me or given me any reason to think that my gruesome, painful death might be imminent. He hasn't laid an inappropriate finger on me, and I have woken up wearing the same clothes that I dressed myself in earlier, seemingly unbothered. All things considered, I don't know whether his apparent innocuousness makes me more terrified than if he were an axe-wielding, wild-eyed lunatic.

What does he want from me? Assuming that, somehow, he could get me to play along with his alternative reality and 'become' Jen, where do we go from here? Am I destined to live out the rest of my days on an island with more elevations measuring above one hundred feet than people?

If what he told me earlier is true, and today is Saturday, then there is a very good chance that my absence will have been noted and highlighted to the appropriate authorities by now. If all of Friday came and went without any contact taking place between my mum and I, then at the very least my parents will have gone to my house to investigate. They have a spare key, for emergencies, and given the close relationship that I have with my family, the absence of at least a text in a twenty-four-hour period (more than that now) will have prompted alarm bells to ring.

I text my mum every day. Usually, if my work schedule allows for it, I check in around ten o'clock, and if it doesn't, then I make contact by lunchtime at the very latest. Even if I forget my mobile phone, as I have done a couple of times, I use my landline at work to let her know that I'm alive and well and will be reunited with my mobile device and the twenty-first century at the end of the working day.

She will have become suspicious of the silence around midday on Friday, I can guarantee it. I can't claim to have

31

the most impressive memory, but keeping in touch with my family is not something that would ever slip my mind. I feel a sharp sensation in the depth of my gut as I imagine how they must be feeling right now.

I lift myself gingerly from the bed and survey the room anew. I start to browse through the drawers that are against the wall, to the right of the bed, and when I open the top drawer I see that it contains ladies' underwear. I move to the second drawer down, and see that it contains t-shirts and tops – again, for a woman – so I start to sift through them, assessing whether any are suitable for me to wear. As I look through the garments, it doesn't take long to register that these are, in fact, my clothes. There's the cute little t-shirt that I bought in Rome last year; the light grey one with the decal depicting a little glass holding a barbell, which says *Gym and tonic* on it. I also find the flowery top that I bought specifically for a date that I was going on a few months ago, but I ended up not wearing it because I thought it made me look fat.

My legs feel like they've turned to jelly, and I sit back on the bed again, defeated. Whoever this man is, who has plucked me from my life and brought me here, has gone to the trouble of bringing my clothes here, too.

I cover my face with the t-shirt that used to make me smile and start to sob into the fabric.

I take some deep breaths, encouraging myself to stop crying. I move to the bathroom, in dire need of a tissue to wipe my tears, and scour over my appearance in the mirror. Contrary to what Jamie may have me believe, it is Natalie's face that I see, just like I saw last night, in the restaurant. My own face, which I've worn for the last thirty-two years, stares back at me from the glass. It is tired-looking, puffy from crying, and decidedly pasty now that it is devoid of the make-up that I wore for my date and made sure to wipe off before bed, but it is still mine. The eyes that express how

I am feeling better than I could possibly say are still blue, with the slightest hint of hazel around each pupil. The nose that has been streaming through all my sobbing is narrow and sharp, as always; the lips neither particularly thin nor plump, but currently downturned with dismay. Jamie might have tried to take my identity away from me, but he hasn't managed to take my face. I splash some water on it, psyching myself up for the mission that lies ahead of me – to break free – and trying to stem the anger that I can feel beginning to surge around my body again. I search around inside the cabinet and find two toothbrushes, both of which appear to have been used. There is no back-up, unopened pack of toothbrushes, which makes me feel more certain than ever that this is not and cannot be my bathroom – I wouldn't be able to sleep at night if there wasn't at least one back-up pack of brand-new toothbrushes available! I may be standing here, scared and apoplectic in possibly equal measure and positively desperate to brush my teeth, but nothing can or will make me use a toothbrush that isn't my own.

'Jamie!' I yell, watching my face move in the mirror. The rage that I am now projecting must be unmistakable. If I were a cartoon character, I would have red steam spouting out of my ears and cheeks the colour of a cricket ball. I hear Jamie bundling through from the living room, as though he were responding to a mayday call.

'Darling, are you okay?' he asks, bursting into the room with a concerned look on his face.

'Yes,' I say, as calmly as I can. 'I need a toothbrush.'

He looks straight at me, puzzled. 'Well, that's yours there, hun,' he says cheerily, reaching over my right shoulder and picking up the pink one. 'The pink one, of course.' He giggles, obviously finding it amusing that the colour of toothbrush we use is apparently driven by gender stereotypes.

I take a deep breath, willing myself just to get through the next few moments, in the hope that I can get my teeth cleaned, get out of here, and get myself into a headspace where I can set about formulating a plan to get back to my own life.

'I need a new one,' I say, trying to stifle my anger as much as possible. I know my own voice well, and I can hear the thinly-veiled frustration in it, which is barely being kept at bay.

'Why? What's wrong with this one?' Jamie asks, waving the pink toothbrush in front of my face. I resist the urge to grab it out of his hand and jab it firmly into one of his eyes. Aside from still not being totally sure that I'm capable of that level of violence, the fact that he is wearing glasses means that the element of surprise would be taken away from me.

'That's not mine,' I say, biting my lip, grasping onto the last shreds of my temper.

'Jen,' Jamie begins, trying to exude the patience of a saint, 'of course it's yours, hun. Why on earth would you think it wasn't?' He tries out a little smile, and it only serves to invite my rage to come pouring out.

'Stop calling me Jen!' I shout, at the top of my voice. 'And stop calling me *hun*!' I grab the pink toothbrush form his hand, which makes him jump. 'Go,' I say, gesturing wildly towards the bathroom door, 'and get me a fucking brand-new, unopened, any old coloured toothbrush so that I can brush my teeth, get dressed, and get the fuck out of here!'

Jamie stares at me, open-mouthed, looking downright gobsmacked. It probably isn't the wisest thing to do, to yell violently at your apparent abductor, but my temper has been tested to its absolute limit, and the words have spilled out before I had the chance to analyse their suitability.

'OK, hu … I mean, Je … I mean, just wait here a sec; I'm sure we'll have a spare pack somewhere.' He rushes off to look for a toothbrush, like a dog with its tail between its legs, and I exhale loudly. I feel slightly better for having let out some of the frustration that I've been feeling, but I'm trembling with sheer emotion.

I'm scared, but I'm also relieved, for the moment. Considering Jamie must be a pretty sick, unhinged individual to do what's he's done to me, so far he hasn't in any way threatened or intimidated me, and for that I suppose I must be grateful. That doesn't mean that I'm safe, though, I warn myself. I cannot be complacent.

As I wait for him to return, my eyes rove over the details of the bathroom, which is kitted out like one you might find in a dirt-cheap bed and breakfast paying homage to the stylings of the nineteen-seventies. The bath, toilet and sink are a sickening shade of blue, and bear the look of units which have not been upgraded in decades. The red towel that hangs over the rail is at odds with the insipid décor: walls painted the same ugly colour as the units; ancient, crummy linoleum covering the floor. In spite of my predicament, a wry chuckle escapes as I marvel at the bare-faced cheek of the man, implying that this place is my home. If I had been living in this hovel for several months, this bathroom would have been ripped out and reconstructed as a matter of priority!

'Here you go,' Jamie says, tentatively coming back into the room. He hands me an unopened pack of two toothbrushes, and I take them from him, silently.

'I want to call my mum,' I say, my thoughts escaping from my mouth.

Jamie seems to hesitate for a second, but after a rather furtive flicker of his eyelids, he replies, 'Sure, whatever you think.' I get the impression that he's realised the folly of addressing me by my fake name, or any of the affectionate nicknames I have forbidden him from using, so that may explain the slight delay in him answering as he forces himself not to say the wrong thing. 'There's no reception here, though, unfortunately. You'll have to try down at the castle.'

More hurdles, of course. But then I didn't really expect him to grant my request without a serving of superfluous bullshit on the side.

'I'll be out when I'm done,' I announce drily, keen to be on my own again, and I reach for the door and start to close it, forcing Jamie to retreat.

'Okay, hu … sure.'

I slam the door shut, in a childish display of temper, but I feel as though it's justified. I brush my teeth, which brings me a massive sense of relief, and then I stand, shivering, replaying the conversation of a few moments ago in my head. Jamie has agreed, albeit unconvincingly, that I can use a phone, and speak to my mum – that can only be a good thing, can't it? I'm loath to get my hopes up, but this is the first remotely positive sensation I've experienced since this whole nightmare began.

A shiver passes over me as an icy draught billows in through the small, stained-glass window at the far side of the room, my eyes brim with tears at the thought of hearing my mum's voice, and I take a towel from the rail and hold it to my face. I recite the number that I'm going to dial in my head, over and over, not wanting to take even the slightest risk of forgetting it.

Why has he agreed to let me call, though? That is certainly suspicious.

When I dial the number, and speak to my mum, and she verifies that I am who I say I am, what will Jamie do then?

6

This island is actually pretty picturesque. Perhaps this is not really the time to be appreciating the landscape, but since everything else about my so-called life today makes my brain hurt like it's being dismantled from the inside, one function at a time, I'm going to take a brief moment to revel in the beauty that surrounds me.

Now that I'm no longer cooped up inside the house, the mountains don't seem quite as scary as they were earlier. They're vast, and majestic, and I'm only just realising that I don't think I've ever seen a real one up this close before. I've seen hills – my parents actually live halfway up some picturesque hills, overlooking the River Clyde – but I think these are the first genuine mountains I've seen, in person. For a Scottish person, that's probably quite inexcusable. We're not exactly short of mountains in Scotland, after all.

Beautiful location or not, it is November, and bearing in mind that we are still technically, geographically in Scotland (or so Jamie tells me; I have no way of verifying exactly where I am) the weather is as expected: freezing cold. The sky is surprisingly clear and strikingly blue, with only the subtlest dusting of wispy clouds, and somehow, I can sense that we're not far from the sea. The very sea that I need to find a way to cross, in order to get back to the mainland, and then home.

Jamie is, at my request, guiding me towards the village hall, where he claims there is a public telephone (more reliable than the scant mobile reception near the castle, he said), and an open-to-the-public, pay-as-you-go internet service. It seems foolish to feel too optimistic about the capabilities of this so-called service – the concept of Wi-Fi, to this island, must seem like sci-fi.

Jamie says there is also a payphone – a proper, retro one, in a red phone box – which I'm very excited to see, and use, for the sheer nostalgia of it, but more importantly because it will allow me to make contact with the real world, and most critically, my family.

I'm going to phone my mum and dad's home number, because, regrettably, I don't know either of their mobile numbers off by heart. I just hope that they're home. They could be out looking for me, although aside from my house, which they could rule out quickly, I can't think where else they might go searching. The thought of speaking to them has awoken an army of excited butterflies inside my tummy, but I feel immense guilt as well at the thought of the turmoil that my absence must be putting them through.

But it won't be long before I can put their minds at ease, I tell myself, trying to stay positive. They will be able to arrange for me to get home – I'm quite sure they will have spoken to the police already and will be able to trigger the rescue mission *tout de suite*.

So, the first priority is a call to home, and if my parents are not home then I will call the police myself.

Jamie has been open to the idea of me using the phone and the internet, but that doesn't mean that he will actually let me go through with it, does it? If he tries to stop me, now that we're out of the house I will scream at the top of my lungs in the hope that there is someone else around to hear me. I doubt that there are police on this island, given that we haven't so much as passed any other houses on the walk so far, but surely there must be other human life somewhere around here? Surely there must be someone who could come to my rescue, and keep me safe from Jamie until I can figure out a way to get home? The village hall, presumably, must be manned by a living, breathing person, and Jamie says it's not far now.

'Any joy?' he asks, as we trudge along. 'Is any of this bringing back any memories?' His face is ruddy from the breeze that has whipped up since we left the house, and his nose is bright red, almost comically so.

I shake my head, preferring to conserve my breath for the lung-busting trek than waste it by talking.

He shakes his too, in apparent consternation. 'I thought you might be feeling better, by now,' he says, sighing wearily, making me feel like I'm a lost cause that he's been burdened with. 'I know,' he says, suddenly animated, 'a story.'

'What?'

'Stories, anecdotes. It's the little things you remember, isn't it? I'm sure you'll remember this one – I love this story.'

I don't want to hear a story. I'm usually a huge fan of fiction, but not when it is being presented to me as my reality.

'You told me this when we were going out at first, when we were exchanging embarrassing stories,' he says, sounding excited, ignoring my indifference. 'Your word was "mortifying" – if there's anything you're bound to remember, it's this!'

Oh, for God's sake, get on with it ...

'So, apparently you were quite the *chanteuse*, back in the day.' He gives me a playful nudge, eliciting a scowl of disapproval that wipes the goofy grin off his face. 'Anyway, you decided to give open mic night a try at the union one night, on a dare from one of your mates, I forget which one ...'

I feel a weird sensation, like a shiver creeping over my brain, as he carries on.

'... you managed the first verse and the chorus, but when it came to the second verse you froze, and you stood there for a good couple of minutes, wracking your brains for the words. The audience started clapping a beat, shouting encouragement, and all of a sudden you just found the words from somewhere, and you ended up bringing the bloody house down! Well, that's what you told me, anyway. I wasn't there unfortunately; I'd have loved to have been.'

I've stopped walking. I did sing *a capella* at an open mic night, just the once, during my time at university; I remember it quite vividly. The reason the memory is so vivid is, ironically, because I did suffer a total mind blank, and I did forget the words after the first verse and chorus. I remember, very clearly, staring out into a sea of expectant faces, struck down by stage fright, and seeing my then-friend, Katie, mouth the words to me. The crowd were superbly supportive, clapping out the rhythm of the song for me. That was enough to snap me out of my fear-induced state, and in the end, I did indeed walk off stage to the sound of deafening applause, from a crowd who clearly appreciated a trier.

But that was over ten years ago, and Jamie wasn't there. And I didn't tell him the story, because I only met him this morning, and why would I tell a mortifying, if somewhat amusing, anecdote to someone who has kidnapped me? *Was* he there, though? Is that how he knows the story? Has he been stalking me for over *ten years*?

'Ah, look, the shop is open,' he says, pointing towards the first building that I've seen in over ten minutes of walking. My confusion over Jamie's recounting of an incident that he couldn't possibly know about is parked for the moment, because if the shop is open, that means that there must be a person, or people in there. I make a dart towards the front door.

There is a light on indoors, and as I push open the door and see an actual, living human being inside who is not Jamie, I whisper my gratitude to whatever deity may be listening.

The human, a small woman of around fifty, dressed in a camel-coloured cardigan and matching skirt, looks up as the door makes an electronic sound to signal that it has been breached.

'Jen,' she greets me, her eyes crinkling as she smiles. 'What can I do you for, my love?'

'W–What?' This, I was not prepared for. This has thrown me, and the sensation of weakness in my legs from earlier this morning has come back.

'Jen, are you okay, darling?' The woman asks, clearly noting my shaky balance. She comes out from behind the counter.

'Why are you calling me that?' I ask her, struggling to get the words out.

She glares at me, puzzled. 'Calling you what? *Darling*? I always call you that, my love.' She laughs, and puts a comforting arm around my shoulder, as though she senses that I'm about to capitulate.

'No,' I say, my mouth as dry as sandpaper, 'why are you calling me Jen? That's not my name.'

The woman throws me the same look that I've been seeing from Jamie all morning, and I feel tears form in my eyes again.

'Sorry, Bessie,' I hear a voice say, and spin round to see Jamie a few feet behind me. 'She's not herself today,' he tells the woman, in that rueful tone that dominates his speech when he talks to me or, clearly, about me. 'Jen, this is Bessie,' he explains, coming towards me. 'Bessie runs the shop.'

I look from him to her, searching for an answer to this madness. The answer to why Jamie has been trying to convince me that I'm someone else is surely, simply, that he is a bad man. He has kidnapped me, and he is trying to control me, by forcing on me the idea that I've lost my mind, temporarily or otherwise. He will be forced to release me when I call the police, and bring them here, and tell them everything that's happened in the last few hours.

41

But why is this woman, this Bessie, going along with his lies? Why is she behaving as though she knows me, when I have been here for less than twenty-four hours, and have never met her before? Why is she in cahoots with a criminal?

'Jamie, is everything alright?' Bessie asks him, her face still a maze of confusion and concern.

'Yes, Bessie,' Jamie assures her, with a friendly tap on her hand. 'Jen's just a little out of sorts today, that's all. I think I just need to get her home, for a wee lie down.'

Bessie nods along in agreement. 'Aye, that's what to do, son,' she instructs him, returning his contact with a squeeze of his arm.

I feel faint, and my legs begin to sway. 'Can I have some water, please?' I croak, the words grating painfully on my parched throat. As Jamie rushes to the cooler to get a bottle of water, a man comes into the store, dressed as though he's en route to a polar expedition. 'Bessie,' he states, by way of a greeting, nodding to the woman, who responds with a somewhat flippant wave. 'Davie,' she murmurs.

The man regards the scene, inquisitively. He looks at Jamie, gives him the same nod that he gave Bessie, then glances at me. Before he even says the words, I just know that he's going to confirm exactly what I fear.

'Jen, are you feeling alright, love? You look a bit peaky.'

7

Jamie leads me out of the shop, and I let him, devoid of all fight at this moment in time. I had pinned my hopes on being able to reach out to a stranger, to plead with them to help me, and those hopes have been shredded. Theories tumble around inside my head as I try to understand what has just happened, and how my mission to try and escape has been so harshly aborted. Bessie and Davie are in cahoots with Jamie; they're in on whatever it is that he is doing. And if there are yet more people on this island, will they unmask themselves as Jamie's co-conspirators too? How has he got these people to go along with tricking me? Has he paid them? I don't understand why anyone would do that, but then I don't understand even a tiny percentage of what has gone on since I opened my eyes this morning, and I'm not even sure that I'm making any sense inside my own head at this moment.

'Let's go home,' Jamie urges, holding me close while we walk in the direction of the house. 'You should really eat something, then have a lie down. Maybe you'll feel a little better after that.'

I want desperately to believe that I will feel better, to the tune of waking up at home – my own home – and finding out that I was right earlier, that this is just a nasty, frighteningly realistic nightmare. Because the alternative doesn't bear thinking about.

A flash of red registers in my peripheral vision, and I realise that it must be the telephone box that Jamie said was around here. I'm desperate to break free from his hold and run towards it, but my body won't comply. My energy, along with my hope of finding someone around to here to help me, has simply evaporated.

It's only a few short minutes before Jamie leads me back inside the house, and the sense of defeat that I feel when I cross the threshold is crushing.

'Why don't you go and have a lie down, and I'll put the kettle on,' he suggests breezily, as though nothing of note has just transpired.

I don't want to lie down. I want to get the hell out of this horrible, draughty house, and get back to Glasgow. I want to see my family and tell the police everything that has happened so that Jamie can be locked up and prevented from doing any harm to me or anyone else.

I grudgingly retreat to the bedroom while he potters around the kitchen, but I'm not going to lie down, I need a plan to get free.

Immediately, at the thought of freedom, my mind fixates on reuniting with my family, and I feel that now-familiar stab of remorse as I think about how they must be feeling right now. Who knows what kind of state my house has been left in, given that my clothes have made it all the way here to Carn with me? What kind of mess have my mum and dad stumbled upon? Will they be dealing with the police right now, letting them into my house to search it for clues as to my whereabouts?

My mind retraces a few steps as I picture the scene at home, and something niggles at its edge as I think about the fact that Jamie has emptied my wardrobe and transported the contents here. What is it that my brain is trying to tell me? I close my eyes to try to focus, and it comes to me.

I rush into the bathroom and grab hold of the towel which hangs over the towel rail attached to the wall. Red. Bearing the Ralph Lauren logo. Exactly like the one I have at home, which came to find its way into my otherwise non-designer bathroom as a result of an ill-advised credit card spending spree that I embarked on in House of Fraser last year, around sale time. This doesn't mean anything, I try telling myself, stifling the panic that I can feel beginning to bubble inside me once more. So, there's a Ralph Lauren towel here, so what? The company produced more than one!

But my eyes latch onto the products that are lined up along the bath, and my feelings are thrown into disarray again. There is a bottle of shampoo, a bottle of conditioner, and a bottle of shower gel. Nothing unusual there, you might think – not exactly out of place in a bathroom. Except that all three are exactly the kinds that I use at home. The shampoo and conditioner bottles are half empty – exactly as mine were at home, the last time I checked. I distinctly remember because when I realised they both contained the same amount of fluid it struck me that it was probably the first time that I've ever managed to achieve exactly equal usage of each substance, as opposed to running out of shampoo long before the conditioner bottle requires even so much as a slight squeeze to give up its contents.

What are they doing here? Yes, it could be a coincidence that Jamie also uses Superdrug's own, cruelty-free brand hair products, and Original Source shower gel (the mint kind that leaves your skin tingling when you use it), but it's one hell of a coincidence. Jamie has practically no hair, and what there is of it surely doesn't require shampoo and conditioner which claim to cure frizz. So, if they are not Jamie's, who do they belong to? Me? That means that when he kidnapped me, as well as packing up my clothes he also went to the trouble of bringing along my toiletries. Why would he do that? To mess with my mind, I offer up quickly, batting away the doubts that are relentlessly creeping into it.

'Don't let him get inside your head,' I warn myself out loud, staring in the mirror again. I know who I am; where I live. I have not 'snapped' and reinvented my reality. I am being manipulated, in a cruel and despicable way, and I need to get away from this dangerous man as soon as possible. But just as I begin to believe this, the story that he told me when we were outside returns to my mind.

My legs feel unsteady again, and I have to perch on the edge of the bath to take the weight off them, feeling very close to being defeated. Whoever this man is, he is going to a lot of effort to make me doubt myself, and my own sanity, and with every item of evidence that backs up his story, another little drop of certainty ebbs away.

I cover my face with the towel that I know instinctively is mine, and let it catch my tears as I sob into it. Is he right? Am I suffering from an *episode*? Have I lost my mind and created a fantasy of what my life really is? 'No!' I murmur into the fabric. 'He's lying.' Saying the words aloud helps ever so slightly to halt the train of thought that was threatening to veer off on a dangerous course, but the fact remains that he has me completely trapped here. Why is he doing this to me?

8

'Well?' the man asks. Gary jumps in surprise. He is already feeling on edge enough without someone creeping up behind him. Especially when that someone is this man, for whom the very word *creep* could have been invented.

'So far, so good,' Gary states, reclining back into his chair, trying to convey that he is relaxed; unperturbed. 'Everything's working fine. The woman is obviously freaked out, and she's tried to make a run for it a couple of times, but right now, she's just sitting on the bath, crying.'

'Good,' the man says, staring straight at the screen, looking mesmerised. He is standing with his arms folded across his chest, mere inches away from the giant screen that is streaming live images from every part of the house. He is able to keep an eye on the proceedings from his own office, but this room is the hub, where all the equipment is, where the large screens are, and where Gary will make sure that all the hardware continues to play ball.

The man gives a little smile, almost imperceptible, as he catches sight of Alex shuffling around the kitchen, killing time.

The man took his own time, mulling over his decision on the lead actor – he needed to be confident that he'd chosen someone who was capable of doing what he needs them to do. On the evidence of what he's seen so far, he is as happy as he can be with his eventual choice. Alex is a good fit, it seems, and the man has high hopes that his lead will be able to keep up his initially impressive performance.

He smiles broadly now, feeling buoyed by the positive start, and the fact that everything up until now has gone without a hitch. He's been itching to bring his plan to life for so long now that he feels like he could quite literally burst with excitement, seeing all his preparation come to fruition. He's sorely tempted to push up the schedule, and ramp up the tension straight away, but his sensible side reminds him that he must be patient, and let things play out as planned, if he is to achieve the results he craves. All of this has taken time and effort to pull off, and he wants to savour it.

'Good man,' he says cheerily, giving Gary a firm squeeze on the shoulder. 'Time for a coffee, I think.'

9

Alex busies himself with the task of making tea. The tiny, almost imperceptible earpiece he lodged inside his left ear has either malfunctioned, or he is being trusted to take care of the next few minutes on his own, without any 'direction'.

Alex knows little to nothing about how the technology in play is being manipulated, but he does know that everything has been planned in great detail, and that the woman has no chance of doing *anything* without the full knowledge – and intervention, if necessary – of the puppet master who croaks into his ear. His assurances about mobile phone signal and internet access are worthless, he knows. The woman has zero chance of reaching the outside world, of making contact with anyone she cares about.

The remote location of the island, the fact that getting to and from it is nigh on impossible without your own transport, and the genuine challenge of maintaining regular contact with anyone not presently on the island are the key reasons that this particular one was chosen for this … event. He was given only scant details about what would actually be going on here, but in order to carry out his role, Alex needed to become knowledgeable about his 'place of work'.

As a result, he knows that even during high season, the island is only accessible by ferry, at quite pitifully infrequent intervals, and it takes at least eighty minutes to reach the corresponding mainland terminal, at Mallaig. The only other option for returning home is making the trip across the water in your own vessel, or perhaps being lucky enough to hitch a lift with the one other person on the island who is in possession of a motor boat, on the off chance that they

49

happen to be popping over for some supplies, or simply for a change of scenery and a taste of modern living. Born of the experience of the last few days, Alex has a hunch that Davie, owner of said vehicle, would not be in a hurry to taxi him back to Mallaig without very good reason, and perhaps not even then.

Alex had no prior knowledge about this island – he had never even heard of it before – nor about the type of work his character supposedly does, but it didn't take more than a quick internet search to swot up on both. Reassuringly, he doesn't have to worry too much about whether he might forget things or be stumped for the correct answer to any questions the woman may ask him. Any information he might possibly need will be fed to him through his earpiece, and he's a good enough actor to hide the fact that he's receiving prompts, if he says so himself.

His instructions, for the moment, are to simply leave the woman on her own for a while. He heard her shuffling around a few moments ago, but he has not been called upon to intervene. Alex has been advised not to go to her unprompted, since *Jamie* is supposed to believe that she is currently resting.

They are directing his every move, just like any other acting job, but unlike any job he has ever done before, he has absolutely no idea when or how this one is going to end.

Alex rubs his beard, pensively, trying to disguise the nervousness that washes over him. He stares at the screen, but his eyes don't focus. He's wondering if there is any chance the job will get any easier, as the days go on. Today is only the first day, and already he feels like a monster.

part two

10

'So, when was the last time you spoke to your daughter, Mrs Byron?' the constable asks, his pen hovering over his notebook. Gillian Byron stares at the notebook, momentarily distracted by the thought that even now, in an age where toddlers are proficient at operating iPads, the police still rely on good, old-fashioned pen and paper.

'Um … Thursday. Thursday evening,' Gillian says, sounding less than certain. She fiddles nervously with her necklace, a rose gold chain with a pear drop diamanté. 'Well, I didn't actually speak to her, then,' she corrects herself. 'She sent a text message, on Thursday night, around six, I think it was. Was it six, would you say, Iain?' Gillian speaks hurriedly, anxiously, wracking her brains for something that will crack the mystery of why Natalie isn't at home and has not been in touch.

Constable Alistair Locke anticipates that he may only have a small window of opportunity to ask his questions before the woman crumples into a heap of tears.

'Uh-huh.' Locke makes a note about the timing of the text message, then poses his initial question once more, re-wording it slightly. 'So, Mrs Byron, when *exactly* was the last time you actually *spoke* to Natalie?'

Gillian's hand instinctively goes to her necklace again, and she absent-mindedly moves the pear drop from side to side, the jewellery producing a low grumbling sound as the pendant clings to the chain.

'Well, she was here, with us, on Wednesday night. She usually comes over on Wednesday nights, straight from work, and she watched the football with us, so I suppose she must have left shortly after the game finished, which would have been around … what time, Iain? Ten?' She looks to her husband to back up her assertion. Iain is perched, quite literally, on the edge of his seat.

'That's right,' he confirms. 'She didn't stay long after the match finished – she had to be up early for work in the morning.' Alistair Locke finishes jotting down the details he's been given. Iain Byron glares at him, impatiently.

'When are you going to start looking for her?' he demands. There is fear barely concealed behind the anger in his voice. In the hours during which there has been a distinctly uncharacteristic lack of contact from his daughter, Iain himself has already investigated every lead that he and his wife can think of. He is not in the mood to be patient; his tolerance is waning for what he sees as time-wasting. He himself has searched her flat from top to bottom three times, hunting for anything that could provide a clue as to her whereabouts. He lingered there for a while, in the hope that whilst he was around she might just materialise, safe from harm, asking, 'Dad, what are you doing here?' She didn't. After more than a whole day of zero contact from Natalie, Iain's head feels like it will explode with frustration at the shocking lack of urgency being displayed by this police officer, considering it took them half a day to get around to sending someone out to speak with them.

'Well, the first thing we have to do is try and piece together Natalie's last known movements, Mr Byron,' the officer advises, sounding uninterested, and as though he could well be reading from a well-rehearsed script. 'It's important that we build a picture of her movements; her habits; any plans that she may have for wanting to get away for a while, any reason that she may have for wanting to be uncontactable …'

'She doesn't have any reasons!' Iain yells, standing up. 'She didn't make plans to go away somewhere without telling us! How many times do we have to tell you? Something must have happened to her!' He is standing over the seated officer, his chest heaving violently from the outburst, his face red and distorted with anger and frustration.

'I understand, Mr Byron,' the constable says calmly, standing up to meet Iain's eyes, and to assert his authority over the situation. He is around the same height as Iain, and similarly built, but his uniform and his steely demeanour give him the edge. He is, naturally, trained for this kind of situation. His tone of voice, however, doesn't provide any indication that he even remotely understands the Byrons' plight. 'But if you could please try to keep calm. I really do want to help you find your daughter, and believe me, I'll do everything I can, but I'm going to need you to calm down, and let me do my job, okay?'

'Please, Iain,' Gillian pleads softly, almost at a whisper. The tears have come now, and she holds a handkerchief to her face. Iain sits back down, reluctantly, and so does the constable, a short distance from Gillian. 'My husband is right, officer,' she concurs, her voice strained, like it hurts her to speak. 'Natalie would never go anywhere and not tell anyone. She's always in contact, every day …' Her voice tails off.

'I understand,' the officer replies, although it still sounds like no more than a stock response; something that he is programmed to say. He steals a glance at Iain, who has reluctantly returned to his seat, and is cradling his head in his hands. Order has been restored, at least for the moment, and the officer continues with his enquires.

'The thing is, the reason that I'm interested in any plans that Natalie may have made,' he explains, 'is that you mentioned that some items appear to be missing from her home, is that right?' He's directing his question towards Iain this time and consults a previous page of his notebook. 'Some clothes, and shoes, I believe?'

'Yes, that's right,' Iain confirms tightly, trying to maintain his composure. He already laboured this point to the person he spoke to on the phone, explaining to them that things were missing. It was one of the first things he mentioned to them, since it seemed so odd. 'But like I told your colleague,' he continues, 'her phone and her purse were still there, and even her keys.' He watches as the officer scribbles some more notes, and feels his temper rising again. 'Look, as we've already told you, there's absolutely no way our daughter would just leave without telling anyone! Even if she had decided to go somewhere on the spur of the moment, she would *never* deliberately miss work, and she would let someone know where she was going; where she was.' His voice falters this time, and he stares at the ground, trying to hold his emotions in check.

There is silence in the room for a few seconds, as Iain and Gillian absorb the gravity of the situation once more.

'I understand how difficult this is for you both,' the officer says, trying his best to sound sympathetic, looking first at Iain, then at Gillian. 'And I appreciate that you have no reason to believe that Natalie's absence is voluntary, but since I'm going to have to file a missing persons report, it's imperative that we cover every possibility, including the one that she, herself, took the said items from her flat and left of her own accord. The fact that some clothing has been removed from the flat, and that you said there are no signs of forced entry, means that we at least have to be mindful of the prospect that perhaps nothing untoward has happened. Believe me, you'd be surprised how many people are reported missing and then turn up, unharmed. Sometimes, people just feel they need to get away from it all for a while.' He offers a smile at the couple, in an attempt to reassure them.

Iain almost erupts again, in fury at what he sees as the officer's flippant treatment of their predicament, as well as covering ground that he already covered on his initial phone call. Gillian pre-empts his outburst and places her hand calmly over his.

'Alright,' she concedes, appreciating that the quickest way to move the process forward is to just answer the officer's questions, fully and honestly.

'What would really be helpful,' the officer states, 'is if you could give me the names of any friends or work colleagues of Natalie's who might be able to help us with our enquiries. And what about her home life; is Natalie married, or does she have a boyfriend?'

Gillian takes a deep breath, but Iain answers before she can reply.

'No, not married, and she doesn't have a boyfriend at the moment,' he states.

The officer starts to make a note on his page.

'But she was going on a date on Thursday night,' Gillian says quietly.

Iain turns his head abruptly, and the officer deduces that this is brand new information that is being imparted to Iain as well as himself.

'Who with?' Iain demands, before the officer has the chance to make the enquiry his own.

'Kevin,' Gillian replies. 'Kevin Lowell. You remember, they used to go out a while ago? He's an architect.'

Iain seems to search his memory for a few seconds, and his expression quickly changes from puzzlement to anger.

'*Him*?' The word seems to be spoken with venom, the officer notes. 'Why the hell would she have anything to do with *him*? And why the hell didn't you tell me before now?' Iain's voice is loaded with rage and disbelief, and the officer infers that Natalie's date with this man, Kevin, is a line of enquiry he will definitely want to pursue, as soon as possible.

Without waiting for Gillian to answer her husband, the officer interjects.

'So, the date was due to take place on Thursday night, you said, Mrs Byron?'

11

The story from her uni days has struck a chord with her, Alex knows. It shook her, but not as much as running into 'Bessie' and 'Davie'. Alex shudders at the memory of her face, the lump of dead weight that he had to hold up when she almost lost her strength and crashed to the ground.

How well do they know this woman? Until now, Alex has been operating under the assumption that she's a totally random victim, and while that was bad enough, he convinced himself that he could deal with it. What choice does he have? But now, evidently, he's telling her stories that are real. He's talking about things that actually happened, and a long time ago at that. So, the woman has been specifically targeted; specially chosen? He's not sure why he automatically assumed that she was selected at random, but now that there are clues that this whole exercise is far more personal than he imagined, he feels a crippling sense of unease, even more so than before.

He's relieved that he seems to have been granted a few moments' peace, enough time for him to figuratively catch his breath. She's still in the bedroom, he knows, and whatever she's currently doing must be of no concern to the disembodied voice that lives in his ear. He tells himself not to think too much about who the woman is, why she was chosen.

He doesn't know her real name, or at least he didn't until she told him. As far as he is concerned, the woman is exactly who he is tasked with convincing her she is.

12

The police constable absented himself over twenty minutes ago, but Gillian and Iain are huddled together on the couch in the same positions that they occupied when he let himself out, holding each other desperately, neither knowing quite what to say.

Iain is silently seething, internalising for the moment feelings of anger at being kept out of the loop with regards to Natalie's rendezvous with Kevin, even after he had given into Gillian's plea to involve the police. Stronger than anger, however, it is hurt that is striking the hardest blow.

Gillian wanted to explain, as soon as the officer exited with the promise of following up on his visit with a report to his superior officers, her reasons for keeping the revelation under wraps. The very second that either of them started to feel suspicious that all may not be well with Natalie would have been the ideal time to drop that particular bombshell, as far as Iain is concerned, but neither of them has voiced their thoughts since they were left alone.

Gillian is certain that Kevin couldn't possibly have anything to do with Natalie's disappearance, and she will assure Iain of that once more when the painful silence they are encased in is broken. She didn't want the date to be taken out of proportion, so powerful is her gut instinct that tells her that there is no link between Thursday night's date and the radio silence from their daughter, but she bitterly regrets keeping the facts from her husband, whose racing heart she can feel beating through his shirt as he hugs her.

She can hear the words that she knows he will say, when he has recovered his own voice. What about his rightful place, as a concerned father? Should he not have been let in on her confidence straight away; should she not have trusted him to make up his own mind about whether the date was of any significance or not? But then, that is exactly why she deemed it best not to say anything. She knew that it would be of the utmost significance to her husband, that he would immediately be inclined to head out to hunt the man down.

'You're damn right I'd be out looking for him!' she could imagine him replying, his voice incredulous. *'I'd be straight out to Kirkie, knocking on every door in the town until I got hold of the little shit!'* He will do whatever he needs to in order to find Natalie, Gillian knows, and if that means driving the fourteen miles to where Kevin lives and subjecting him to an inquisition, then so be it.

Once he has calmed down, once Natalie has been located and returned safely to the bosom of her family, perhaps he will feel differently, Gillian muses, about what she did. Perhaps he will be able to see it from her perspective, and to understand that she couldn't let him go on a wild goose chase, leaving her to deal with the police on her own.

Iain seems to return to the present, as though he has been hypnotized but is now back in the room, ready to focus on the matter in hand, for the time being putting aside his bruised feelings. Up until now, Iain and Gillian have owned all of the worry themselves; it has been shared exclusively between husband and wife, mother and father. But now that Natalie has not been heard from in over twenty-four hours and the police are on the verge of declaring her a missing person, they have no choice but to inform their other daughters, and their son. A task made more difficult than it already is by the fact that two of their children are on holiday, on opposite sides of the globe, while the other is occupied attending her son's Saturday afternoon football match.

Since Thursday evening, only Gemma has returned to the family group chat on WhatsApp. Natalie's last comment, at six-thirty that evening, when she replied to Gemma's message confirming that she and Mark had arrived in Los Angeles, saying, *Glad you made it safely, sis. Have an awesome time, y'all!*, remains the last crumb of contact for close to two days.

Disturbing Gemma and Max's vacations with such distressing news is hard for Gillian and Iain to contemplate, but they resolve not to keep Max in the dark any longer. They will have to wait several hours before they can inform Gemma, because on the west coast of the United States, she and Mark will be asleep. As for Anna, Gillian types out a vague text message with trembling hands (*Hi A, call me when you get a chance. xx*). As she hits the send button she wonders where she will be able to draw the strength from to explain the meaning behind it. She wonders if she should try to call Anna straight away, but Iain implores her to wait. Max will be the first to find out what is transpiring, providing he answers, and Iain hugs his wife tightly, psyching himself up to make the call. For a few moments, there is silence in the room again, broken only by the sound of the gas fire roaring intermittently whenever the wind picks up speed. Both are thinking exactly the same thing: that, in this moment, there is nothing they could want more in the world than to have all four of their children there with them.

13

Kevin checks his phone for messages again, for about the tenth time in twenty minutes. It would take a seismic shift in personality for him to admit it to anyone, but he can't shake his disappointment at not having heard back from Natalie, since their date on Thursday night. At least, to his mind, it was a date.

The evening bore all the hallmarks of a typical date, he reminds himself, mentally ticking off the qualifying criteria. Dinner, which he duly offered to settle the entire bill for, like a gentleman, but which Natalie insisted on paying her share of: check. Drinks – not too many, because it was a school night, but enough to get them both tipsy and giggly: check. Flirtatious behaviour across the table, check, followed by a long, passionate kiss just before they each went their separate ways at the end of the night: check. It had gone really well, or so he had thought, but the more time dragged on with no affirmation, the less convinced he became.

What could he possibly have missed? Should he have insisted a little harder on covering the cost of the meal? No, Natalie's not the type to get annoyed about stuff like that. Is she? If she didn't have a good time, or want to see him again, why did she agree to meet up again next weekend, when he floated the idea after their kiss at the train station?

An unwelcome, uneasy thought pops into his head as he tries to make sense of the situation. Is there a chance that she agreed to go out with him again to get back at him for the way he ended it when they went out before? He put his hands up and admitted that he was out of order, a year ago, when he'd called things off without really giving her much of an explanation (in actual fact, he had started seeing someone else, but that had failed spectacularly, and he'd been left rueing the way he had cast Natalie aside). But had he misjudged her so drastically that he had failed to suspect that she might be the kind of person to exact petty revenge on him, by making him think he was being given another chance?

'Nah,' he answers his own question, shaking his head in denial at the insinuation.

She wouldn't do that, he assures himself. She's not like that. And he knows she enjoyed herself the other night – she really did. That kiss … that couldn't be fake. Could it?

Kevin dismisses the idea again, his ego baulking at the attempted slight. There does remain, however, the small matter of zero contact since they exchanged a few goodnight messages upon arriving home on Thursday night. The last one from her was sent at about twenty minutes past eleven, and if she was putting on a show over dinner, then she was maintaining the charade even after they parted company, by confirming via WhatsApp that she had a lovely time and was looking forward to seeing him again, possibly the following weekend.

Maybe there's something wrong with her phone, he speculates, again, for the umpteenth time. Maybe she dropped it, and it's broken, and she doesn't know his number off by heart. But this is the twenty-first century. There are more means of making contact with another person than ever before, and if it came down to it, she could get a message to him using Facebook, or Snapchat, or Instagram. She could even go proper old school, and send him an email, if all else failed!

But she hasn't done any of those things. She hasn't connected to WhatsApp since she sent that last message. She hasn't been on Facebook Messenger for three days. She hasn't posted on Instagram, or Snapchat, and Kevin's

Outlook inbox is conspicuously empty of unread mails.

Even if she were playing games with him, which he doesn't want to believe that she is, would she really go to the extreme of abstaining herself from all forms of social media, just to avoid him? Of course not, he decides. That would be ridiculous. And how long would she keep it up for? There has to be some other explanation for her absence from the digital world.

With all available hypotheses exhausted, Kevin can't shirk the niggling sensation that plagues him, that something is not quite right about this state of affairs. But his avenues of recourse are limited. If she won't (or can't) answer her phone, or any other kind of message, then he doesn't really have a platform from which to start asking around: her family probably wouldn't welcome him back into the fold after previous events. And her friends, well, again, he's not exactly Mr Popular in that circle. Would she even have told anyone that she was going out with him?

Technically, they've only been on two dates. Given the events of a year ago, and although it doesn't make him feel good to think it, he reckons that the news of their reunion probably wouldn't feature prominently in her conversations with anyone who had heard his name in the past.

He sighs. His ego has taken a bit of a beating, but more than that, he genuinely does want to see her again. And if she doesn't feel the same, then he will take it on the chin, but he doesn't want to just leave things like this. He doesn't like unfinished business, even if it's unsuccessful business. A little closure is all he wants.

He checks his phone one more time, out of habit more so than expectation, and decides to take the bull by the horns and just call her. Direct action is the way to go, he thinks. There are no rings on the line though – it goes straight to voicemail. Natalie hasn't bothered to record her own personalised message, so the voice on the other end is the generic, robotic one selected by the provider that tells him, 'You have reached the voicemail of ...' and then rhymes off the number.

He hangs up, and sighs again, dejected. He slumps back onto his pillow, hoping that when she sees the missed call, Natalie will feel compelled to call him back, or at least initiate some kind of contact, so that he can have a chance to lay his cards on the table. He has grown up a lot since the last time she knew him, and he wants a shot at making her happy. One more chance. That surely can't be too much to ask.

14

My eyes are tired and sore, from crying for what feels like hours. It could have been only minutes, but I have lost all track of time. I feel like I should be able to draw some courage from the anger that I'm feeling, but it's hard to feel courageous when I feel physically and mentally exhausted.

A tiny sliver of light appears at the end of the tunnel I feel like I'm staring into, when I think back to earlier, when Jamie was guiding me back to the house. Did he purposefully steer me away from the telephone box? He certainly seemed very keen to get me back here. It's got to be worth a try, surely.

I take a look outside and see that it's still light, so I can't have been lost in my tears for as long as I thought. However long it's been, Jamie hasn't returned to the bedroom, and the house is silent apart from the occasional burst of wind rattling the windows. I make a quick decision: I'm going to go back out, on my own this time, and I'm going to call home. I'll need to be quiet, and quick, but I think I can do it.

I sneak into the hallway on tiptoe, looking and listening for any signs of Jamie approaching. Nothing. He must be in the living room, or the small draughty kitchen. I don't really care – all that matters is that he is not forming a barrier between me and the door. I pad slowly, silently down the hallway, and for the first time I notice that there is a small shelf beside the door. There is a small pile of coins there – exactly what I need! I scoop them into my hand without allowing them to make any sound, and I feel my pulse start to speed up as I contemplate the call connecting. Slipping them into my jacket pocket, again noiselessly, I take a peek behind me to check that Jamie hasn't crept up behind me, but still there is no sign of him. I open the door to a huge gust of wind that I should have expected, but it catches me a little off guard and I have to make a grab for the door before it slams and alerts Jamie to my imminent exit. I catch it just in time and gently close it, with only the softest of clicks betraying my plan. I don't waste any time waiting to see if Jamie is any the wiser – now that I know where I'm going, I break into a sprint and head for the phone box, the coins jangling in my jacket pocket.

I'm there within a few minutes, and almost smash my face in the glass on account of running so hard to get there. The door is heavy, and my energy is depleted from the run, so it takes me a few long, agonising seconds to get inside the box and feed the coins into the slot.

'Come on, come on,' I urge, as I hear a sound that I never thought I'd be so thankful to hear in all my life: it's ringing.

15

The phone beeps its inappropriately upbeat alert, and Iain grasps for the receiver so desperately that he loses his grip and sees it crash onto the floor. 'Shit!' he yells, crouching down to pick it up, blood rushing to his head.

'Hello?' he says, with unbridled hope.

'Dad?' It's Anna's voice on the line, but it is so similar to Natalie's that for a split second he allows himself to think it might be her. 'I got your message, is everything alright?'

Iain's heart went into overdrive when he heard the phone ring, and now it hurts him as it sinks, like a stone, at the realisation that all the prayers he has been offering up remain unanswered. He gives a bleak shake of his head to Gillian, who leapt from her chair a fraction of a second after him, and is standing at his shoulder, straining to hear what is being said at the other end of the line. She slumps back down onto the couch, defeated, and Iain joins her, placing a comforting arm around her shoulder.

'Dad?' Anna's voice betrays a hint of impatience.

'Where are you?' Iain asks his first-born child, bringing his hand from Gillian's shoulder to his forehead and rubbing it, in an attempt to displace some of the tension that has converged there.

'We just got home,' Anna answers promptly. 'We went shopping after the match. What is it, what's wrong?'

Iain takes a deep breath, planning his next words with trepidation.

'It's Natalie,' he says, standing up and making his way into the hallway, as though, somehow, he can shield Gillian from any additional pain by not making her suffer through hearing once again those words that taste like poison in his mouth. 'She's gone missing.'

16

'Hello?'

'Mum!' I yell, as though I have no control over the volume of my voice, stamping my feet in excitement, like a hyperactive child. 'Mum! Mum, it's me! It's Nat!' My voice is screechy now; any higher and it would only be audible to dogs. There is a pause on the line.

'Jen? Is that you, love?' the woman asks, sounding a little confused. Now that I can really hear her voice, I realise that it does not belong to my mum.

'What ...?' I start to ask a question, but the muscles in my face feel like they've gone into temporary paralysis, and I can't complete it. All I can do is stand here, holding the receiver to my ear, hoping that, by some miracle, something has been lost in translation between my ear and my brain and the balance will be restored soon.

'Jen, love, is that you? Are you okay? Is Jamie there with you?' The woman sounds perfectly lovely, and genuinely concerned, but nonetheless, there has been no misunderstanding. She is definitely not my mum.

If I ever wondered where my solar plexus was, I needn't wonder any more. I've taken a violent, fully-loaded punch straight to it. I let the receiver drop down to my side, and start to sob like a baby, leaning against the glass of the phone box for support. Jamie appears out of nowhere, reaches for the phone with one hand, and puts the other on my shoulder, to try and comfort me.

'Ange?' he checks. 'Yeah, it's me. Hi. Listen, Ange, she's not feeling at her best today ... Yeah, I think so – it certainly seems that way ... I know. I've said we should get her to see the doctor, but you know what it's like here – it'll be Thursday at the earliest ...'

I can't stand to listen to any more of this. I push past Jamie, and out of the phone box, barely able to see where I'm going through the tears that are clouding my eyes. I stumble outside, with no clue which direction I should head in. All directions, it seems, lead to dead ends. There is no one here on this island who will help me, and now I know that Jamie's web of conspiracy extends much farther than I could have ever contemplated. I let my knees bend, and sink to the ground. I'm doomed.

17

Anna yells at the car in front, urging it to move faster. She curses the driver for sticking rigidly to the speed limit, oblivious to her need for urgency. She curses the road planners for making the shortest route from her house to her parents' single carriageway, with a desperately inconvenient thirty miles per hour limit. She curses herself for not looking at her phone earlier, for not sensing that something wasn't right. She feels as though she has ingested pure adrenalin, and sitting behind the wheel at the mercy of traffic lights and other road users is becoming more and more difficult to do.

Natalie can't really be missing, can she? This all must be some mistake, she assures herself. There's no way her sister can have just disappeared.

Anna re-read some of the recent messages that Natalie sent, the last being only a few days ago. Should she have found it unusual that Natalie hadn't been in touch since then? No, not necessarily, she assures herself. They don't chat every day. Usually every few days, and Thursday evening to Saturday afternoon certainly isn't an alarming amount of time to go without contact.

She delved into the content of the messages, looking for any hint of anything that might explain what's going on. Nothing. There was nothing different, nothing new, nothing sinister. They talked about a TV show they had both been following, exchanging theories and predictions about how it might end. Their messages were littered with emojis and acronyms, like 'lol', just like always. There were no undertones, or hidden messages, nor cries for help.

She shouldn't feel the need to check, anyway, she tells

herself, angry at the insinuation of the policeman that visited her parents and didn't take their concerns seriously, from what she's heard. He doesn't know what he's talking about, or rather *who* he's talking about, she thinks to herself. Natalie, of all people, would never run off without telling anyone.

Tears start to fall down Anna's face as she wonders what could have possibly happened to her sister, making the drive even more difficult. None of the answers that her mind has conjured up so far make her feel any better, and although it's unthinkable, she can't help fearing that she may never see Natalie again.

18

'Would you like to tell me what the fuck just happened?' the man demands, bursting into the room, his face distorted with anger. 'Can he hear you, or what? You told me this couldn't happen, Gary, what the fuck?'

Gary hold his hands up in a gesture of defence. 'It's sorted now,' he insists, checking to ensure that no part of this conversation is being accidentally transmitted to Alex through his earpiece. 'I don't know what happened, exactly, but we only lost contact for a couple of minutes, tops. We've got him back online, now. He can hear me perfectly, I promise.'

The man stares at Gary, still furious at him and the other loser whom he hired to be his proxy, then glares at the screen, willing himself to regain his composure.

This wasn't supposed to happen. Everything was supposed to be under control. How can he succeed if he doesn't have total control?

He takes a moment to assess the damage. They may not have been able to direct Alex's every move in the last few minutes, but at least he managed to save the situation. In fact, as he regards the scene playing out in front of him, the man feels quite satisfied with the way things are progressing, despite the fact that Alex didn't have a fucking clue that she had gone, and only discovered her missing when he finally woke up from his daydream and went to check on her. Thankfully, there is a finite number of places that she could be, and he guessed right at the first attempt. The loss of transmission bothers the man greatly, though, even if it was only short-lived. Failures like that cannot be allowed to happen, not if everything is going to go exactly as he wants – needs – it to.

'A couple of minutes isn't fucking good enough,' he snarls at Gary, who is perspiring so much he looks like he could have just stepped off a squash court. 'You make sure nothing like that happens again, do you hear me?' He lowers his face to be in line with Gary's, to amplify the intimidation. 'No more mistakes, got it?'

'Got it,' Gary replies, his eyes facing straight ahead. He is eager for his boss to leave so that he can get back to his task without distractions, but more so because of the intense discomfort he feels whenever the other man is around. The sensation that his skin is crawling with unease.

Gary watches as the man who dictates his every task looks back to the screen and gives a little sinister chuckle. He is over the worst of his ire, it would seem. On the basis of the man's quite frequent mood swings, Gary suspects that he may be bipolar, or at the very least just very, very odd.

'So, she's been introduced to another of her new friends, has she?' he asks, then gives out a cackle that sends a chill down Gary's spine.

19

Alex is thankful to be back at the house, and especially glad that his earpiece seems to be fully operational again. He doesn't think he made any wrong moves whilst he was out of the loop, but having to think on his feet, without reassurance that the voice would step in and save him if he started to veer off course, was far too stressful for his liking. Everything about this job – if he can even call it that – is incredibly stressful, and he feels totally worn out.

He takes a sip of the coffee that he has made for himself, now that Jen (he has started to think of her as Jen, as opposed to the faceless, nameless woman that she was prior to today) has gone to lie down again. It's only instant coffee, and it tastes little better than what he imagines muddy water must taste like, but it will have to do. If nothing else, it will give him a caffeine boost, of which he feels in desperate need, considering the day he's had so far. He puts the cup down on the table and once again wracks his brain for a way to get himself out of this mess. He can only surmise what kind of people he is dealing with here, but from the interactions he's had with them so far, he is wise enough to know that doing anything to piss them off is not likely to result in a rosy outcome for him.

He holds his head in his hands, his heart beating a little faster due to the presence of the caffeine, asking himself again how he could have been so stupid as to get wrapped up in something like this.

An ad in a local paper, for Christ's sake. How could something so innocuous lead to something like this? And what possessed him to even answer the ad? He doesn't even read the bloody local paper, usually. He was kept waiting for his dentist appointment, and out of sheer boredom he picked up the only reading material available. How he wishes now that he had found some mind-numbing game or something on his phone to occupy himself with instead.

He desperately needed the money, of course, but, surely, he could have found another way. *Except you couldn't,* he is reminded by the voice inside his head. He spent weeks, months, trying to come up with some other way to get himself out of the mire, and by that point he had come up with exactly diddly squat.

Why the hell had he not come to his senses and backed out at the first twinge of unease? How could he have been so stupid as to sign on the dotted line, after that random so-called audition they made him do? And while he was on that matter, why had he been stupid enough to let his debts get so out of hand that he wasn't sure how long his kneecaps would remain intact?

It's too late now, he knows. He made the wrong choices, caught between two evils, and he might as well have sold his soul to the devil – perhaps he has. He has signed a contract, and a non-disclosure agreement. He doesn't have the faintest clue about the legality of such things, but he doesn't fancy his chances of trying to wrangle free of this one, trying to put up a fight with people who could do something as heinous as this to an innocent woman. At least, he can only assume she is innocent. What could she possibly have done to merit this type of treatment?

He feels deceived, tricked into being a part of their sick game, all under the pretence of an acting opportunity. But more than that, he feels stupid. Gullible. As thick as two short planks, his father would say. Weren't there clues that he should have spotted? Weren't there huge, bright red flags, cropping up at every point in the process he went through to get here, to this place where he feels like there's no turning back? He knows he was blinded by the money, so hopelessly needful of it was he, but now he can't even say that it was worth it.

There are so many questions that he is desperate to ask, mostly about exactly what will be expected of him going forward, but he is forbidden from making contact with them whilst there is any chance that Jen could become aware of it. Even if he were to ask, he doubts he would get any real answers, anyway. They're not obliged to tell him the truth, are they? And not bloody likely to, on the evidence of what's gone on so far.

He drinks some more coffee, a bigger gulp this time. His head is pounding. He's heard other people talk of their suffering with migraines, although he's never actually experienced one, and from his symptoms he suspects he may be about to know what the condition feels like. He resolves to go and look for some painkillers after he finishes his coffee. Perhaps they will be in the little Aladdin's cave of supplies under the sink, along with the spare toothbrushes.

He can't predict how this will all end, for either himself or Jen, but he longs for something much stronger and more effective than caffeine to help him through it.

20

I'm so tired. Tired of asking questions, and receiving answers that hurt like physical injuries. I'm home now – at least, the only version of home I have at the moment – and I'm lying in bed, staring out of the window at the mountains, and wondering whether I really have gone mad. I have no tears left at this moment, following my mini-breakdown inside the phone box, but my eyes feel full of grit. My eyelids are striving so hard to snap shut that there could be magnets inside them.

I keep running over in my mind what Jamie told me on the way back to the house. He's invented a whole new story for me, an alternate life with a whole new family, and a narrative that doesn't belong to me.

They are all in this together: him, Bessie and Davie, and now this abhorrent woman that I spoke to on the phone as well. They're all trying to convince me that I'm Jennifer Mayhew, resident of the Isle of Carn (albeit temporarily), and girlfriend of Jamie.

Brian Mayhew, father of Jen, is sadly deceased, Jamie informed me with a mournful voice, and reportedly has been for seven years, since before Jamie and I got together. The woman on the phone was, of course, Angela, he insisted, as though I should already know this.

Jamie assured me that I am not an only child; that I have a sibling, Leanne. She is thirty-six, he claims, and she has lived in Germany for the last nine years. The reason for this is that she married a German man, whose name escapes me now, and she teaches English in Frankfurt.

Jamie says he has met Leanne. From memory he thinks

they have crossed paths perhaps three times, on the big family occasions he's been invited to over the last two years or so, in the days since our relationship was adjudged serious enough to warrant him being welcomed into the family.

He says he is particularly fond of Angela, whom he insists invited him into *my* family with open arms and treats him more like a son than a son-in-law-to-be. About Leanne, he had very little to say, other than 'She's … nice. Different from you, though. Very different.' I felt too mentally exhausted to ask what he meant by that, but from his tone, I got the impression that the two didn't really get on all that well.

What am I even talking about? There is no Leanne! I am not Jen!

I am Natalie. I have two sisters and one brother: Gemma, who is four years older than me; Anna, only two years my junior; and Max, who, at twenty-four, is the youngest of us all. Where on earth has Jamie dug up all this bullshit that he's been telling me? Is it coming from his own warped imagination?

The way he talks about 'me' makes me wonder whether Jen is a real person, whether he loved and lost her, and whether that led him to take a wrong turn into *Crazyville* and project her onto me.

But then, just when I think I've reached a conclusion about the motivation behind all his craziness, he will throw a red herring into the mix, and make me doubt everything I know.

Like when he described, in great detail, that night when I choked in front of the crowd and the microphone that drained my memory temporarily. As I listened to him describing an event that he shouldn't know anything about, it felt as though he had found a way to climb inside my brain, collect random memories about an event that happened in my past, and throw them back at me, each one like a tiny weapon wreaking psychological scars.

I've been trying to think rationally and retain faith that my mind is feeding me the truth when I ask it to produce facts and memories, but with each new confusing interaction or outright untruth that is thrown at me, the harder it is getting to reassure myself that I haven't simply gone loopy. Now that there are more people in the mix, independently verifying Jamie's claims, I feel as though I have no choice but to take a step back and examine my state of mind. I need to determine whether there is the slightest possibility that my own brain could be playing a very cruel, absolutely terrifying trick on me.

I think about everything that has happened today and try to piece it together in a way that makes sense to me.

Jamie told me this … state has befallen me before. Worryingly, he knows things about me, that he could only really know if I had told him. The story of the open mic night is case in point. Only a handful of people know about that night, and I very rarely keep in touch with anyone who was there at the time. It was before the days of Facebook and Instagram were integral parts of any night out, so there was no sharing of information like that in the way there is today. So how the hell does he know about it if I didn't tell him, and he wasn't there? He also knows how I like my tea, but I'm not so concerned about that.

Then there is the fact that my clothes, and shoes, and accessories are here. The toiletries in the bathroom are ones I like, and tend to buy, down to my favourite perfume; the one that I wore on my date with Kevin only the other night.

Most unnerving of all is the fact that the woman that I spoke to briefly on the phone, wanted me to believe that I am her daughter, Jen, even though I'm certain the number I dialled was the number that has served my parents' home for more than fifteen years.

Every person that I've come into contact with today asserts that I am Jennifer Mayhew. Natalie Byron does not exist, according to them, and Jamie would have me believe that I have invented her very existence from my own imagination.

Reviewing all of this, I conclude that one of two things must be happening here.

The first possibility is that I have been kidnapped, presumably knocked out somehow, (although I don't want to think about the ins and outs of that too much), and transported, somehow, to an island which may well be the least densely-populated part of the United Kingdom – if we're even still in the United Kingdom. Again, I'm relying on Jamie's testimony on that point.

To assist him in whatever goal he is pursuing, my kidnapper has recruited others to collude with him and perpetuate the horrible lies that he's told me about myself, and my life. Somehow, he has managed to hijack my mum and dad's home phone line and misdirect the call that I thought I was making to them, to yet another accomplice who is posing as my mother.

The second possibility is that I woke up this morning having lost all sense of reality, and have actually dreamt up an alternative life in my head, which I believe to be my true existence. In this scenario, my family, my friends, all my memories, and even my own personality, are a figment of my imagination, and I am faced with the prospect of having to learn who I am, whom I love, and what my whole life is, and has been, about, from scratch.

My eyelids clamp shut, unable to put up any resistance against the force that draws them together any more. I revel in the darkness, willing my brain to shut off now, for a while, to give me some respite.

Of the two scenarios that I'm faced with, I can't tell which one terrifies me more.

21

Detective Inspector Gordon Jackson stares once more at the photograph of the missing woman, biting on his lower lip. It's something that he does unconsciously, when he's concentrating deeply.

A full search of the woman's property has been carried out but has reaped little reward other than verifying what her father told the responding officer – that clothes, shoes, and some other incidentals appear to have been removed.

The father's claim that the wardrobe and drawers, whilst not entirely empty, are considerably barer than they would normally be, is hardly a useful lead upon which to build a hypothesis about what may have occurred, but it is certainly true that nothing much has been left behind, Jackson concurs.

Her 'date' of Thursday night is the key, Jackson has insisted to his team. With a bit of luck, they will find that the mystery man and the missing woman experienced a rush of blood to the head at some point during dinner, decided to take off on a spur of the moment flight of fancy, and by the time the weekend is drawing to a close and the reality of Monday looms large, both will have resurfaced and Jackson will be able to draw the curtains on the case that never was. They have the man's name, and a vague notion of his residential address, from the woman's mother. It won't be long before they track him down.

Jackson's theory adds up. Or, at least it would, if they hadn't found a handbag on the couch, containing all the usual bits and pieces that you would expect to find in there: hairbrush, purse, chewing gum, keys – house and car. Why would she leave without those things, when she apparently

83

found time to pack clothes and shoes?

Then there's the mobile phone, still plugged into the charger on the bedside cabinet. Several missed calls, and texts, from her parents, visible from the home screen without even having to unlock the device. The team will be able to circumvent the pass code and take a more detailed look at the contents, which can yield so much in cases like this, in Jackson's experience.

The king-size bed was unmade, as though it had been recently slept in, but just how recently is mere conjecture. There is DNA to be tested, which may introduce new lines of enquiry, but then again, it may not.

If the missing shoes and clothes are indicative of a possible hastily-arranged getaway, the items left behind – arguably the essentials that a young woman might be loath to leave home without – seem to pour scorn on that hypothesis. At the same time as the keys, phone and means of accessing funds were abandoned, the bathroom was apparently cleared of its contents. All those items that you would expect to find in there are conspicuously absent: toothbrush, toothpaste, shampoo, conditioner, deodorant, make-up – all are missing, leaving gaping voids where each once stood. There isn't even so much as a towel in there.

The almost clinical spotlessness of the bathroom is undoubtedly odd. If the working theory is that she decided to slope off into the sunset with lover boy on a whim, then grabbing a few handfuls of clothing and toiletries makes sense, but it doesn't explain why she didn't even take her keys with her, let alone her phone or her purse.

Naturally, the family insists vehemently that Jackson and his colleagues are barking up the wrong tree with their suspicions of a wilful absence, that she would never dream of going AWOL. There's no history of mental illness in her medical records, they claim, but Jackson knows well that symptoms can go unnoticed, and often the loved ones are the last ones to know that there is a problem. Jackson is a veteran of the Missing Persons Unit, with twenty-seven years' experience under his belt. He's been solving cases almost as long as the missing woman has been alive, long enough to know that hardly anyone ever actually suspects that their loved one might be on the verge of doing a runner, whether it be for a few days, a few weeks, or in some cases, even several years. Natalie Byron is one of more than a hundred thousand adults who 'go missing' in the UK every year, and Jackson feels inclined to stick with his hunch that she will be safely tucked up at home, probably with a red face and some explaining and apologising to do, by the end of the week at the latest. Just like the vast majority of similar cases.

Jackson was instantly sceptical when the details of the case were passed to him, classed as medium risk by the Constable who wrote up the initial report. There are no signs of forced entry into the house. There are no signs of struggle; no blood. Clothes, shoes and toiletries are missing – not unusual for someone going on a trip.

Her current, valid passport was found in a drawer, which is helpful – already the search radius is logically limited to the UK. Her car is parked outside, in the driveway – unsurprising considering that the key is in the house.

If she doesn't want to be found, or contacted, ditching the phone is understandable, but also points to an element of pre-planning, and deceit, not to mention wasting police time.

The local hospitals have been checked – none reported any admissions matching Natalie Byron's description since her last known check-in: a text to her mother on Thursday evening around seven. Her photo has been distributed to all the hot spots up and down the country: police stations, airports, ports. Jackson and his team will be alerted if any hits turn up.

The techs will make light work of the phone, and whatever secrets are stored in there will provide a clearer picture of her last known movements, Jackson hopes. Financial records will take a little longer, but the most onerous task is that of trawling through CCTV. He has tasked Marie Slater, an old-fashioned sleuth in her methods, with yielding some results in that area.

By all accounts, Thursday night is the watershed they are working from. 'The city centre' is all they've got to go on, courtesy of her mother, in terms of where she had planned to go for her date, and while this encompasses a not inconsiderable area, the social media pleas for information that Jackson will authorise when he gets back to the station will hopefully throw up a few leads.

He reviews the photograph again, the one that was provided by the family. The only semi-recent one they could find, it's of Natalie with a young kid – he assumes a relative's kid, since she's not a mother herself. The child is pulling a silly face while Natalie smiles into the camera. Gordon Jackson wonders to himself whether he will get the chance to see that smile in person.

There's nothing sinister here, he insists, placing a bet with himself on his initial instinct, hoping that he's got it right. It's very rare that he's off the mark with his hunches, and beyond his own experience and capabilities, he has a good team of professional, dedicated officers around him. There's no reason why they won't be able to track this woman down, and soon.

22

I wake up with a violent start, and whereas yesterday I had to work up to opening my eyes, today I'm desperate to do it. I'm hoping that when I look around, I'll discover that the whole of the last day was actually just a horrid dream, and that I'm now back where I'm supposed to be. I'll most likely be in dire need of rehydration and will have to scramble to make it in to work on time, but other than that I'll be alright.

It's barely daylight, and the curtains are drawn, so I can't see much, but what I can see sucks any hope I woke up with right out of me. There are bare walls all around. The window is to my left. Jamie is to my right, snoring lightly; one bare, freckled arm draped over the outside of the duvet.

I jump, taken aback by the sight of him lying there, close beside me and shirtless, as though he has the right to do that. How dare he? He squirms a little, and it seems like he might open his eyes, but then he turns onto his other side, still asleep. He is now facing the other side of the room, away from me.

I drive my hands through my hair and leave them there for a few seconds, staring intensely at the intricate pattern on the duvet cover as I try to decide what I should do. I thought a lot yesterday. I thought about the two possible explanations that there could be for where I find myself, and after a great deal of psychological turmoil, I narrowed them down to the only feasible one. I've been abducted.

It's terrifying. I don't know what this man has in store for me; what I'm up against. At this point, I haven't quite worked out what my game plan will be, how I might be able to escape, but I am absolutely, unequivocally sure that I have not lost my mind.

I've made a promise to myself, that I will not, for even one second, doubt myself again. All of my energy and focus must go into trying to get away from this man, and his cohorts (however many of them there may turn out to be), and to getting off this bloody island.

I get up from the bed, taking care not to wake Jamie, and tiptoe across the room. Thankfully, the bedroom door is lying slightly ajar, so no additional sound is produced as I make my way into the hall. I register a stark shock through the soles of my feet like I did yesterday, as they make contact with the cold stone, and wish I had thought to grab some socks from the drawer first, before leaving the bedroom. Never mind. It's not worth going back in now and taking the risk that I might wake Jamie.

I almost jog into the living room, on my tip-toes, and take a quick scan to see if I can spot anything that I might find useful. Everything seems exactly as it was yesterday, only this time I'm alone, and I have a chance to investigate without Jamie watching my every move. I look over my shoulder, just to check, but he is not there. Yet.

I examine the room more closely, trying to see as best I can in the dim light, and I am disappointed to realise there doesn't seem to be much that it can tell me, although I'm not sure what I was hoping to find.

In terms of furniture, there is only the couch, the desk, and a small wooden coffee table. Jamie's laptop is still out, lying on the desk, and the case that he presumably carries and stores it in lies beside it. I lower myself quietly onto the chair at the desk, still trying to move as noiselessly as possible, and check if the laptop is switched on. I know that there is little to no chance that I will be able to work out what the password is, but I power it up anyway, not wanting to waste any possible opportunities that I may have to at least gather some additional information.

As the laptop goes through its start-up procedure, I take a look in the carry case, and there is nothing of interest in there – only some Scottish Natural Heritage paperwork that seems to focus mostly on red deer. I'm reminded about the portrait of the deer that hangs above the fire, and when I raise my head to look at it, I can't help thinking that its startled expression epitomises how I feel, exactly. We are kindred spirits, I realise, feeling for the first time like I have an ally. Of sorts.

I notice that the desk has three drawers under it, but I assume that they will be locked. To my surprise, the top one opens with no resistance. I sift curiously through the items that it contains. There is more paperwork relating to Jamie's so-called research, some stationery, a half-eaten packet of biscuits (presumably emergency, energy level-boosting snacks for when Jamie can't be bothered getting up to go to the kitchen), and, most significantly, some photographs. Photographs of me, with Jamie. Photographs taken on this very island, by the look of things.

I recognise this house in the background of the first photo, a selfie that is mostly dominated by Jamie's outstretched arm. I look at another photo – this one was clearly taken by someone else – in which Jamie and I stand at the water's edge, hugging each other tightly and grinning happily. There are several taken on parts of the island, as far as I can tell, and some others that appear to have been taken in other, livelier places, like pubs, or restaurants. Which means they most likely weren't taken on this island.

I feel a wave of nausea creeping up inside me and take a deep breath to try to keep it under control. Photos can be doctored easily, I remind myself. Considering the technology that is available now (in the real world), given the right equipment I'm sure even I could take a collection of someone's treasured moments and manipulate them beyond all recognition. The photos don't mean anything –

other than perhaps that Jamie has gone to much more effort than I had even thought about in order to make his deceit seem plausible. I try to stay calm, and close the first drawer, hoping to find something useful in the other two, although again, I can't really say what it is that I'm looking for.

The second drawer also allows me to pull it open, and I almost let out a squeal of delight when I see a mobile phone lying inside, on top of more paperwork. I put a hand over my mouth, to stifle any accidental outbursts of joy. I switch the phone on, and once again I can hardly contain my excitement when I see that it is not secured with a pin.

The screensaver is yet another photo of Jamie and me but owing to the extremely girly phone cover (white leather, with multi-coloured owls on it), I assume the phone doesn't belong to Jamie. It's the same model as my own phone and has all my usual preferred apps: music, email, Goodreads, various social media apps. I'll check the social media sites in a second, if I can, but my first priority is to check the contacts list. I remember that Jamie told me there's no reception here, at the house, but I'll be damned if I don't at least try to make a call.

I navigate to the *Contacts* menu, and the first thing I notice is that *my* number is not one I recognise. Undeterred, I start to scroll through the list, looking for the names of the people I am missing so much. Mum is there, but there is no number for Dad. In Jamie's description of *Jen's* life, of course, her father is dead. I feel a sharp sensation in my gut, like being stabbed, when I think of my own dad. I can only imagine what he and my mum are going through right now. They will most definitely have reported me missing by this point, and the thought of the anguish they must be feeling makes the stabbing pain even worse.

I open the contacts record called *Mum* first and wish I could remember what her mobile number really is. I try to call the number, but as expected there is not a hint of reception and it doesn't even ring, never mind connect to another phone. All I get is a succession of irritating beeps.

The home number that I dialled from the phone box yesterday is not in the contacts list, either. I'm disappointed with myself that I've never made any attempt to commit anyone's mobile number to memory, but I've just never had any reason to. Technology really has made us lazy, I realise. I go back to the main menu and scroll through the list again, thinking that if I can make a note of the important numbers, I can try to get another chance to make a call from the phone box.

I look under *A*, for *Anna*, but her name is not there. There is an *Amy*, and an *Alistair*, and then the list moves onto names beginning with *B*, none of which are familiar to me. 'No!' I cry, thumping my fist on the desk, much harder and louder than I intended. I remain still, and silent for a few seconds, listening out for any movement from the bedroom, but there doesn't seem to be any.

None of the names in this contacts list mean anything to me, other than *Mum*, and what are the chances that calling this number will get me through to my real mum?

I browse through the recent text and call history and find messages between *Mum* and whoever this phone belongs to. The style and overall content of the messages is exactly the same as the ones I would usually exchange with my own mum, except that every time Mum would call me *Nat*, I see that the messages all contain *Jen*. I look at other texts and see the kind of messages that normally fly back and forth between me and my friends, Evelyn and Carol, except that in this phone they're *Rachel* and *Anita*.

I could never be friends with someone called Anita. There was a girl with that very name who stole my boyfriend in primary school, and I've never forgiven her for it, hence the embargo that I've stuck to all this time, on ever letting anyone with that unfortunate moniker into my inner circle. Now that I come to think of it, I don't think I've ever come across another Anita, so the issue has never presented itself.

I cover my face with my hands, frustration making them tremble, but I don't want to give up, and waste time, not while I'm currently unsupervised. I navigate to the *Settings* menu and turn on the mobile data, but I already know there is no chance that it will work, not here, and sure enough I am proved right.

I take a pen and a notepad from the top drawer and make a note of the number that's listed in the phone under *Mum*. I'm going to keep this pen and paper, I decide, and I'm going to make a note of everything I know about myself, and everything Jamie tells me about myself, so that I can try to catch him in a lie. It's only a tiny flicker of an idea, but if I can get him to crack, perhaps I can unearth some leverage or something. Anything, however outlandish, has to be worth a try.

My mind is racing, but I latch onto the thought that throughout my life, nothing bad has ever come of me being armed with notes. I'm about to snoop in the third drawer when I become aware of Jamie's presence in the room. He's standing in the doorway, wearing grey jogging bottoms, but nothing on the top half of his body, and rubbing his eyes, like a child.

'Jen, are you okay?' he asks, sounding half-asleep. 'It's still dark. How come you're up?' The room is very dark, but still, the sight of this strange man standing in front of me, in a state of undress, is making me uncomfortable.

'I couldn't sleep,' I say, deeply disappointed that I seem to have run out of time and opportunity to search for a way out of this mess. 'I'm fine, honestly. Why don't you go back to bed?' I try to make the suggestion sound breezy, hoping that he'll agree that going back to bed is a great idea, but he comes towards me, and I close the laptop. He crouches down beside me, and I realise this is the first time that I've seen him not wearing his glasses.

'What are you doing?' he asks. His tone is inquisitive, but thankfully not overly suspicious.

'I was just making some notes,' I reply, gesturing towards the notebook. 'I thought it might be a good idea, you know, to try and jog my memory.' I give my most convincing smile, hoping that a lot of my deceit, along with what I have actually written down, will be disguised by the poor light.

He focuses firmly on my face for a second, then his own face breaks into a grin, and he says, 'I think that's a brilliant idea.' He starts to yawn, and I take the opportunity to suggest once more that he should go back to bed and leave me to further my plan to escape.

'Why don't you come with me?' he asks, reaching out to take my hand. I pull it sharply away from him, and he looks surprised. 'I only meant for you to lie down,' he insists, holding up his hands in a defensive gesture. 'It's Sunday, and it's obviously still really early. I just thought you might want to get some more rest.'

He sounds hurt, but I don't care. This man is dangerous, I remind myself. He has brought me here, against my will, and escaping from him is going to be very difficult, if not impossible. I can't afford to waste time worrying about my manners and whether I might have offended him by recoiling at his suggestion of going to bed with him.

'Really, I'm fine here,' I reply, insistently. 'I really think making these notes will help me.' I stare straight at his face, not blinking, and after a few seconds he appears to concede. 'No worries,' he says, a little dejected. 'I'm going to try to catch another hour or two, but wake me if you need me.'

I watch him leave the room, feeling proud of myself for standing my ground. I turn the laptop back on and tap my fingers impatiently on the desk as I wait for it to power up. I'm even more determined than ever that I'm going to get out of here. I'm going to get home.

23

Alex lies with his eyes closed, wishing he could go back to sleep, for real. He did actually sleep through Jen getting out of bed, and had to be awoken by a harsh, ridiculously loud noise in his ear, which he feels was disproportionate, and from which he is still recovering. He's supposed to be alert to her actions at all times, but he's human; he's got to sleep, hasn't he? It took him ages to finally get to sleep, on account of all the guilt and anxiety he feels like he's drowning in, so by the time he did drift off he was mentally exhausted.

The voice in his ear didn't instruct him to stop her doing whatever she's doing – she won't find anything she's not permitted to see – but only to make it clear that he was aware of her being up and snooping around.

He feels weary, not only from being woken so rudely after only about five hours' sleep, but from the sheer pressure he's under. He may be the one out of the pair of them in the house who is in the know, to a degree, but it's still far from easy to play a part like this.

Not for the first time, he tells himself he would give anything to go back in time and turn down the offer of this so-called job.

He wonders what Jen's next move will be. She has made it through one whole day, so far, although quite a considerable chunk of that was spent sleeping. He doesn't blame her – if he was being mentally tortured he would much rather be unconscious, too. He can tell she doesn't really believe anything he's told her, but there have been moments when he's seen real fear in her eyes, and he can't tell whether it's fear of believing what he says or fear of never getting away from him, or from this place that he himself detests.

Given her lack of options for getting off the island, and the fact that she now must assume she has no allies here, he struggles to imagine what she could possibly try next. His remit, for the moment, is still to comply with anything she asks, although he knows that if her demands were to veer into unacceptable territory he would be advised accordingly.

She was behaving a little suspiciously in the living room, but Alex reminds himself that she can't even access the laptop without the password, and that its contents pose no threat. He wonders if she's found the photos yet. They're so frighteningly well-produced that even he almost believed that he'd actually been there, making those poses, when he saw them for the first time. He hasn't seen the originals, of course, but he suspects the images of the woman, at least, came from actual, genuine snapshots of her life.

In all of the photos, she is, of course, smiling, and, to Alex, she looks genuinely happy. Seeing her face radiate so much joy made him feel guilty and uncomfortable at seeing his own face dropped into snapshots depicting events he didn't even witness.

If she did see the photos, she didn't show any signs that they have had any major impact on her. In fact, aside from behaving in a way he can only describe as shifty, she was probably as calm as he's seen her, so far. She made it absolutely clear that she just wanted to be left alone, and out of sheer curiosity he wants to know what she's currently getting up to in there.

His eyes feel heavy, and he lets them close for a few seconds. He knows that if – or when – he's needed, he will be called upon.

24

The laptop, as I suspected, is secured with a password. I rest my chin on my fist, wishing I was some kind of mastermind hacker, capable of decrypting the password and delving deep into the hard drive, to search for answers. I wrack my brains, trying to think what the password could possibly be, hoping for a flash of inspiration. This is probably Jamie's work laptop, so would he have set the password as something connected to his research? I scan some of the paperwork that I found in the drawer, but I give up after a couple of seconds when I realise there are infinite possibilities, and I don't have a chance in hell of simply making a lucky guess. No, the laptop is a dead end, I realise. Or is it? I remember that there is a *Switch User* option, and manage to log in as a guest user, which does not require me to enter a password.

The background, when the home page boots up, is a photo of a beach at sunset, and I'm thankful that I'm not being forced to look at another fake photo of Jamie and I.

I try to connect to the Internet, but even as I click on the little icon in the left-hand corner I know it's pointless. What was I expecting? There's no Wi-Fi here! It's like I've stepped back in time, to the land that technology forgot, and good taste completely bypassed, judging by the deeply depressing décor in this house.

Whatever Jamie uses the laptop for must not require Internet access. Report writing, maybe? I suppose he could do that offline.

All thoughts of me accessing the internet at the village hall were aborted yesterday. After coming face to face with more fellow island-dwellers in the way that I did, all

I wanted to do was get back to the house. Still reeling from the events at the shop, and the sham phone conversation I had with the woman who claimed to be my mother, I could find neither the energy nor the motivation to go back to the hall to check the validity of Jamie's claim that there is actual genuine connectivity here.

He told me that the hall is open to the public only between the hours of midday and two o'clock at this time of the year, since it's out of season. I would love to believe that, in season, this place turns into a much more current millennium version of itself, but my imagination doesn't stretch that far.

I click into folders, finding more photos that make my heart sink. Jamie and I in New Zealand, posing outside the Auckland ice bar, wearing newly-purchased bar merchandise. Jamie and I in Paris, standing under the Eiffel Tower, grinning like idiots in our Frank Spencer-esque berets. Jamie and I in Tenerife, both of us embarrassingly, irresponsibly sunburnt, having woefully underestimated the power of the late September sun. Except Jamie didn't go to any of those places with me. Those photos are all from trips that I went on with my ex, Steven, with whom I was in a relationship for four years. Call it sentimentality, or sheer stupidity, but I've never had the heart to just get rid of all the photos that survived beyond the end of our relationship. I keep them stored in an *Archive* folder on my laptop, and in the five years since Steven and I broke up, I think I've felt compelled to look through those photos only once.

I accidentally bumped into Steven, quite literally, in the supermarket, about a year ago. I was hovering around one end of the magazine aisle, my gaze falling a little longer than strictly appropriate on the cover of *Men's Health* magazine due to the appeal of Ryan Reynolds' impressive top half, just as Steven was turning into the aisle, and we collided. We literally crashed into each other, like the two protagonists in a cheesy romantic movie. Once we had gotten over the initial mortification, we had a chat that was very brief, perfectly civil, and carefully hedged within the boundaries of banal small talk, the kind you might exchange with a neighbour, or a work colleague from several years and jobs ago that you had all but forgotten existed.

It was a strange sensation, considering that I hadn't given Steven a second thought for goodness knows how long, but bumping into him left me feeling horribly unsettled for the rest of that day.

I remember now that I booted up my laptop that evening, pretending to myself that my reason for doing so was to browse for some new music (and perhaps to steal a read of that *Men's Health* cover story), but knowing full well that I was deceiving myself.

I probably did download a tune or two, but I also spent the best part of an hour mournfully clicking through that archived collection, daring to wonder what might have been, had we made a success of our relationship. Sensibly, no alcohol was involved, otherwise what would have been would not have been pretty.

By the time I woke up the next morning, those feelings were resigned to the archives again, but I still didn't feel ready to get rid of the evidence of those memories. And now, Jamie has gone and stolen them, violated them, and inserted himself artificially into my past. That makes me exorbitantly angry, but it also intensifies my freak-out level, which I had been trying so hard to keep under control.

I try to put my resurging panic on the back burner and continue clicking through the files that are stored here in the 'Guest user' area of this computer. There is nothing that stands out as being useful to me. There are plenty of music files, and the tracks are ones which could well have been plucked from my own iTunes library. That makes sense: since Jamie has gone to the trouble of hacking into my laptop, he has obviously stolen all the things that he must know I will recognise. The frail sense of victory that I felt a few moments ago at being able to explore this computer while he is unaware has faded, and it strikes me that if I had asked, he probably would have told me to 'feel free'.

There is a CV here, in the name of Jennifer Mayhew. I skim-read it and find that it contains the details of my supposed qualifications and experience as a translator of literary works. I have a degree, according to this file, and my specialism is translating works of fiction from Spanish into English. As much as that all sounds very impressive, and I wouldn't necessarily mind being able to take credit for those things, the document itself is a work of fiction. Aside from knowing how to order limited food items and ask how much things cost when I go on holiday to Spanish-speaking destinations, my skills in the area fall woefully short. And as far as the Bachelor of Arts degree from the University of Glasgow is concerned, again, I wouldn't be opposed to that being true, but it is categorically, unfortunately, not. University life and I did not go well together, and my time spent there was not a period of my life that I like to dwell on.

I focus my attention back to the CV and note that a home address is listed at the top. Not on Carn, but in Glasgow. At least, in an area with a 'G' prefix in the post code, which means it must lie within the Glasgow boundary.

There are some telephone numbers listed which don't strike any chords with me, and some blurb relating to 'Jennifer's' hobbies and interests, which would more likely roll off the tongue of a beauty pageant contestant than be found on a so-called professional's CV.

I search a few more folders, but there is nothing else worth bothering with. Clearly, what I need, in order to make any kind of progress, is Internet access. Today being Sunday, however, the day when apparently everything is on complete, as opposed to partial, shutdown means that's not going to happen. I don't know that I'm entirely convinced about Jamie's assertion that the ferry doesn't operate on a Sunday, or, indeed, this time of year. Surely it has to be a year-round service, or as close to it as possible? If I had access to the Internet I could, presumably, find the answer to this question, but I'm so isolated in my ignorance here. How did we ever survive before the invention of the World Wide Web?

Perhaps, I could find the ferry terminal on my own, I think, trying to place confidence in my own ingenuity. Perhaps, there will even be someone there, someone whom I can ask for help. The main snag with that idea is that I have no money to buy a ticket. Although, surely, if I can make it there, and explain to the people who operate the ferry what's happened to me, they would take me to the mainland, to the police, wouldn't they? As long as they are not also Jamie's partners in crime.

I can feel ideas budding inside my head. I start to make notes, formulating plans. Now that I think about it, Plan A should really be to find the payphone again, and phone the police. I will need to make sure that I keep calm this time, and explain everything to them in such a way that doesn't have them thinking I'm just the unhinged, delirious person that Jamie has tried to make me believe that I am. Right, so that is most definitely Plan A. But what will I do if there's something wrong with the phone?

In that case, Plan B will have to be to find the ferry port. Alone? But how will I know which direction to head for? I tap the pen against my forehead, urging myself to think clearly. This island can't be all that huge, I hope, given that hardly anyone lives here. And there's only one village, so Jamie says – the one we went to yesterday, although a shop, a village hall that opens for two hours a day and a phone box are not my idea of a village. The ferry terminal can't be that far, I tell myself. I'm willing to give it a try, anyway, and see what I can find.

If I make it onto the ferry, I imagine they would let me make a call to the police from there. They must have means to contact the police, or some kind of emergency service, while they're crossing, mustn't they? Does the Coast Guard actually exist in real life, or only in movies?

I'm scribbling frantically, making note of all the additional factors I need to be mindful of. How will I be able to get dressed, and leave the house, without waking Jamie? What if the phone is out of use, and I get lost, looking for the ferry port? What if there really is no ferry service, and no one else around, and I have to come back here, with my head hung in shame, following *another* failed escape attempt?

My stomach grumbles loudly, in protest at the fact I haven't eaten anything since yesterday afternoon. Jamie made some boiled eggs on toast for me that I barely nibbled at, because I was too traumatised to eat. I realise that's one more thing I'll have to try to do without disturbing Jamie – have breakfast. This is nowhere near the normal time that I'd be thinking about breakfast on a Sunday (usually I'm lucky if I see breakfast – Sunday brunch is much more in keeping with my routine), but all of a sudden I'm ravenously hungry, and no matter how keen I am to get going and execute my plans, I am in desperate need of substantial fuel to keep me going throughout my mission. Besides, Jamie only went back to bed a few moments ago, so I should probably give him a chance to get back to sleep again before I attempt my getaway.

I shut down the laptop and take a peek into the third drawer of the desk – the one I didn't have a chance to examine before Jamie appeared, earlier. This appears to be the drawer where official documents are stored. There are bank statements, and utility bills in Jamie's name – his surname is Baxter, I discover. There is a registration document for a vehicle,

101

again in Jamie's name, showing an address in Glasgow that's completely unfamiliar, even the post code.

Apparently, there are no cars allowed on this island – there are certainly no roads to speak of, that I've seen – so if Jamie still owns this car, a red Renault Clio, then it must be parked or locked away somewhere in Glasgow.

I make a note of the address on the document, resolving to give it to the police when I get to talk to them in case it's useful. It's not a part of Glasgow that I know of, but if I were to take a guess judging by the post code, I would estimate it's on the other side of the city, to the east. It's not even an educated guess, but the fact that I have no idea where it is gives me some comfort that when this is all over, and I'm back home in my own home, there shouldn't be much chance of me accidentally running into this monster again, if he should ever be set free.

Surely, if he ever did get out to roam the streets again, I would be able to have him banned from ever coming near me, wouldn't I? I don't know much about how restraining orders usually work, but when this is all over I'll be insisting that he's forbidden from coming within a mile of me, no matter how far away he might live!

There are some more bills in the drawer, and ultimately nothing of any great usefulness, it seems. But then, I uncover two passports.

I open the first one, and see Jamie's blank, expressionless face staring back at me. A chill runs down my spine – bizarrely, he looks more frightening in the photo than he does in real life. My hands tremble slightly as I open the second passport at the photo page. Although I've made a promise to myself not to doubt my mental strength, I'm afraid of what I might see when I open this document. Could he have forged my passport? Of course, it can be done, I know that, but would he really go that far?

I squeeze my eyes shut, like a child anticipating a surprise, but what I see when I open them is far from pleasant. Name: Jennifer Mayhew. Born: twenty-ninth of July nineteen eighty-three. Place of birth: Glasgow. Nationality: British. Face: mine.

My own face. In the very same passport photo that I remember sitting stiffly, awkwardly for, five years ago, which is exactly when this passport was issued, if I'm to believe what's staring me in the face.

How could he do this? He must have taken my own passport, and made a doctored copy, but how? Why? When? Forging photos is one thing, but creating an entirely false passport? Who the hell is this man?

I can't even allow myself to think about him being in my house, without me knowing.

'It's not true. It's not true. It's fake. It's fake.' I repeat the words over and over, quietly, like some kind of mantra.

I stash everything back in the drawer and gather together all the notes I've made; my plan. I'm going to eat something, out of sheer necessity, and then I'm going to get the hell away from this man, for good!

25

DCI Jackson arrives at the station to learn that there is nothing particularly helpful or fruitful amongst the results of the initial checks that have been ticked off.

Natalie Byron has not passed through any of the hospitals or police stations in the city, and the search has been widened to the whole of the UK, in light of the fact that she could have travelled the length and breadth of the kingdom several times over in the time since anyone last heard from her.

Her call and text histories are being sifted through with a fine-tooth comb, but to date there have been no red flags, no cries of 'Boss, you're going to want to see this,' from any of his team.

DNA samples from her hairbrush are being checked against hairs found in the bed, as well as the familial samples which were collected as a matter of priority. Fingerprints were pulled from the house, and results are pending.

In keeping with the original assumption that there was no violent altercation in the property, forensic officers failed to uncover any blood evidence, either visible or concealed.

The family members, with the exception of a sister and brother who are both out of the country on holiday, have been questioned to within a whisker of their patience limits. Three of the five occupants of the houses in her street have been interviewed, none of the enquiries as yet yielding any results of significance.

Complicity and culpability of relatives should never be ruled out, Jackson knows only too well, especially at this early stage in the game, but he doesn't see any benefit in devoting too many man hours to poring over their statements again. His gut instinct is telling him that none of them know any more than they've let on already.

They offered up the names of two close friends but were unable to confirm exact addresses for them, only street names. The police will find them, and Jackson's team will interview them in the next few hours, but the not-quite boyfriend that Natalie arranged to meet is still Jackson's number one priority.

Her mother wasn't able to confirm whether the date that was arranged had actually taken place, but a message sent from Natalie's phone at 23:19 suggests that it most certainly did. Her disclosure that she had made it home safely and that she had enjoyed herself was answered with a similar reply less than a minute later, from her suitor confirming that he had enjoyed the evening, too, and was looking forward to them meeting up again. Did they make a decision thereafter to meet up again sooner rather than later, and go gallivanting God knows where?

Unless further texts or calls arranging such a plan were erased later, the phone holds no evidence of any exchange that would imply that an agreement of that nature was made. A deep dive on the records will confirm whether there was any additional contact, but assuming that there wasn't, Natalie's state of mind and her movements beyond eleven-twenty remain a grey area.

The state of mind angle is a decent one to pursue, Jackson decides, progressing leads in his head. Hopefully, someone within her inner circle will be able – and willing – to breathe life into the theory that he continues to nurse: that Natalie could well be taking a sabbatical from her life.

Close to sixty hours have now passed since that last message was sent, and if Kevin Lowell isn't on a jaunt with the AWOL woman and can corroborate what Gillian Byron believes to be the case, then just short of sixty hours have passed since Natalie was last seen. She hasn't accessed any

105

of her social media accounts during that time, nor either of her bank accounts. Jackson suspected as much regarding the cash, given the discovery of the purse in the house.

Her car, like her keys, were left behind. Abduction? The investigation, naturally, must consider it as a possibility, but Jackson doesn't yet want to cave to his instinct to believe in the worst-case scenario. Not until such time as every other explanation has been exhausted and disregarded.

Nonetheless, he paints pictures of hypothetical forceful appropriation in his head, assessing them for likelihood.

No signs of forced entry into the property means that either she invited her abductor in, or she was abducted from another location. Her message puts her at home shortly after eleven, and her mobile phone provider should be able to confirm or deny that at least the phone itself was there when the message was sent. If it was, it's reasonable to assume that she was at home shortly before midnight, and then she failed to turn up for work at eight o'clock the following morning. If she left the house intending to go to work, she did so without taking her keys or her mobile phone, but took several of her other earthly belongings with her. Unlikely.

So, scenario A: she invited the perpetrator into her home. Who? Did she invite Kevin Lowell home with her? If so, why would they exchange those messages to one another?

Or did he perhaps follow her home? Did he wait for her to send the message confirming she was safe, then knock on the door and say, 'Surprise!'

And if not him, who would she open her door to at that time of night, unannounced?

The location of the house, Jackson grudgingly acknowledges, could provide a relatively easy and undetected getaway, if someone were so inclined. It is the last in a row of detached properties, and with a five-feet tall hedge surrounding the garden on all sides; goings-on inside would not be easily noticed by anyone around, at

106

least not at street level. There is a narrow, poorly-lit lane to the east of Natalie's home which leads to an underground tunnel connecting her street to the main road, approximately five minutes' walk from her front door. To the north of the property is the railway line that serves Glasgow to the east and all the way up to the highlands to the west, and a little further east from Natalie's property is the rear entrance to an industrial park. The entrance serves pedestrians and cyclists only, owing to the three stone bollards which prevent vehicular access.

CCTV coverage in the area is woefully spartan, but if she arrived home by train that night, they should at least be able to place her at Dalmuir station, and to check whether she was alone when she was there. From the station, the walk to her address would take in the region of ten minutes, or fifteen at the most if factoring in heels and/or a relaxed gait. Jackson makes a note to check with local taxi companies in case she baulked at the thought of the half-mile journey on foot and flagged one down. It is unlikely and might have taken longer for her to catch a cab than to cover the distance herself, but it's worth checking out. The street is not a major thoroughfare, and traffic would have been minimal at that time of night, so perhaps one of the neighbours who have not yet been interviewed will recall seeing or hearing a car.

There is little in the way of nightlife in the area, but there would have been two or three fast food takeaway joints open within a few hundred yards' walk, and enquiries will be made to each of them as to whether she popped in, when they re-open for the day in a matter of hours.

'Any joy on tracking down this Lowell?' Jackson asks of Detective Constable Graeme Nixon, his second in command on this case, who is peering into his computer screen, deep in concentration.

'Yes, sir,' Nixon replies, 'I was just waiting for you to come in. Thought you'd want to come with me.'

Jackson nods his agreement. 'Absolutely,' he says. 'Let's go.'

He's heard what Gillian Byron had to say about this Kevin Lowell: that he's an ex-boyfriend of Natalie's, that she and her husband found him to be agreeable when they met him, and understandably changed their opinion of him when he broke up with their daughter under a cloud of mystery. Apparently, however, Gillian Byron was at pains to stress that she is certain that this guy has no involvement in whatever has happened with Natalie.

Jackson will reserve judgement until he has interviewed the guy, assuming that he's at home and not accompanying Natalie on a jolly around the home nations. Decent guy or not, Kevin Lowell is very possibly the last person to have seen Natalie, and that makes him the prime suspect.

26

Gillian Byron hasn't slept a wink all night. She has barely closed her eyes since it became apparent that something wasn't right, around Friday afternoon.

There's a pattern, a routine to Natalie's interaction. For the most part, Gillian could set her watch by Natalie's morning text messages, which arrive unfailingly around the ten o'clock mark.

Gillian could count on the fingers of one hand the number of times that midday has come and gone without so much as a, *Hi Mum. How are you?* And those times would have been explained away by a forgotten phone, or a training course or such like. But the message or the call always arrives, eventually. But there was something different about Friday.

Call it sixth sense, call it women's intuition, call it 'a mother just knows'. Gillian knew there was something odd about the fact that she was about to head into a three o'clock meeting and she still hadn't heard from her daughter. Natalie doesn't often forget her phone, but when she does, she'll call from her work phone, just to let Gillian know. Gillian checked with the girls in the office, just in case she'd missed it and they had taken a message, but none of them had spoken to Natalie. She had tried to focus on her meeting, to put the feeling of unease on the back burner, but it persisted.

'Text her,' Iain had advised, when both he and Gillian had returned home from work without hearing a word, puzzled as to why Gillian hadn't just done so already.

'You know I don't like to when she's at work,' she'd insisted, but by five-thirty Natalie should have finished and be heading home.

'Maybe she's on a training course or something,' Iain offered. 'Did she mention anything?'

'No,' Gillian answered. Natalie hadn't mentioned anything. Not about work, anyway. Why hadn't Gillian just told Iain about the business with Kevin? Natalie hadn't explicitly asked her mother to keep it under wraps, but both women had a fair idea of what Iain's reaction was likely to be, and as it turned out, Gillian had been far more understanding about her decision to give Kevin another chance than Iain had. But then, he was dealing with the news at the worst possible time, she conceded, feeling guilty again. If Natalie was safe and sound at home, Iain probably wouldn't have had such strong feelings about the subject.

'She would have called or texted on a break, or her lunch hour,' Gillian insisted.

'Well, maybe she left her phone in the house,' Iain offered, exhausting all the obvious explanations.

Gillian shook her head. 'She would have called,' she told him. 'She would have used another phone. I'm telling you, Iain, something's not right.'

Still not entirely convinced of the need, following several unanswered calls and text messages, Iain had agreed to carry out a reconnaissance mission on Friday evening to check whether Natalie was, in fact, at home. He returned to report that there were no visible signs of life, and that he was standing by his original hypothesis that she had left her phone at home, and had simply gone out after work. All would be right by the morning, he assured his wife. Natalie would call, or come round to the house, apologetic about causing any worry.

By ten-thirty on Saturday morning his certainty had faded and his level of concern echoed that of his wife, who had remained unconvinced by his explanation. He drove the ten minutes to Natalie's home and this time, he let himself in when there was still no reply to his knock on the door.

Everything that has happened since then has been surreal. Gillian feels like she's in a daze, enveloped in a fog that won't lift until she hears Natalie's voice again.

Trying to sleep is pointless. She glances at Iain, watching the steady rise and fall of his chest. She envies his ability to switch off, to give in to the exhaustion. As she watches him, she feels anger and resentment bubbling inside her. How can he possibly sleep so soundly when his daughter is missing? Doesn't he care the way she does? Instantly she feels remorseful for thinking such a thing. Of course, Iain cares. He's been like a cat on a hot tin roof, pacing back and forth, desperate for any new, untried task that will keep him busy and make him feel like he's doing something.

He is the one doing the right thing, Gillian concedes. It will do no-one any good if they run themselves into the ground through lack of sleep and constant worrying. Iain has always been the pragmatic one in their partnership, and that is what is needed right now. He is terrified of what might have happened to Natalie, of course he is, but his default mode is to act. To search, and ask questions, and do whatever it takes to find her and bring her home. Panicking, and staying awake all night concocting worst-case scenarios will not achieve anything, is what he would tell her if he woke up at this moment and found her doing just that.

What Iain wants to do is go and track down Kevin, of course, but Gillian won't allow it. She would wager her house on the fact that Kevin has nothing to do with Natalie's disappearance. He's immature, and possibly not the ideal boyfriend in light of how he treated Natalie a year ago, but he's not a threat, Gillian is certain of it. And if Iain were to go storming round to his house, interrogating him and God knows what else, well, it would only end in disaster. The last thing they all need is for Iain's temper, fuelled by frustration, to land him in a police cell.

Besides, the police are quite possibly questioning him

right now. They've already confirmed that Natalie sent a message confirming she had arrived home on Thursday night. So, what happened after that?

Gillian checks the time and decides she can't stay in bed any longer. She wonders if it's too early to call the police and ask for an update. Her voice of reason tells her that someone from the force would have called them, or come around, if there had been any developments, but like Iain, she needs to feel as though she is doing something, even if that something is chasing up the people who are currently devoting their waking hours to tracing her daughter. Even if it's just to remind them that she and her family are in pain, waiting, with bated breath, for news of any progress that might be made with the case.

She climbs out of bed, taking care not to disturb Iain, and pulls on her fleece dressing gown, hugging it tight around her body. She makes her way quietly downstairs, and adjusts the central heating dial at the bottom, waking the boiler from its slumber.

In the living room, photographs of Natalie remain scattered on the coffee table. Gillian picks up one taken probably two decades ago, when the Byron family included two larger than life German Shepherds, both females, called Lily and Lola.

Natalie, never more content than when she was surrounded by those dogs, is smiling at the camera, with her left arm around Lily and her right around Lola. Gillian picks up the photo, kisses it gently, and holds it close to her chest, sobbing quietly.

Iain stands in the doorway, willing his heartbeat to return to normal in the wake of finding Gillian gone from the bed when he woke with a start. She clearly is unaware of his presence, or she doesn't want to break from her reverie.

He goes to enter the living room, but hesitates. His instinct is to go to his wife, and hold her, and offer words of comfort. But he has none.

27

Trying to make breakfast without making any noise is extremely difficult, if not impossible. I've been back and forth over this decision, wondering whether breakfast is absolutely necessary, but the conclusion I've come to is that there is no way I can even contemplate embarking on my mission without food.

Who knows how long it might be before the police can get here, or a ferry appears, to take me back to safety (not to mention the twenty-first century)? And there's little or no chance that I'll be able to source any food from the village, even if I manage to snaffle some cash that Jamie might have left lying around. Seeing as the shop apparently only opens for a total of four hours a day during the week, it would be a real turn up for the books if it were to be open and ready for business at seven o'clock on a Sunday morning. I think it's safe to assume that it won't be. In any case, I don't particularly want to lay eyes on Bessie again if I can avoid it.

I'm going to take the phone that I found in the drawer with me, and try calling the police with it, as well as any other numbers I might be able to muster up from the dark recesses of my brain. If the mobile doesn't work, I'm sure you can call the emergency services for free from public phone boxes, so I'm banking on being able to get through to someone who can help me, by any means necessary.

I closed the door to the kitchen when I came in here, and hopefully it's far enough away from the bedroom that Jamie won't be able to hear, but the eighties-style kettle is the noisiest small appliance I've ever come across. It also may be the slowest, and I've been hopping impatiently from one foot to the other, cajoling it to heat up quicker. What's that saying? '*A watched pot never boils.*' Well, this little trooper has finally huffed and puffed its way to boiling the water, and I've made myself a steaming hot cup of tea – exactly the way I like it. I found some wholemeal bread and some strawberry jam in one of the cupboards, and have made myself four slices of toast, which should afford me sufficient fuel for a few hours, I hope.

There is no sign of Jamie getting back up again, thankfully, but as I shove toast down my throat at a rate which cannot be conducive to a healthy digestion process, I feel under pressure to get out of here as soon as possible. There is still the small matter of how to retrieve some clothes from the bedroom to contend with, but I'll handle that predicament better once I've had some food. The toast tastes like cardboard, in spite of the sweetness of the jam, because I'm so tense and anxious. Even the few sips of tea that I take to try to aid it going down a little easier offer no help or comfort. I wish I had a fast-forward button that I could use to skip past all the difficult parts of my plan and transport me to the business end, where I am tearfully reunited with my family. The thought of that happy event is what is keeping me focused, even though unearthing the doctored version of my passport threw me for a moment. Yesterday, a discovery like that would have left me in complete disarray, but I'm feeling stronger today; more resolute, and more certain than ever that this is all an elaborate and deeply disturbing hoax.

I swallow the last of the toast, and gulp down the tea, and I'm ready to go. There is only one problem: I'm dressed in jammies. If I head for the ferry port wearing only pyjamas and running trainers, I fear that my chances of being taken seriously will be diminished somewhat. On the other hand, maybe it would add some credibility to my story? If I were to explain that I had to leave at the first chance I got, hence the unconventional outfit, would that make them more likely to believe me?

I take a peek out of the window and decide that I don't want to take my chances out in the wild-looking weather that seems to have struck the island overnight. The last thing I need is to fall victim to hypothermia. I'm going to have to use stealth, and cunning, to retrieve proper clothing without waking Jamie, but I believe I can do it.

There are relatively loud snoring noises coming from the bedroom, which heartens me, as I take it as a sign that Jamie is sleeping deeply, and unlikely to be easily woken. I peek into the room, and see him sprawled on his front, looking like he is out for the count. I quickly but quietly grab the jeans that I wore yesterday, and a long-sleeved top from the drawer. My trainers are at the front door, where I left them, and my jacket is hanging on a hook in the hallway, so all I need now is some clean underwear and I'm all set. I pick some up from the top drawer, and sneak back out of the bedroom, releasing the breath that I've been holding since I entered the room.

I hate to have to sacrifice hygiene, but I don't think it's wise to delay any further, and risk being found out mid-wash, so I hastily put on the clean clothes and hope I don't smell too offensive, for the sake of anyone who may end up in close confinement with me.

I already brushed my teeth before heading into the kitchen to make breakfast – that, I will not compromise on – so at least I don't feel totally inhuman.

I grab the mobile phone from the living room, check that I have all my notes, and rummage around in the pockets of Jamie's jeans, hoping to find some money. It feels wrong, and I feel guilty, but then I remember the injustice of what he has inflicted on me, and I feel wholly vindicated. I find a few pounds worth of change, and although it's not ideal by any stretch of the imagination, I think my haul of supplies should go some way to helping me to succeed. I do a quick check of what I'm taking with me: phone, notes, money. What else can I take? Not the passport – that would be counter-productive. Not the photos, nor the laptop either – those would only cast doubt over my version of events. No, I think I'm good to go.

I creep down the hallway, on tiptoe, and put on my trainers as noiselessly as possible. I retrieve my jacket from the hook, but I can afford to wait until I'm outside before I put it on. I take a look back down the hallway, and see that, still, the coast is clear. I open the front door, and thankfully it doesn't make any squeals of protest, the way my own front door at home does. Initially, I'm not going to bother about closing it behind me, but then I remember that it will likely bang shut from the force of the wind if I don't, so I carefully ease it back to where it was.

A gust of wind batters my face as I take the first step outside, but I'm expecting it this time, getting used to it, and whereas I would normally be cursing the typical Scottish weather, I feel more grateful than I've ever been to have my breath taken away by a gale force gust. I put on my jacket, and with one last look behind me, I set off, breaking into a jog after the first few paces, taking my first few steps towards freedom.

The tale of *Hansel and Gretel* is what is going through my mind as I settle into a steady-paced jog. I wolfed down breakfast, and I realise I may need to conserve energy for a potentially taxing day ahead, so after my initial exuberance when I first tasted freedom, I've decided I should keep my pace under control.

I wish I'd had some means to mark out the route we took yesterday, just like those two crafty kids did in the fairy tale, so that I wouldn't have to waste any time trying to figure out how to get back to the phone box. This island may have only a handful of occupants, but in the grand scheme of things it's by no means as tiny an area as I would like.

116

I thought I remembered the way and the amount of time to the phone box yesterday, but since all I can see at the moment are mountains, which naturally all look pretty much the same as each other, I can't be sure I'm on the right course. I'm starting to think I should have brought a slice or two of bread with me, so that I could leave a trail which would guide me back to the house.

Going back there, to where Jamie is, is absolutely the last thing I want to do, but if, somehow, I can't call the police, and there really is no ferry service, what will I do then? My only option would be to try knocking on the doors of any of the other houses in the village, but since Bessie and Davie are clearly in on Jamie's plot to make me think I'm Jen, with diminished mental capacity, I can't be sure that I would be any safer with anyone else I might find than I am with him.

I listen to the sound of my feet pounding the harsh, rocky earth beneath them, and I'm transported back to the last time I went running outside, at home, about two weeks ago. I'd forgotten to take my headphones with me, and when I realised I would have to rely on nothing but my own thoughts to distract me from the physical discomfort, I thought that would be game over. Barely having made it through my five-minute warm-up, I was prepared to write off that day's session altogether. Somehow, though, I actually managed to jog for a full three kilometres without stopping – something I hadn't achieved in about a year, since that time I participated in a ten-kilometre race (I finished, without being disqualified for slowness. Other than that, the less said about my performance that day, the better).

I counted my paces, sang songs in my head, tried to calculate my average speed as I ran, and before I knew it, my ever-so-clever little smart phone was vibrating and figuratively high-fiving me on achieving my goal. Of course, I'm well aware that three kilometres is far from an impressive distance, and I'm not going to be declaring

117

myself *one to watch* for the next Olympic Games any time soon, but to me it felt like an achievement worthy of *Rocky's* celebratory run up those famous steps, and I had to restrain myself from trying to recreate that moment on the steps of my local library.

Running without having music to take my mind off the fatigue and inevitable pain had been difficult, but also strangely liberating. Being at one with my own thoughts had led me to dig deep, and to find some strength and stamina from somewhere, to keep going. I take heart from that memory now, as my lungs start to remind me that I'm not what you would call an accomplished athlete.

I guess that I've been out of the house for about five minutes now, and I chance a look behind me, just to make sure that Jamie hasn't been following me all the way. There is no-one there. In fact, there is not much of anything at all around me.

I slow down to a fast walk and try in earnest to establish which course I should follow in order to get back to the relative civilisation of the little village we ventured into yesterday. As if being removed from my home against my will wasn't bad enough, why on earth did he have to bring me to a place where the notion of the modern life that I'm used to is like something out of a George Orwell novel? I think I'm able to answer my own question: to keep me hidden.

It's quite genius, actually, I now start to realise – evil genius. How would anyone ever find me here? Unless Jamie really did leave a Hansel and Gretel-like trail of clues to follow, I can't imagine how the police (or anyone else who may be looking for me) could possibly track me down here.

I slow down even further, suddenly struggling for breath. I've realised that I'm pinning all my hopes on being able to talk to the police, and having them take my plight seriously, and come here and rescue me. I've been so focused on that being my most likely-to-work plan that I hadn't really considered what might happen if it actually doesn't work out.

The reality is, if I can't contact the police, or my family, or anyone else who might be able to save me from this nightmare, then I could be stuck here, forever. The thought of it makes me suddenly feel like I'm going to be sick, and I lean forward, placing my hands on my thighs as I take deep, heaving breaths.

28

Alex is fully awake now, having been forcibly woken for the second time, this morning. This time the noise blasted through the earpiece was even louder, and more distressing than the first, and he can still hear a ringing in his ears. The earpiece is so uncomfortable; he would give anything to leave it out for a while, but that would not be acceptable, he knows. He did try to stay awake, after his half-hearted attempt at an intervention in the living room earlier, but despite his best efforts, clearly, he dosed off again, and was in a deep sleep within minutes.

He's been told that Jen is no longer in the house. His initial reaction was to panic, but they explained there is no cause for alarm at the moment; *they* have the situation under control. This is actually good, he thinks to himself, as he fills the kettle with cold water. He likes the prospect of having some more time on his own, just to gather his thoughts, without having to be Jamie, without having to act.

His instructions are to sit tight, until further notice. They told him he probably won't be needed for an hour or so, so he plans to make himself some breakfast and a full pot of tea, and simply relax for a while. If it's possible to relax, that is.

He sits down at the kitchen table as he waits for the kettle to boil, and rubs the back of his neck, trying to undo some of the knots of tension that have appeared over the course of the last few days. Maybe he's not cut out for this, after all, he thinks. He made the decision to enter into this on the spur of the moment, and he knows he didn't think it through properly. It may be the fatigue of the last seventy-two hours catching up with him, but now he can't rid his mind of the little voice screaming 'Don't do it!' when he came to sign the papers. Why didn't he pay more heed to that voice? Things are always so much clearer with the benefit of hindsight, and this is the perfect example of that.

He still doesn't know why they chose him. Surely, he wasn't the only one taken in by their ad? He's his own harshest critic, but even allowing for a certain amount of natural self-deprecation, he knows that as actors go, he's mediocre at best. He really should have given up a long time ago, and started looking for a proper job, and a career to boot, but acting is all he has ever wanted to do.

In reality, minor parts in local theatre and some truly uninspiring roles as an extra in a long-running television series don't pay the bills for long, and certainly don't open doors to the fame and fortune that he always dreamt of. On the odd occasion that he's asked to state his occupation for any reason, he regretfully concedes that jotting down *Actor* is probably something of an overstatement.

This role just seemed like it would be so perfect for him, when he first saw the advert. Why on earth didn't it occur to him at the time that it was just too good to be true? He's made some stupid mistakes, reckless decisions in his life, to date, but this one truly takes the biscuit. At least, if there's any consolation, so far, they've allowed him to be himself – albeit speaking their words – on occasion. He hopes it will remain that way. Whatever else he is – gullible, foolish, a little impulsive – essentially, he's a good guy. He really doesn't want to have to compromise that.

29

I don't think I've ever had a full-blown panic attack before, but I may have just experienced my first taste. I'm feeling slightly better now, after a couple of minutes, but for an instant there I feared that I might actually pass out or have a heart attack. The pains in my chest were very real, and very scary, but since I'm still conscious and the symptoms are subsiding, I'm starting to believe that I'm going to be alright.

I'm trying to regulate my breathing by taking deep, exaggerated breaths, and I'm giving myself yet another little pep-talk inside my head. I still feel a little nauseous, and I seem to have developed a slight tremble in my hands, but I'm determined not to let this thing get the better of me. In fact, I'm feeling determined not to let anything get the better of me.

I tell myself not to be silly; that of course I'm going to make it home, back to my family, and friends, and even my middle-of-the-road job. What could possibly prevent me from contacting the police? I already know that the payphone works – I used it yesterday. This doesn't strike me as the kind of community where vandalism is rife, so there shouldn't be any reason why the phone won't still be in perfect working order. I have coins, if needed, and it's not like I've forgotten the number for the emergency services!

I've stacked up enough evidence to suggest that I can succeed. All I need to do is find the phone, and everything will be alright, then. I'll be on my way to putting this whole nightmare behind me.

I hope the police will be able to come and get me today,

but even if I did have to stay put here, for one more night, I'm sure I could deal with Jamie for a few more hours, as long as I don't do anything to tip him off about my impending rescue.

I look up to the sky and take in a lungful of fresh air – probably the freshest, least-polluted air I've ever breathed in my life. There isn't much about this island that appeals to me, but not having to breathe in all the toxins and germs that inhabit city air is a positive in an ocean of negatives. I test out my legs, by taking a few tentative steps, and thankfully, they're back in play. I think I'll walk the rest of the way, just in case trying to run causes me to have a relapse. The phone box can't be far.

30

Any other Saturday night, Gemma and Mark would likely still be out at this time, enjoying a few drinks with friends and, more importantly, their friends' adorable pug, Daisy. The fact that they are on holiday, in Los Angeles of all places, makes it all the more ridiculous that they had already been in bed for the best part of two hours. They have a flight to catch at the crack of dawn, and although they debated toughing it out and staying up all night, in the end they opted to *try* and get some sleep. Not that Gemma is doing any sleeping.

Mark has dozed off, but her eyes are wide open, her mind wide awake. Mark hadn't initially been in favour of ditching their long-awaited trip of a lifetime and flying home at the earliest opportunity, but Gemma had insisted, and they were booked on the six o'clock departure. How could they stay here and enjoy themselves in the sun when her sister was missing? How could Mark even contemplate such a thing? He hadn't grumbled much since the flight had been booked, to his credit; he seemed to have accepted that there was no choice: they have to go home.

Gemma turns to her left, feeling her pillow wet with tears that she hadn't noticed were falling. She thinks of the journey to come, the torture of the flight during which she will be able to receive no news, either good or bad. She admonishes herself for even allowing the possibility of the bad, but how many times do people just go missing and then return home safely? Hardly ever. On the news it's always the opposite: people who go missing are found dead. Or never found at all. What will the rest of her life be like if that is what becomes of her sister? What will life be like for all of them – her parents, her sister, her brother? Her poor nephew, far too young to have to bear a tragedy such at this. She begins to sob at the thought of it, and Mark is awoken by the movement beside him.

'Hey,' he says, pulling her towards him, 'shh, it's okay. They'll find her.'

31

I've found it! I've found the phone box! Right now, I wish there were some steps that I could sprint to the top of, à la *Rocky*, to celebrate this achievement.

I throw the heavy door open with all the strength I have left, which is, worryingly, not much at all. My nerves are jangling; my hands shaking. I pick up the receiver and check that there is a dial tone like there was yesterday. There is. I lean against the glass to compose myself for a second, retrieving my notes and planning what I will say, and how I will be able to convince the police that I am not just some crazy person who is intent on wasting their time.

While I'm playing out the conversation in my head, I am reminded that there is absolutely no way that I can verify the location of this place. I mean, I don't even know if there really is an island called Carn! My geography knowledge is worse than pitiful, actually, and in this moment, I'm suddenly very concerned that Jamie has spoon-fed me nothing but misinformation, which I'm now about to rely on, and relay to the police.

What I know for sure is that the people I've encountered all sound Scottish. The weather is characteristically very Scottish, and this phone seemed to connect to a UK landline yesterday in exactly the way it would do if we were, indeed, still in any part of the UK. The sum of those three facts I've plucked out of my little bag of hopes could technically add up to me being stranded on any one of a frightening number of remote Scottish islands, but since Carn is the only name I've got, that is what I'm going to tell the police.

Surely, they'll be able to trace the call that I make,

anyway? I'm pretty sure the real police can actually do all that fancy stuff they do on television detective shows, can't they? They'd better be able to, or else I could be in deep trouble.

The phone's own number is shown here, I notice, and I whisper '*Thank God*' under my breath. I insert a coin, just in case, although I'm quite certain there is no charge for calls to any of the emergency services. I've never actually called the police before – I've never had to.

My finger seems to be moving in slow motion as it touches the number nine button three times, and my heart starts racing as I wait for the call to be answered.

'Emergency, which service do you require?'

I start to cry when I hear the man's voice. They are tears of relief, but I really need to choke them back right now, at least until I've said what I need to say.

'Yes, hello ...' I manage, 'police, please.' The split second of silence that follows has me panicking that something might be wrong, but my fears seem unfounded as the voice returns.

'Connecting you to the police now,' he says. I let out a massive breath, reminding myself not to blurt out unintelligible nonsense.

'Police Scotland, what is your emergency?'

My mouth has gone ridiculously dry, and I wish I'd had the presence of mind to bring some water with me.

'I need your help,' I say, the words struggling to force their way out of my parched throat. 'I've been kidnapped.'

32

The boss man was always going to do this part himself. Gary was the initial call handler, because Natalie needed to hear two distinctive voices. The boss has adopted an accent to disguise his own and added a gruff quality to his voice. He's putting on his most sincere, caring voice as he runs through his researched list of questions, and for a split second he feels slightly surprised at how detached he has managed to become. The sensation fades in an instant, and the rush returns. He knows he is giving her hope, reassuring her that the police will follow up on her assertions straight away, that he will arrange for her call to be traced to her exact location. He's urging her to find a safe place to wait for help to arrive, and even suggests that she try again to check for mobile reception. He implies that they might be able to track her and contact her while she is on the move. He doesn't mention the fact that he is tracking her through that very means, but for a very different reason.

The relief in her voice is palpable, as is the emotion. She was tearful at the start of the call, and although she's managed to pull herself together during the last few minutes, no doubt buoyed by the prospect of emergency services personnel scrambling to her aid, there is still some faltering and a lot of sniffing. She's so grateful that he almost feels guilty. Almost.

Gary has counted the number of times she thanked the man, thinking all the while that she is talking to someone who is going to arrange for her to be rescued; to be returned to her family. He tries to swallow down a lump that has developed in his throat, but it doesn't seem to want to comply, and so he tries to clear it with a little cough. When that doesn't work, he takes a gulp of water, and holds it in his mouth for a few seconds.

He must take care not to betray any emotion in front of the man in charge, but the knowledge that the woman is pitifully grateful to someone who is hell bent on ruining her life makes him feel like he could cry for her.

33

I still hold the receiver in my hand, though the man is no longer on the line. The relief and adrenalin that are coursing through my veins is like nothing I have ever experienced before, and I feel like my body is frozen in place.

I feel an urgency to snap out of it, pronto, and to swing into action, but my brain is trying to do too many things at the same time, and I can't figure out what kind of action is appropriate to take. Sending the required signals to my legs to have them carry out their primary function seems quite far down the list of priorities for my brain, and I slump lazily against the glass of the phone box.

I'm busy thinking about how I'm going to manage to keep myself out of Jamie's sight, if he comes looking for me, until such time as the police get here. I'm also thinking about how long it will take for me to get back home and wondering how much pomp and protocol will have to be waded through before I get to be reunited with all the people that I care about. No doubt the police will want to trawl painstakingly through all the intimate details of the past few days, but they won't insist on doing it all today, will they? At the very least, they'll have to let me see my parents, let them come to wherever I'm going to be debriefed. Surely.

My need to speak to them, to hug them, is like an itch that is driving me to distraction.

I wonder, too, what will happen to Jamie, once the police have taken him to task for what he's done. Not that I care about him, nor will I feel in any way bad for him when he's caught, but I would prefer that they get me off this island and safe in the custody of the police before they deal with him.

I finally place the receiver back where it belongs, and step out of the phone box, with a whole new lease of life. My situation has changed now. I am the one in control. Now, every step I take is a step closer to home.

*

'What's the plan now, Boss?' Gary asks. The other man hasn't spoken in a few minutes, since he ended the call. He's just been staring at the screen, wide-eyed, wearing a smile that, to Gary, is nothing short of disturbing. Gary isn't even sure whether his question has been received and understood.

The woman stood still for about two minutes with the phone receiver in her hand, her eyes dancing uncontrollably as though she was struggling to think straight. She looks overjoyed, understandably, but Gary seems to sense that she's not taking anything for granted; not just yet.

Shit! Is he starting to get to know her? He is, he suspects. How can you not when your number one task is to watch a person during every waking moment of your day? It's like watching *Big Brother* and feeling by the end of the run like you know the people, inside out, but at least those people willingly signed up for that kind of intrusion into the minutiae of their lives. Natalie didn't.

Shit! He's calling her by her real name! In his head, at least. He's beginning to think he can interpret her facial expressions, her body language; and a wave of panic hits him as he realises that he's in her corner; he's rooting for her. His face suddenly feels hot, and he can sense that his skin is turning red. He feels like he's been caught doing something he shouldn't, and the more he tries to dampen down his visible symptoms, the worse they become.

Mercifully, the boss is apparently still in a world of his own, barely even blinking as he follows the lone figure on

131

the screen. She's on the move now, following her helper's instructions to try and find a phone signal, completely unaware that her actions are ultimately pointless.

Gary clears his throat, now that his mild anxiety attack seems to have subsided a little and attempts to ask his question again. 'Boss?' The man stirs, as though he's been broken from his reverie.

'Hmm?' Gary is about to repeat the whole question, but he is cut off. 'What's next, Gary,' the man says, his eyes unnaturally wide, 'is that we remind some people how hard they need to work for their money.'

34

Kevin opens his eyes gingerly. His head is thumping, but he's stuck in a catch-22 situation: his head hurts so much that he can't possibly contemplate getting out of bed to go and acquire some paracetamol from the cupboard in the kitchen where they live.

He hasn't been this hungover in a long time, and he curses himself for putting his body through hell like this. And hell is exactly what it feels like.

He's sweating, but his one arm which is resting on top of his duvet is freezing cold, sending an unpleasant shiver through his body. He pulls it under the covers, wincing from the effort the movement requires, and buries his face in his pillow.

He definitely can't handle alcohol the way he used to be able to. At the relatively tender age of twenty-nine, this is something of a depressing revelation, but it is undeniable.

Back in his student days, he could happily down a few weeks' worth of units in one night and still be raring to go for a repeat performance the following evening.

Quantity-wise, he didn't drink all that much last night, but he should have known far better than to give into Pete's insistence that the evening be peppered with multiple shots. Beer, he can deal with. But downing shots at the rate that Pete dictates can only achieve one thing: annihilation.

He can remember random portions of the night with remarkable clarity, considering, but the journey home has been blotted out of his memory like temporary marker being scrubbed from a whiteboard. He must have taken a taxi home from the city centre, which will have set him back around thirty quid or so, and as the thought of checking his bank balance on Monday pings into his head, it sends an additional jab of pain to mingle with the rest. He has no recollection of withdrawing the cash, nor the trip in the cab, nor of handing over the extortionate fare, but he very much doubts having slummed it and waited for the night bus.

From what he is able to remember, it was a pretty good night, but it's the parts that have gone astray from his memory that he fears. He hopes he didn't do anything embarrassing.

A mini wave of recall dances in front of his eyes, making him wince again.

He kissed someone. It was a drunk, meaningless kiss, but the fact that he has no idea who the girl was or how they came to part ways makes him feel a little seedy. He offers up a quiet thanks to anyone who may be listening that he wasn't daft enough to bring a random woman home with him. That's not his style, anyway. Pete's, yes, but not Kevin's.

Nonetheless, he has all but given up on Natalie, since she has ignored every attempt that he has made to contact her since they had dinner and shared a meaningful (or so he thought) kiss almost three days ago. It still strikes him as odd that she wouldn't reply, even if only to tell him to back off (he's sent seven texts, and tried to call her twice), but what more can he do? He doesn't want to venture into stalker territory. He already feels like he has, a little, by stealing glances at her Facebook and Instagram, but neither have been updated since before they went out on Thursday, and if she doesn't want to answer him, then that's up to her. She must have her reasons, and he's decided to accept it, as much as it annoys him that she couldn't just be a grown-up about the whole thing and warn him off to his face.

Hence the impromptu snogging of the mystery girl last night, that he can barely remember anything about. Not that Natalie is likely to find out about it, but it proves that he's prepared to move on and forget about her, like she has him.

He's thankful that he doesn't have a single thing to do today. It's just as well, because the amount of alcohol still loitering around in his blood stream won't allow for legal driving for quite some hours yet, and public transport in his neck of the woods on a Sunday just isn't worth the hassle.

He's not sure what time it is – still pretty early, he deduces from the colour of the sky, but when the time does come when he can muster up the energy and strength to go and find some painkillers, it's comforting to know that he can simply fall back into bed and stay there for as long as he wants.

He glances around the bedroom, noticing that his clothes are scattered untidily all over the floor – nothing unusual there. He spots his mobile phone, lying face down on the carpet, and slides across the bed, into a position where he can reach out and grab it without having to actually lift his body. There are no missed calls, or messages, and he gives a wry chuckle at the realisation that none of his so-called friends were concerned enough to check that he made it home safely, considering the fact that he must have been pretty off his face by the time he said his goodbyes to them. The rest of the boys were most likely pretty mangled too, he concedes, and he wonders if any of them will have even surfaced by this time. Perhaps he should check on them?

He notes that the time is fourteen minutes past eight – far too early for Pete or any of the others to be making a comeback into the real world. He resolves to text them later. He could guiltlessly sleep for about another four hours, he estimates. Midday is a reasonable time to be thinking about getting up, taking into account his fragile state. Maybe, by that time, he'll be feeling a little more human, and will be able to consider eating something – the greasier, the better. He knows there are definitely some sausages in the fridge, and a rule that he unfalteringly lives by is that he never allows the bread count to fall below half a loaf before

135

replenishing. Sausage sandwiches: that's a plan, he thinks to himself, resting his head again on an inviting pillow, and closing his eyes.

A loud, aggressive knock on the door rouses him after what feels like a matter of mere seconds. 'Who the fuck can that be?' His question reverberates around the small room. His initial strategy is to bury his head under the duvet, ignore the knocking and hope that whoever thinks they can disturb him at eight o'clock on a Sunday morning will get the message that they can't, and give up. Anyone who might need to get hold of him urgently would call his mobile or his landline before coming over, and since he hasn't missed any calls on either (even in a drunken or hungover state, the shrill ring of the house phone is impossible to miss), he concludes that the mysterious caller is not someone he knows. He throws his head defiantly back on the pillow and wills his harasser to hurry up and leave.

'Kevin Lowell?' he hears a loud, deep voice enquire. 'Police. Open up, please.'

35

This old castle, on further inspection, looks very grand indeed. I managed to find it without much difficulty, thankfully, after I spoke to the police. Well, the police call handler, I suppose he must have been; probably not an actual policeman. I don't really know how these things work. Like I said, I've never actually had to call the police before.

I would estimate that the castle is only about a kilometre away from the landmarks I'm familiar with now – the phone box, the shop – so thankfully it didn't take me long to make my way here. My legs were pretty useless for the first few seconds, wobbling like jelly after I left the phone box, but they came to my aid fairly quickly, and have managed to get me to where I need to be.

The castle is much bigger than I was expecting, although I'm not sure where my preconceptions could have come from. I've seen quite a few castles in my time, owing to the fact that Steven and I went through a phase of visiting the really *interesting* ones a few years ago. To be fair, he was considerably more interested in the process than I was. Don't get me wrong, it's practically impossible not be blown away by the fact that some of the sites are so impressively intact, after hundreds and hundreds of years, and the history you can literally breathe in when you stand in one Great Hall or another is a very special experience. I just didn't share his enthusiasm when it came to the less stately, less windproof ruins that he managed to convince me to spend an excessive amount of time perusing.

As I take a brief rest on the lawn, wishing desperately that I was trudging up the Royal Mile towards Edinburgh Castle instead of loitering hopefully outside of this as yet nameless castle, I wonder if any notable, history book-worthy events have taken place here. At least, I think to myself, Jamie didn't lie about this place being here. Maybe this really is the Isle of Carn, as he claims. That would certainly be a boon, considering that's where I've told the police I am.

Obviously, I can't see what the interior of the castle looks like – I assume it's not necessarily within the law to break into a stately home and take a peek, even if it is most likely vacant – but the exterior of the building is rather fancy. It's all turrets and archways, and reminds me of something I would have sketched as a child, if someone had said to me: 'Draw a castle.' I have no idea how long ago it was built, but I don't imagine it's been all that common to commission the building of castles in recent years, has it? I resolve to read up about it when I get home; broaden my knowledge. My geography is in definite need of a boost, that's something I've learned in the last few days.

I've walked the whole way around the outside of the castle, which is a perfect square, as far as I can gather (maths was never my strong suit at school, but thankfully I managed to get my head around basic shapes, and retain that knowledge), searching for the mystical place where mobile phone reception is apparently a thing. So far, I have had no joy. There was one point, about ten minutes ago, when one of the little bubbles taunted me, threatening to change from transparent circle to solid white bubble, but it flashed so quickly, I can't be certain I even saw it, or whether I was simply so utterly desperate for it to be true that I imagined it.

My mind starts to drift towards my impending rescue. How will the police do it? Will they race towards the shore on one of their speedboats, tossing up surf as they tear through the water? Or will it be an even more dramatic affair, where officers touch down in a navy-blue helicopter, like a scene straight out of an action movie, all ready for

138

a showdown, just in case? Looking around here, I can't be sure whether there is a particularly suitable spot for a helicopter to attempt a landing. There are no official roads here, only rocky, uneven paths, and as yet I haven't seen a single car, so I suppose it would be most unusual if there were to be a helipad somewhere in the vicinity. They'll be able to figure all that out, though, won't they? They'll have access to satellite images, and Google Earth maps, and all that technologically-advanced stuff that seems like it could be from a completely different universe as I look around the vast wilderness that surrounds me.

'Jen?' A man's voice rouses me from my daydream, and my first thought is that it must be Jamie, and that I've been rumbled, and the game is officially over. My heart sinks to the pit of my stomach. I look up, almost in slow motion, and see Davie, the man I encountered in Bessie's shop yesterday, he of the boat which may or may not exist. He's towering over me as I sit, cross-legged on the grass, and he's smiling. 'Morning, lovey,' he says. His voice seems kinder than it did yesterday, but then I did only hang around long enough to hear him say one damning sentence, before making tracks out of that shop like Roadrunner on amphetamines.

'What brings you down here at this time of the morning?' he asks. 'Jamie not with you?'

I notice for the first time that he has a little dog with him, a tiny, over-excited Jack Russell who seems to have found something worth investigating on the sole of my shoe. It distracts me for a second.

'I'm … eh … no, he's, eh …' What should I tell him? He's in on this thing with Jamie, too, remember? If I tell him I'm waiting for the police, won't he just alert Jamie? Or worse still, what if he tries to make me go back to the house, by force? Like Jamie, the man is far taller than me. Unlike Jamie, he is built like someone whose main hobby could be competing in the Highland Games, perhaps in a caber-tossing contest, or some other feat that requires the strength of three regular, Jamie-sized men. His warm smile and friendly voice don't seem to belie violent tendencies, but just as I am with Jamie, I am wary of what I might trigger in this man if I suddenly become non-compliant with whatever they have in store for me.

'I just fancied a walk,' I say, unconvincingly. 'I thought it might do me good, you know. Clear my head.' I point to my head, in case there is any doubt about what body part I'm referring to. I want Davie to believe that I've fully recovered from yesterday's episode, and that I'm simply enjoying some alone time. He regards me closely, with a hint of suspicion, but after a brief moment his face creases into a smile. 'Well, this wind'll certainly clear your head,' he declares, with a loud guffaw, as his dog starts to gnaw on the end of my shoelace.

'Yeah, it sure will,' I agree, forcing out a mirthless laugh. I'm quickly becoming tired of the scrutiny, and the small talk, and the tiny terror who seems determined to have my trainer off me.

'Percy, stop that!' Davie thunders, the volume of his voice taking me aback. Percy pays him no heed whatsoever and continues to snarl and snap at my foot. 'It's okay,' I offer weakly, 'he's not doing any harm.' He is, actually, but I can't bring myself to shoo him, he's only little.

I love dogs. I always have done, ever since I met the Shetland sheepdog who endured the entire duration of my childhood in our family home. I say endured, because I can vaguely remember subjecting her to many attempts to fold her ears forwards, and make them stay in that position, which of course they didn't. It was a testament to her good nature that she never once snapped or growled at the annoying, persistent three-year-old me, even though my misguided attempts to mould her appearance into my vision of what it should be must have been very wearing. There was no malicious intent on my part, of course, and as I grew older I became as protective and adoring of her as she was of me.

Percy is a cute, if over-exuberant, little chap, and I don't feel that I should admonish him. 'Hey, Percy,' I say fondly, 'what are you looking for there, eh?' I reach down to give him a playful tickle, and he turns his attention away from my foot to my hands, which he begins to sniff at furiously, then proceeds to lick with great enthusiasm. Davie looks on, amused. 'Well, are you finished your walk?' he asks. Given that he found me seated on the ground, staring into space, it's a fair assumption to make. *Damn.*

'Eh, no,' I say, wishing my brain would provide much better back-up to my mouth than it has done since Davie appeared. 'I was just taking a rest. I'll set off again in a minute, I think. Might as well take advantage of this mind-clearing wind.' I try to make the last sentence sound humorous by giving a little forced chuckle, but it doesn't quite hit the spot.

'Fancy some company?' Davie asks. 'Percy needs another good half hour or so outdoors, or else he'll just be a wee bag of energy all day.' He smiles at me, and as if on cue, Percy rests his head on my lap, and starts to snuggle, as though he's saying, *'Please, let me come with you. Pretty please!'*

Can I simply say no? By nature, I don't like to be rude to people, but this is a very particular set of circumstances that I find myself in, and I really need Davie and his adorable little dog just to leave me alone. The police could be on their way here right now, and if I move away from here, how will they know where to find me? Granted, so far, I've been unable to latch onto any viable reception, but I'm still hopeful of finding that elusive spot where this island collides head-on with present day technology. But wait, they'll be able to trace the phone itself, though, won't they? Through GPS or whatever? You see it all the time in movies and television shows, where they follow the little flashing dot right up until they home in on the precise location. Maybe the best thing to do is just agree to go on a short walk, to avoid raising any suspicion, and then make my excuses and find my way back here, if the police haven't already swooped in by then.

'Percy won't take no for an answer,' Davie quips, reaching out his hand for me to grab, and haul myself up.

I'm guessing he doesn't really mean Percy. 'Well, I wouldn't want to disappoint Percy, would I?' I reply, rising to my feet. I take a look around, in all directions, to check for potential shining knights in police-issue body armour, but none are apparent. I let out a sigh, hoping that Davie doesn't pick up on it.

'He would never forgive you,' Davie says, flashing a cringe-worthy wink in my direction, and Percy plays along, wagging his tail at a speed I've never witnessed on a dog before.

'Up to you to lead the way, then, Percy Boy!' Davie instructs, as though he's at the helm of a chariot. With a final glance around me, and a niggling doubt in the back of my mind that maybe I'm not doing the right thing, I start to follow.

36

'Sorry, what's this about?' Kevin asks, rubbing his eyes, his head pounding even harder now that he's had to get up out of bed and make his way downstairs. The light that's pouring in through the open door is not exactly dazzling sunshine, but his eyes are feeling fragile this morning, and he has to squint to see the men's faces.

There are two of them. A taller, older one, who is screwing up his face at Kevin, either in disapproval or in order to breathe in less of the pure alcohol that is emanating from Kevin's body, and one who is a few inches shorter and probably twenty years younger. His face is neutral.

'Detective Inspector Gordon Jackson and Detective Constable Graeme Nixon,' the older man declares, and both wave their warrant cards.

Detectives? What the hell?

'Can we come in, Mr Lowell?' the taller man asks, although it's more of a statement of intent than a question and he takes a step forward.

'Eh … sure,' Kevin answers uncertainly, opening the door wider to allow the men to pass him.

'You might want to put some clothes on, son,' the tall man suggests, reminding Kevin that in his haste to make the noise stop – and his panic at realising it was being made by the police – he answered the door dressed only in his boxer shorts.

'Right,' he agrees, his mind sluggish, 'I'll be back in a second.'

He tries to sprint upstairs, but there is a wrecking ball inside his head, swinging from side to side and making harsh contact with the inside of his skull, and he is forced to move more slowly. He pulls a pair of jogging trousers, a t-shirt and a pair of socks from his drawer. His mind clamours desperately for clues as to why the police want to speak to him so urgently. And not just the beat bobbies that deal with any old shit – these guys are detectives!

His attempts to think clearly are impeded by his hangover. Even though it's Baltic outside, and only a moment ago he was standing in the doorway almost naked, the hangover and the anxiety that's rising in him makes him start to sweat.

Did he do something last night that he can't remember? He had a fair amount of shots, but he's not the type to get aggressive when he's drunk. He's never been in a fight in his life. Before he pulls his clothes on, he makes a quick check of his body in the mirror, and finds no cuts, or bruises, nor signs of altercation.

He remembers the kiss, with the nameless woman, but only vaguely. *Oh God.* Did he go too far? He dismisses the idea almost as soon as it pops into his head. That's absolutely not the kind of man he is. He would never dream of taking advantage of a woman – even when he's under the influence, his morals in that respect remain strict and unyielding. But what if the woman has accused him of something he didn't do? He starts to feel nauseous and has to rush to the bathroom to take some gulps of water. He longs to be able to go back to bed, but he knows there's no possibility of that until the police have concluded whatever business they have with him. Which is what?

He stares at his face in the mirror, searching his eyes for clues of what he might have done that would bring two detectives to his home at this time on a Sunday morning. But there's nothing. His brain hurts from the effort of trying to unlock memories that are buried beneath a smog of alcohol, or don't exist at all, and he gives up trying. He'll find out, soon enough.

He splashes some water on his face, and holds a towel against it for a few seconds, taking deep breaths. He takes one last glance in the mirror. His face is not the face of someone who could hurt someone. Least of all a woman.

The detectives are waiting for him in the living room when he comes back downstairs. Both are sitting on the couch, and the older one looks even sterner than he did before.

'Take a seat, son,' he orders, in an authoritative voice that matches his stature and demeanour. The man is about six-feet, or just over, which makes him only a couple of inches taller than Kevin, but even when the man is seated Kevin feels like David to his Goliath, and instinctively he is wary of getting on the wrong side of this man. Kevin perches himself on the edge of an armchair, maintaining a distance of a few feet between himself and the policemen.

'Can you tell me why you're here?' he asks, his voice croaky and quiet. He hasn't spoken much since he woke up, and his vocal chords are still in the process of warming up.

'We'd just like to ask you a few questions,' says the man who introduced himself as DI Jackson, the one who is clearly in charge. He stares unwaveringly at Kevin, making him feel even more uneasy. The other man, who still hasn't spoken a word yet, glares at him too, his pen poised ready to take notes.

If this is a good cop, bad cop situation, then the thus far mute guy will be good cop, Kevin surmises. He hopes that Bad Cop isn't actually as scary as he comes across.

'You met Natalie Byron for dinner last Thursday, the ninth of November, is that right?' DI Jackson enquires.

Natalie? They're here about Natalie? Kevin's mind shifts into high gear as it joins the dots between his repeated attempts to contact Natalie over the last few days and the sudden visit from the police, asking questions about his date with her. *Oh shit!* Has she reported him for harassment or something? Surely not. Does she actually think that he's

145

turned into some kind of stalker? And would they really send two detectives to his house just to tell him to back off? Why wouldn't she just tell him herself?

'Mr Lowell?' DI Jackson's voice interrupts his thoughts, and Kevin finds himself grateful for the intervention. His head was swimming from the all the questions that were whizzing around, like clothes tumbling around inside a washing machine.

'Yes. Yeah, I did,' he manages. 'We went out for dinner on Thursday night. We went to the Dhabba, in Merchant City.' He's trying to act normal, but his nerves make him fidget, which in turn makes him more nervous, as he worries his squirming might be read as an indication of guilt. But what do they think he might be guilty of?

'And when was the last time that you saw Ms Byron, Mr Lowell? Kevin – can I call you Kevin?'

'Sure,' Kevin replies, answering the second question first. 'Kevin is fine.'

The two men stare at him, and he realises he hasn't addressed the earlier question.

'Eh, well, Thursday night was the last time I saw her,' he replies, rubbing the back of his neck with his left hand. It's a nervous habit, a reflex which kicks in when he's put on the spot. 'We went for dinner, like I said, then a couple of drinks, then I walked her to the train station, and she got the train home. That's the last time I saw her.'

Silent cop makes some scribbles on his notepad, and Kevin cranes his neck to try to make out what's being written about him.

'Which station?' he asks, taking Kevin by surprise.

'Eh … Central,' Kevin replies, second-guessing himself. Was it Central, or was it Queen Street? No, it was Central. He remembers now, because he remembers noticing that the clock on the main concourse was lit up in red. He had never noticed that before, and wondered whether it had always been like that, or whether it was a recent development.

'And where did you go for drinks?'

Kevin notices that the second policeman has an accent. Possibly Edinburgh, although Kevin doesn't have much of a knack for recognising them. Natalie has a talent for mimicking them, he remembers fondly. Her Liverpudlian one, plucked straight from that old movie *Shirley Valentine*, is hilarious.

'Kevin?' The baton has been passed back to DI Jackson, who seems to be getting a little impatient. Kevin has to try to find a way to stop his mind from drifting off on a tangent whenever he is asked a question.

'Eh … a few places,' he answers, trying to recall which places. The only names of venues that are popping into his head are the names of pubs and clubs that he and his friends went to last night – too many, in truth – and those are of no use to him at all.

'Let me think,' he implores the men, bringing his hands to his temples, hoping that having them there will help him to think clearly.

'Can I just grab a glass of water?' he asks feebly, like a bashful child in a classroom. His mouth feels dangerously bereft of any moisture, and it's no wonder, given the amount of perspiration that must have seeped out of his body in the last few minutes. 'I was out pretty late last night, and I just woke up …' he carries on, his throat like sandpaper.

'Allow me,' says the younger cop – Kevin can't remember his name – standing up. 'Kitchen through there, is it?' He gestures towards the door to his right, and Kevin nods, conserving the limited amount of saliva he has left in order to make it through the next few seconds without choking. He suspects that the cop might want to use the opportunity to have a quick snoop around while he's in there, but Kevin doesn't really care. He doesn't have anything to hide. Not in the kitchen; not anywhere.

147

'Good night, was it?' DI Jackson asks quietly, almost conspiratorially. The expression he wears seems like a mixture of sympathy and annoyance. Kevin nods again, feeling smaller and more afraid than he has for a very long time. The other cop returns from the kitchen, bringing Kevin a tall glass full of water. Kevin accepts it from him gratefully, and gulps down more than half of the contents quickly, without a break, as though he's been stranded in the desert for days on end.

'Are you alright to continue?' his saviour asks, resuming his position on the couch, to the right of DI Jackson. This gives context to the term *right-hand man*, Kevin thinks to himself.

'Yeah, I'm fine,' he answers. His thirst is only partially quenched, but at least now he can speak without feeling like the words might catch in his throat.

'So, can you tell us where you and Natalie went, after you left the restaurant?'

Kevin takes another sip of water. 'We went to a couple of places in Merchant City,' glad that relevant words are starting to flow from his brain to his mouth again. '*Home*, first, for one drink, but it was mega-busy, and we couldn't hear each other so we left there and went to *O'Neill's*, then *Bar 91*.' His thirst has returned with a vengeance after all those fully-formed sentences, and he gulps down even more water, noting that there is barely any left in the glass. He notices a furtive glance passing between the detectives.

'When you say "*Home*"?' Good Cop prompts. Apparently, he is now the one doing all the talking.

'I mean the bar, *Home*,' Kevin replies. 'It's the one on … wait, what's that street called again? I can never remember all the streets around there. It's around the corner from Merchant Square. No, wait. Is it? It's opposite a club, I think. I've never been in it, that club, but I'm pretty sure it's just across from *Home* …'

'Okay, thank you,' DI Jackson interrupts, clearly unwilling to tolerate any more of Kevin's unintelligible rambling. 'So, *Bar 91* was the last place you went to? What happened after that?'

'Yeah, that was the last place. We stayed there until about half-ten, I think. Yeah, that's right, because Natalie's train was due about quarter-to-eleven, so I walked her to the station and waited with her until she got on the train.'

Good Cop looks up from his notebook. 'You saw Natalie get on the train?'

'Yeah, definitely,' Kevin insists. 'My train wasn't due until five-past, so I had plenty of time to get around to Queen Street and catch it. I didn't want to leave her there on her own. Especially on the lower level, at that time of night.'

The two policemen exchange glances again, and Kevin wishes they would just fast forward to the point.

'And then what did you do?'

'I walked to Queen Street, got on my train, and came home. I was in the house for about quarter to twelve at the latest.'

'And since then, have you had any contact with Natalie?' DI Jackson seems to have retaken the reigns, with his sidekick demoted to scribe for the moment.

'No,' Kevin answers promptly. 'Well, yeah,' he corrects himself, rubbing the back of his neck again. 'She texted me to let me know she got home alright – I asked her to. But that was it. I haven't heard from her since.' He wonders if they're already abreast of this, if they're setting him up for a fall in respect of his attempts to contact her.

'And were you ... expecting to hear from her again?'

Kevin pauses for a second before giving his answer. He decides to lay his cards on the table. There's no sense in denying that he's been trying to get hold of Natalie. For all he knows, they already know about every text, call and voicemail message anyway. And it's not as though he's actually done anything illegal, is it?

'Well, yeah, I was,' he replies frankly. 'I've been trying to contact her all weekend actually, but I think she's blanking me.'

The men look at each other again, but this time their glance lasts longer than the times before, and their expressions have turned more serious. Kevin suddenly feels a surge of bravery from somewhere inside of him, and his next words come out in a voice which is less feeble, more borderline aggressive.

'Look, will you please just tell me what's going on?'

DI Jackson frowns. 'Mind if we take a quick look around, son?'

37

Without me being aware of it and, strictly speaking, without my explicit agreement, it appears I've been led to Davie's house. We've been so busy chatting about a wide variety of things – or, should I say, I've been so busy trying to keep up with his seemingly endless hyperbole – that I can't recall much about the route we took to get here, from the castle. I really should have paid more attention, but between trying to give Davie the impression that I was fascinated with what he was saying and trying to discreetly check the phone and my immediate surroundings every five seconds for signs of the cavalry coming, the journey here has become a blur of mountains, trees and murky sky inside my head. Percy did indeed lead the way, as Davie commanded, and I suppose it makes sense that he would lead us to a place he knows – his home.

'Come on in for a cuppa,' Davie urges, as we near the front door. The house looks almost identical to the one I woke up in yesterday morning, the one I refuse to call my home, although whereas the door of that house is green in colour, this one here is a drab, unattractive shade of brown, and the paint is old and flaky. The curtains are open in the rooms facing the front of the house, and although the light at the moment is not ideal for distinguishing shades, the curtains also appear to be dark, and carrying a rather hideous pattern.

'I really should get back,' I say weakly, trying to edge backwards, away from the door. 'Jamie will be wondering where I am.' It must be almost an hour now since I spoke to the police, which means it's over an hour since I left Jamie asleep. I'm worried that, by now, he will have woken up, realised I'm not in the living room, where he left me, and started hunting me down.

'Ach, if I know that boy, he'll still be snoring his head off,' Davie declares, dismissing my attempt to excuse myself with a wave of his enormous arm. 'Not exactly a morning person, is he?' he chuckles, and inserts his key into the lock, as though the notion that I'm coming inside for cup of tea with him is a done deal. I laugh along, making use of my best fake laugh for about the fifteenth time since he accosted me earlier, and wondering what I can say to get out of this, and get away from him, back to a spot where I can be rescued without risk of intervention or complications.

I'm obviously supposed to know whether Jamie is a morning person or not, since that is certainly something his live-in girlfriend would know, but I have absolutely no idea whether he is or he isn't, on account of him being a complete stranger to me. I ponder, briefly, how Davie would know such a thing about Jamie. I didn't ask any questions yesterday about how Jamie and Davie and Bessie all know each other, but the first thing that comes to mind is that maybe Davie and Jamie work together? Since Bessie obviously operates the only commercial business that I've been introduced to on this island, of which there seems to be very little need, it's not a giant leap to assume that everyone who lives here probably knows her through frequenting her shop. Davie may or may not have mentioned Bessie, or even Jamie, while we were walking, but since my game plan was simply to say 'Mm-hm', and laugh in all the right places until I could be free of him, I have absolutely no idea whether he did or not.

I remind myself that none of that is really relevant, and that whatever bullshit story any of them may tell me is just that – bullshit.

'Even so,' I counter, 'I should really get back. Sunday mornings are kind of our thing.' As I say it, I have no idea what that might mean, or what Davie may take it to mean

– something sexual, maybe? I shudder at the thought. It's very vague, but at the same time it sounds like a reasonable excuse to get me away from here, and that's all that matters. 'Thanks for the walk, though,' I say to Davie. 'And you, of course, Percy.' I kneel down and give the dog a little scratch on the top of his head. 'Thanks for being such a good guide.' Percy laps up the attention, his tail wagging furiously. I'm about to turn and walk away, feeling satisfied that I've been able to decline Davie's offer in a polite yet assertive manner, when he takes hold of my arm. 'I'll not take no for an answer,' he states, and I believe him. His grip is strong, and although he still wears a smile, it doesn't look genuine or friendly. I'm scared.

'Come away in, love, and I'll make you a wee cuppa,' he says, directing me into the house. 'I've got bacon, as well, if you fancy a wee buttie.' Percy's ears seem to prick up at the mention of bacon, and a little growl of encouragement seems to rise from within his throat. My better judgement is screaming at me that I should simply break out my reserves of courage that I've been storing for an event such as this, but the words don't come out.

I'm in the house now, with Davie's hand in the small of my back, gently guiding me through the hallway. The décor is strikingly similar to the house that I've been living in, the main difference being that in this house, there are a few photographs hung on the walls, of Davie and a woman. He hasn't mentioned a wife, and so far, there is no-one else to be found in the house. Maybe he's divorced. Or maybe another cretin is about to make an appearance to join in the merry dance that Jamie and Co. are leading me in. The hall carpet is an eyesore of a thing, with stripes of dark grey, beige, white, and – of course – brown. I'm mesmerised by the hideousness of it, and as Davie moves ahead of me into the living room, I suddenly feel like I just need to get out of here, and fast. I feel like although he is good-natured (on

153

the face of it), he is steamrollering me into a situation that I don't want to be in, and it's beginning to feel like I've been kidnapped all over again. My fear is shirked off, and I make an abrupt turn, only to trip over Percy and make a commotion that alerts Davie to my plan.

'I … really, I should go,' I say, failing to offer any further explanation. I edge past Percy carefully this time, and Davie thankfully makes no attempt to stop me. I don't turn around to see how he has reacted to my departure. I do steal a little glance at Percy, and give him a little parting smile, the way you would if you were excusing yourself prematurely from a dinner table. He whines a little in return, perhaps wondering if I've scuppered his chances of enjoying some bacon.

'Are you okay, love?' I hear Davie ask, but I'm at the door now, and I simply yell back, 'Yeah, I'm fine,' feeling anything but fine as I turn the handle and make my way out. When I'm back outside, I take a deep breath of fresh air, and expel a sigh of relief that they haven't tried to stop me. Now that I'm outdoors, I feel quite foolish for getting myself into a bit of a state. What did I actually think Davie was going to do? Hold me there, against my will, and force-feed me bacon and tea? I don't know, and now that it's no longer an issue I don't care. I need to focus all my energy now on getting back to the castle, and my surely-imminent rendezvous with the police. Where the hell are they, anyway? Shouldn't they be here by now? I check the phone and see that it's now been well over an hour since I made that call, and I start to wonder if maybe I should go back to the phone box and call them again from there.

I look around, trying to get my bearings, to figure out which way leads back to the castle. I actually let out a little yelp of despair when I see Jamie, advancing towards me and now only a few feet away, grinning. 'There you are, babe,' he states, reaching out his arms with the clear intention of wrapping them around my waist. 'I've been looking all over for you.'

38

'What do you think, Boss?' Graeme Nixon asks, as he and DI Jackson make the short walk back to the car after interviewing Kevin Lowell. Jackson, deep in thought, aims the fob at the car a little belatedly, which leaves Nixon tugging on the handle a fraction of a second before the door remotely unlocks, making him go through the process a second time to open the passenger door.

Jackson is distractedly chewing on his lower lip again, running over key elements of the interview in his head. The shock that registered on Lowell's face when they broke the news seemed genuine enough, but Jackson has borne witness to plenty of Oscar-worthy performances during his tenure, and he knows only too well that sob-stories and outpourings of grief can be manufactured, and very convincingly. He sinks into the driver's seat with a heavy thud, feeling tired in his body as well as weary in his mind. The first rumblings of a nasty headache have appeared, and he searches his pockets for some painkillers, but comes up empty. He knows that it's impossible, but he feels as though Kevin Lowell has managed to infect him with his hangover symptoms. Either that or he's picked up another cold or bug from the pool of ever-present maladies that circulate around the station on a loop. He realises he hasn't answered the question Nixon asked him, and that his colleague is staring at him, waiting to hear his opinion on what transpired inside the house.

Jackson likes having Nixon work alongside him. As Detective Sergeants go, Graeme Nixon has all the qualities Jackson would ask for if he got to hand-pick his team members from a finite list.

Nixon is fiercely intelligent, confident in his own abilities, and will leave no stone unturned in the search of answers and justice. Something of a late convert to the force, Nixon gained a degree in forensic psychology before deciding that he would prefer to get his hands dirty, as it were, so he knows his stuff. He's not one to shy away from hard graft; married to the job, but he doesn't bring with him the arrogance and cocksure attitude that Jackson has seen in other graduates who have passed through his department, and his amiable nature makes him well-liked amongst his peers and his superiors.

Jackson wouldn't be surprised to see his protégé promoted in the not too distant future, and if that happened to coincide with his own retirement, then Jackson would be hard-pushed to think of anyone better suited to fill his shoes.

Nixon will, Jackson knows, have his own opinions on events, and won't shy away from revealing them, but as always, he will listen to what his superior officer has to say before offering his own angle.

'He seems genuine enough to me,' Jackson concedes with a sigh, taking a sip of water from a bottle that has been lying around the squad car for longer than he dares to think about. He can't even be sure that it belongs to him, but before he has time to consider it, he's already taken a swig. It's slightly warm, and unpleasant, and does nothing to refresh him, but it will have to suffice until they can stop at a shop or a petrol station to buy a fresh, chilled bottle. 'A bit edgy though,' he carries on. 'What's your gut feeling?'

'Agreed, Boss,' the younger detective concurs. Nixon always addresses Jackson as *Boss*, and it's another reason why Jackson holds him in such high regard. Jackson himself isn't pernickety about pomp and ceremony within the force, but he appreciates a fellow officer who shows respect to their superiors. 'He was jittery from the second we walked in,' Nixon elaborates. 'I know he said he's coming to after a serious night out, but to me he looked shit-scared about something.'

'Hmm,' Jackson responds, seemingly in agreement. 'So, what's he got to be shit-scared of?' He stares ahead, pensively. He absentmindedly takes a second swig of the lukewarm water and screws up his face at the taste of it. 'Urgh. Do me a favour, check in with Slater and find out where we are with the CCTV from Thursday night, will you?' he asks. 'Let her know what Lowell said about the train from Central at ten-forty-five and have her check it out.'

'Will do, Boss,' Nixon replies, already dialling his colleague, Marie Slater's, extension.

39

Natalie's *missing*? How the hell can she be missing?

Kevin has barely caught his breath since the two detectives left. He's pacing, without realising it, his hangover put to one side. He's drunk about two litres of water in the last twenty minutes, but his body has seemed to have sprouted holes – he still feels dangerously dehydrated. Stress is making him perspire uncontrollably.

Now that they've questioned him, and poked their noses around every room in his house, they can't possibly think that he's got anything to do with Natalie disappearing, can they? Is that what they thought in the first place? Why would he have been trying to get hold of her for the last few days, if he knew where she was?

He probably didn't do himself any favours by behaving like a half-cut nervous wreck when the police were here, but who wouldn't be rattled after being awoken by the Old Bill knocking on their door at the break of dawn on a Sunday morning?

He was worried they might not have believed him when he said he doesn't have a clue where she's gone, or why she hasn't been in touch, but they didn't suggest that he accompany them down to the station, so presumably they're not going to waste any more time barking up the wrong tree.

How could she just vanish? They wouldn't tell him much, other than the fact that he was the last person to see her, as far as they know. Which means no-one else has seen her since Thursday night. *Shit.*

He lets his body flop down on the couch and cradles his head in his clammy hands. His t-shirt sticks to his back, the cold sweat sending a shiver down his spine.

His mind rakes over the details of Thursday night, his head hurting from the intense concentration involved in trying to remember the sequence of events.

Dinner. Drinks. The kiss at the train station. The messages exchanged when they got home. Everything happened exactly as he described it to the police. He didn't leave anything out, or tell any little white lies, because he has no reason to. He has nothing to hide.

He watched Natalie get on the train and waited for it to leave so that he could wave her off.

He asked her to let him know when she got home, because he wanted to know she was safe. He always used to do that, before, when they went out. Wait, did he tell the police that they used to go out? Does it matter? His head feels mangled.

What he needs is a shower, a strong, hot coffee, and that greasy food that he had his heart set on earlier. He doesn't really feel in the mood to eat, but the noises coming from his stomach are a distraction, and hunger is one less thing he wants to have to deal with at this point.

He starts to peel off his t-shirt as he makes his way upstairs, goose-bumps appearing as his bare skin is exposed to the cool air. He really hopes the shower will kick-start his sluggish brain, because once he's washed, eaten and had a hit of caffeine, he wants to do whatever he can to help find Natalie. Anything at all.

40

MISSING WOMAN – DALMUIR

Police Scotland is appealing for help to trace a woman from Dalmuir who has not been seen since exiting Dalmuir train station at 23:12 on Thursday, 9th November.

Detective Inspector Gordon Jackson from Clydebank Police Office said: 'For Natalie not to contact her friends or family is completely out of character, and her loved ones are extremely distressed and concerned about her well-being.

'Officers are carrying out enquiries to find Natalie as soon as possible, but we need help from members of the public.

Natalie is 5' 4", of medium build, with shoulder-length brown hair and blue eyes.

'I would appeal to everyone to share this appeal and if anyone has heard from Natalie, or has information on her whereabouts, please contact officers at Clydebank Police Office on 101.'

41

'Right, gather round,' Jackson commands, removing his jacket as he walks into the incident room, with Nixon following closely behind.

'Slater, tell me you've got something from the stations,' Jackson urges.

'I have, sir,' Marie Slater replies, 'all of the stations. Natalie and Lowell are seen entering Central via the Gordon Street entrance at 22:37 and heading in the direction of the lower level platforms. To look at the body language, there is no suggestion of anything untoward between them – both are smiling; she seems comfortable with him.'

Jackson nods, and DC Slater carries on. 'Natalie then catches the 22:47 to Dalmuir, and again she can be seen leaving the station via the Duntocher Road exit at 23:12, alone. Kevin Lowell is seen entering Queen Street station at 22:57, and he gets on the 23:06 service to Lenzie. He's seen exiting the station at 23:26, and then the camera on Station Road picks him up thirteen minutes later, supporting his assertion that he went straight home.'

Jackson inhales deeply, then asks a question. 'So, Dalmuir station is the last we see of her?'

'Yes, sir.'

CCTV is a wonderful invention, as Jackson knows well. Often the footage can be the lynchpin of a case, the difference between solved and unsolved. But when the outcome is solved without a happy ending, it can be hard to make peace with the fact that sometimes, the last time a family gets to lay eyes on their loved one, it's courtesy of a grainy, impersonal image on a computer monitor, that has probably already been plastered all over the papers and social media for the world to see and scrutinise.

'There are no more cameras from there to her house,' Nixon interjects. 'We're assuming she walked home from the station – there aren't really any other options apart from a taxi, and it's unlikely that she would have flagged down a cab for such a short journey. It probably took her ten minutes, tops. We've checked with several cab companies but, so far, nothing.'

'And what about the train, was it busy? Did many people get off at Dalmuir?'

'Four or five at the most,' Slater answers. 'And everyone else exited on the Clyde Court side. The streets would have been pretty deserted at that point, but Duntocher Road especially.'

'So probably not the safest, then,' Jackson mutters, repeatedly sickened by a world where untold dangers descend with the darkness. 'Local businesses with cameras?'

'We're checking them, too, sir,' Slater confirms. 'The takeaways won't open for another few hours, but we'll check them all. We've put the appeal out on the usual social media outlets.'

'Good,' Jackson answers. 'Keep me posted. Kyle, where are we on interviewing the friends?'

He directs the question to Kyle McClure, the youngest and newest member of the team.

'We've dug up the addresses for the two friends the family mentioned – going to try and catch them at home now.'

'Okay, good,' Jackson says. 'Let's get somewhere with this, okay?'

'Sir, I've got something that might be worth looking into,' Slater adds. 'I was doing some digging and I found out that Natalie left university under a bit of a cloud.'

'How so?'

'The details are a bit woolly, but it seems she made an accusation against someone and it backfired. She left suddenly. We'll need a warrant to access the full records.'

'Hmm. Definitely worth checking out,' Jackson says. 'I want to go and speak to the family anyway, I'll ask them about it. See about getting that warrant sorted. Good work.'

'Thanks, sir,' Slater answers, and she and Kyle McClure grab their coats and leave the office.

'So,' Jackson says to Nixon, 'we've got her leaving the station, but nothing after that. We've got her – at least, we assume it was her – sending messages saying she's home. We've got her phone, her bag and her keys all making it home.' Nixon once more nods his agreement in silence. 'So, let's say she gets home, sends the messages, sets her alarm, puts her phone on charge, intending to go to work on Friday morning. Then what?'

42

Kyle McClure knocks heavily on the door, his two presses of the doorbell having prompted no response from indoors.

'Julie Coulter?' he asks the bleary-eyed woman who answers the door a few seconds later.

'Yes,' she replies tentatively.'

'Detective Constable Kyle McClure, Detective Constable Marie Slater. We'd like to ask you a few questions. Could we come in?'

'Questions about what?' Julie asks, her brow furrowed in concern.

'Do you mind if we come in and talk, Ms. Coulter?' Slater asks with a polite smile, 'it's a bit chilly out here.'

Julie Coulter waves the officers in, leaving DC McClure to close the door as she leads them down the hallway and into her living room. She is dressed in cotton pyjamas, and slippers in the shape of bunny rabbits. It's obvious that she was asleep when the detectives announced their arrival at her door.

'Have a seat.' She gestures towards a cream fabric sofa, remaining standing. 'What is it you want to talk to me about?

'We believe you're a friend of Natalie Byron's, is that right?' Slater asks, duly seating herself on the couch closest to the door.

'That's right,' Julie answers. 'I've known Natalie since we were at primary school. Why?'

'And when was the last time you heard from her?' Nixon asks.

'Thursday. She was supposed to be going on a date. I called her when I finished work to check if she was still going ahead with it, and she said she was.'

'Why were you checking if she was still going to go on the date?' Slater enquires.

Julie Coulter sighs. 'She used to go out with the guy a while back, and he's a bit of a dick, to be honest – pardon my French.'

'In what way?' McClure asks.

'Just … I don't know, I just didn't get a good vibe off him when I met him. She wasn't with him long, so I probably only met the guy a handful of times, but he just wasn't my kind of person.'

'And did you say that to her when you spoke?'

'Not in so many words. I just asked her if she was sure she wanted to go down that road again, seeing as it didn't work out well with him the last time. She said she was going to give him a chance, and if he messed up again then that would be it.'

'And you haven't spoken to her since then?'

Julie shakes her head. 'I'm on nights this week, haven't had the chance. We've arranged to meet up tomorrow night for a coffee, at the Beardmore.' She reviews the police officers' expressions. 'You're worrying me,' she tells them. 'What's happened?'

DC McClure clears his throat. 'Natalie's parents have reported her as a missing person,' he declares. 'She hasn't been seen since Thursday night, after going on the date.'

Julie Coulter's hands reflexively cover her mouth. 'Oh my God,' she says. 'Missing?'

The detectives nod solemnly, in tandem. 'Have you heard from her?'

'I told you, I haven't spoken to her since Thursday, before she met Kevin.'

'Is there anything you can tell us that might shed some light on her whereabouts?' McClure enquires. 'Did she mention that she was thinking of going away anywhere?'

'What? No,' Julie replies, confused. 'I thought you said she was missing. If she was going away, she'd tell me. She'd tell her family, for God's sake.'

'And what about Kevin, what else can you tell us about him?'

Julie seems lost in her thoughts, and takes a moment to respond, eventually blinking back to the present. 'Sorry?' Slater repeats the question. 'I don't really know much about him, to be honest,' Julie admits. 'He's an engineer or something like that. He was always a bit cocky, kind of overbearing sometimes. She never saw it though.'

'Any idea why they split up?'

'After a few months he kind of went a bit funny, started stringing her along,' Julie answers, finally sitting down. 'He kept her hanging, making all kinds of excuses as to why he couldn't see her, but every time he cancelled on her, he'd be like, *"I'm so sorry, babe. I promise I'll make it up to you."* Turns out, he was already seeing someone else.' She screws up her face, making her feelings about the man abundantly clear.

'And how did Natalie find out?'

Julie looks away momentarily, as though she is deliberating how to answer the question. She sighs, her shoulders rising and dropping dramatically.

'She didn't,' she finally admits. 'I mean, she knows that he ended it, obviously, but she doesn't know why. At least, I don't think she does. I asked him not to tell her.'

'*You* asked him?' Slater prompts.

She sighs again. 'The girl he was seeing came up as a suggested friend on my Facebook,' Julie explains. 'He – Kevin – didn't use Facebook at the time, but he was too dim to realise that his new girlfriend was posting pics of the two of them together, left, right and centre. She came up as a suggested friend, and I saw his stupid face in her profile picture. I messaged him through Instagram and told him I knew, and that he'd better break it off with Nat asap, or else I would tell her the truth. I told him not to hurt her, and, as far as I know, she never found out that he was cheating on her.'

'So, you weren't impressed when she told you she was going out with him again?' McClure points out the obvious. 'Did you contact him again, try to warn him off?'

Julie responds with a shake of her head. 'I was going to. That was my first thought when she told me she was planning to go on another date with him. But something stopped me. I thought, you know what? Maybe he's changed; maybe he's grown up a bit since then. And maybe it's not my place to interfere. I didn't know what to do,' she admits. 'On the one hand, I wanted to tell her everything, so that she would steer clear of him. But I didn't want her to know that I'd kept it from her all this time. To be honest, I was hoping she would go on this date, realise what a plank that guy is, and decide that she didn't want to see him again anyway. If she didn't, I thought I might tell her tomorrow night. I just needed a bit of time to decide what was best.'

McClure nods, unconvinced. 'But you said she was having doubts, prior to Thursday, about going out with him. Why do you think that was?'

'She really was, and I laid it on really thick about how it's never a good idea to go back, hoping that she would give up on the idea altogether, but when I called her on Thursday she sounded so ... excited. I was on the verge of telling her everything, but I didn't want to bring her down, and anyway, it's not the kind of thing you tell someone over the phone, is it? And part of me thought, he must have known that she'd tell me about meeting him. Surely, he wouldn't be stupid enough to pull the same kind of stunt again? Oh God, you don't think he's got anything to do with this, do you?' Julie looks horrified at the thought.

'At this point, we're just making enquiries,' Slater answers.

'But have you asked *him*? What did he say? Did she go out with him?'

'We have spoken to Mr Lowell,' Slater replies authoritatively. 'What we are particularly interested in doing is tracing Natalie's movements prior to the date. Have you noticed anything out of the ordinary in terms of her behaviour recently?'

'No, nothing,' Julie answers abruptly. 'She's been fine, the same as always. What do you mean?'

'Like I said, we're just trying to paint a picture, to try and understand what might have happened.'

'You're asking me if there's been anything different about her, like you think maybe she's just left and not said anything,' Julie observes. 'Is that what you think? Because she would never do that. I know her; I've known her since I was six. Are you sure Kevin Lowell doesn't know where she is? She didn't let him come home with her, did she?'

'We're satisfied that Natalie made her way home alone on Thursday night, separately from Mr Lowell.'

'Oh God,' Julie says again, allowing her body to sink into the couch cushions behind her back. 'So, what do you think has happened to her?'

'That's what we're trying to find out.'

43

Nice place, Jackson thinks to himself, as he manoeuvres his service vehicle into the driveway to the side of the Byrons' home. The house is a detached bungalow, with a large garden to the rear of the property. Taking a closer look as he gets out of the car, Jackson notices that the house has probably had a very recent paint job – it's perfectly white, unblemished.

There are trees of various types and sizes in the garden, at least one of them bearing apples, and a collection of assorted ceramic woodland animals is dotted around the space. The grass seems freshly cut, and Jackson wonders briefly whether the Byron family employs a gardener to look after the not inconsiderable yardage, or whether one or more of them has green fingers. He pauses for a moment before going to knock on the door, taking in the view from where he stands in the driveway. It is stunning. The property sits on a hill, a couple of hundred feet above sea level, overlooking the River Clyde. Jackson can see the outline of the whole city from this vantage point. The Erskine Bridge looms large and proud in his immediate line of vision, but beyond that he can make out the complex landscape of the city he has called home for every one of his fifty-seven years. It may be November, but the sun is harsh on his eyes, despite the briskness of the air. A piercing gust of wind catches his breath as he takes a moment to just admire the surroundings. After the frustratingly slow drive back from the city centre, he could do with a moment of calm.

A noise behind him makes him turn around sharply, and he sees a petite, exhausted-looking woman standing in the doorway.

'Detective Inspector Gordon Jackson,' he states, by way of introduction. He approaches the house, fumbling inside his jacket pocket for his warrant card as he takes the few steps towards the front door. 'Mrs Byron?' he enquires, holding the card aloft for the woman to scrutinise. 'Gillian Byron?'

The woman glances furtively at the card and gives a nod in return. The worry and distress written all over her face are proof that there was no real reason for him to ask for confirmation of her identity – he knows straight away that this is the face of a woman who is living in fear for the life of her child. Jackson has met with countless distraught, desperate family members during his career, not least when working the missing persons cases. This part of the job never gets any easier, no matter the age or the status of the missing person, no matter how many times he goes through the motions. At least, he reminds himself, he hasn't come here to carry out the worst task of them all. He hasn't come to impart the worst news of all, the most devastating news that anyone can prepare for. No news is good news, that's what they say. In other people's line of work, maybe. In general, in everyday life, that might be true. But when you're a DI heading up a missing persons case, no news is torture, worst case scenario. And for the family struggling to get through every moment of every day without news of their loved one, the experience is one of the most difficult there is.

'Is it alright if I come in, please, Mrs Byron?'

Gillian Byron opens her mouth as though she is going to say something, possibly to object to his proposal, but she seems to change her mind, and no words come out. Her eyes drop to the ground, and she opens the door further to allow Jackson to enter, before showing him into the living room.

'Have you found her?' The woman's voice is strained, barely louder than a whisper. There is no hint of hope or anticipation in it. It's loaded with fear, and dread, and Jackson

170

guesses that it took all the energy she had just to say the words. He thinks now that she was about to ask the question when he asked if he could come in but decided instead to wait until they were inside before hearing his answer. Inside the house, presumably, she feels ever so slightly braver, just a little bit safer.

'No, I'm afraid I don't have anything new to tell you at this stage, Mrs Byron.'

The woman's shoulders drop dramatically, and she exhales loudly, as though she has been holding her breath in anticipation of his response. She was bracing herself for the worst, Jackson knows, and he only wishes that he had something more positive to pass on, than the fact that they are still no further forward in their search. At least, for the moment, she will not have to confront her biggest fear, and that seems enough to temporarily release the tension that she so obviously carries in her every muscle. She sits down gently, gracefully on the couch that hugs the wall to the right of the room, and Jackson takes a seat on the other couch, closer to the window.

Gillian adjusts the cardigan that she is wearing, pulling it tighter around her torso and folding her arms across her chest, as though to hold the garment in place. Jackson recognises the protective gesture and rues the fact that he cannot offer more comfort than she can draw from the clothes that she is wearing.

Gillian Byron is a petite woman, probably around five feet tall, and in stature she is diminutive. She has a pretty face, but there are worry lines etched into it like unsolicited tattoos. Her eyes are tired, and red, from no doubt hours of insomnia and crying. Underneath her cardigan she is wearing a white blouse, tailored black trousers which are baggy on her, and Jackson wonders whether her clothes usually dwarf her the way they do today, or whether the pain she is clearly in has shrunk her. Her light brown hair hangs

171

neatly at her shoulders, and she wears no make-up.

'Why are you here, then, if you've got nothing to tell us?' she asks accusingly, choking back tears.

Jackson clears his throat, feeling the guilt of having come to try and source information rather than provide it. 'Well, I wanted to introduce myself, as the lead detective on the case, Mrs Byron. I know you and your family have spoken to members of my team already, but I was out of the office on the day that the case was opened, so I just wanted to come here and let you know that I am heading up the investigation into your daughter's – Natalie's – disappearance. I wanted to-'

'I knew a Gordon Jackson once,' Gillian interrupts him, 'when I was young. He was a policeman. He had a brother, Chris; their mother was Lexie Jackson. They lived not far from us in Garscadden, when I was growing up. That's not you though, obviously.'

A small smile is all Jackson can manage.

'I'd have recognised you, even if it was over thirty years ago, the last time I saw you.' She smiles ruefully, staring ahead at nothing in particular. She focused on a spot on the floor ahead of her the whole time she was speaking, Jackson notes. Her eyes are glazed over, as though they are unaware that they should be playing a role in the show that she is putting on for his benefit. It is a show that Jackson is painfully familiar with. People who are terrified, as Gillian undoubtedly is, cling to safe, familiar things, to keep themselves from focusing on the thing that they are so afraid of. Talking about her past, about easier times in her life, must give her a small sense of stability and calm, at least for a brief moment.

'No, that's not me,' he confirms with a tender smile. 'I grew up in Dennistoun actually. And my mother was Irene, not Lexie.'

Gillian's lips curl up at the sides in a distracted smile, but again, her eyes don't seem to get the memo.

'Can I get you a cup of tea?' she asks, rising from her chair.

'If you're having one, that would be lovely, thank you,' Jackson answers politely.

Gillian potters into the kitchen without acknowledging his reply.

Jackson takes a look around while Gillian busies herself. The living room is not small, but neither is it massive. There is enough space for a three-seater sofa and a two-seater to match, and a coffee table in the centre of the room. A large flat screen television rests upon a wooden stand, and there is a tall wooden storage unit comprising of several shelves, hosting a large Bluetooth speaker and various ornaments.

There are more ornaments on the fireplace, and a vase full of fresh flowers on a small end-table at the far end of the couch. Photographs of the Byron family are hung on the walls, and Natalie's face beams from one of them, triggering a pang of guilt in Jackson.

The room is spotless, and from where Jackson stands he can see that the kitchen looks impeccable too. Gillian moves almost noiselessly, re-adjusting her cardigan every few seconds to avoid it ever becoming too loose. She makes the tea as though she is in auto-pilot mode, and Jackson suspects that perhaps she is in a somewhat medicated state.

'What do you take in your tea?' she asks from the other room. This is the loudest that Jackson has heard her speak so far.

'Just a splash of milk, thank you,' he answers, considering going into the kitchen to offer some help or even ask some questions, but deciding against it. She might feel cornered if he follows her in. She is already feeling fragile enough.

'Here you are,' she says, handing him a mug in the shape of a bulldog.

'Thank you.' He goes to take a sip but decides to hold

off for a moment or two, to allow the tea to cool down just a little. Gillian sits back down, gripping her mug with two hands in front of her.

'Natalie bought that mug,' she states, staring straight ahead again, 'for her brother.'

Jackson bows his head and blows gently on his tea before taking a sip. 'That's nice,' he murmurs.

Gillian does not carry on. She sits frozen in place, and Jackson decides to take the bull by the horns and kick off his questioning. 'Like I was saying earlier, Mrs Byron, I just wanted to come around and introduce myself, to let you know that I am the senior officer in charge of the case. And I wondered if I could ask you a few more questions. Is your husband not at home?'

'He's gone to pick up our other daughter and her boyfriend from the airport,' she tells him, with a sigh. 'They were in California on holiday. I told Gemma not to cut it short, to wait and see what happened, but she wanted to be home.'

'That's entirely understandable. Well, I won't keep you long,' Jackson explains. 'If I could just go over a few things, make sure that there's nothing we might have missed, so far.'

'Like what?' Gillian asks suspiciously.

'Well, I understand that Natalie is very close to her family, especially you, Mrs Byron.'

'That's right. We've already told your colleagues all this.'

'Did you notice anything different about her in recent weeks? Any changes at all in her manner, her behaviour, her routine?'

Gillian sighs loudly and shakes her head. Jackson thinks he witnessed a flicker of anger across her face.

'No,' she says decisively.

'And ... I don't mean to be indelicate, Mrs Byron, but does Natalie have any history of mental illness? Stress, anxiety, depression?'

'What?'

174

'It's just that we've become aware of an … incident that happened when Natalie was younger. An incident that led to her leaving university-'

Gillian's face changes again, and this time her anger is unmistakable.

'How many times do we have to tell you people?' she yells, slamming her cup of tea on the table in front of her with enough force to cause almost half of the liquid to spill out. 'What are you expecting us to say? First you make it clear that me and my whole family are prime suspects, subjecting us to hours and hours of questions and insinuations, and now this! What are you suggesting now, that she's suicidal?'

'No, I'm not saying that, I just …'

'Don't you think if we knew, or even so much as suspected there was something wrong, we'd have told you? Don't you think if me or my family had any idea where she is, who she's with, or what she's doing, we'd have told you, the very first time you asked?'

'Mrs Byron, I …'

Gillian is standing now, not seeming to care that her cardigan is no longer wrapped tight around her. 'No, you listen to me,' she demands, projecting a far greater stature than her size allows for. 'It's been almost three days since I last spoke to my daughter. Three days! And what have you people done so far? My husband, my son, me, we've all answered all your questions, and we've all told you the same thing: Natalie would *never* go anywhere without letting us know! No matter what! I know my daughter, Gordon Jackson, and I know that there is not a day that goes by that I don't hear from her. I know that she was not depressed or suicidal, and I know that there is absolutely no chance she would even *think* of running away, and making it look like something else. You don't know this, because you don't know my daughter, but why won't you *listen*?'

Her voice breaks, and rage gives way to grief. She sinks

back onto the couch, almost falling, as though all her strength has deserted her. Her shoulders move in time with her sobs of despair, and Jackson feels awful for compounding her already significant grief.

The human side of him feels tempted to go to her, and offer a comforting hand on her shoulder, but his professionalism keeps him from doing so.

'I'm very sorry, Mrs Byron,' he says softly. 'I appreciate that this is a very difficult time for you, and your family.'

Gillian continues to cry, painful, hacking sobs. She has pulled her cardigan around herself once more, and it could almost cover her slight frame twice over.

'Please be assured that myself and my team are following all lines of enquiry and are doing everything we can to find your daughter.'

He pauses but gets no response. 'Would you like a glass of water?'

Gillian sniffs loudly and wipes the tears away from her face with a tissue that she had in her pocket.

'I'd like you to leave,' she says, coldly.

Jackson rises to his feet. 'I really am very sorry, Mrs Byron,' he repeats. He starts to make his way to the front door, to show himself out when he remembers the other reason for his visit. 'Just one more thing, Mrs Byron, we've issued a public appeal for information. Natalie's name and photo will be distributed via news outlets, social media, places like that, just so you're aware.'

Gillian looks up, her eyes scarlet, her face bearing a look of exhaustion.

'About bloody time,' is all she says.

44

I'm having the most wonderful dream. I know it's a dream, because I'm with my family, and I feel all warm and fuzzy inside. I feel happy.

I'm pleading with my brain to keep me here, in this dream, because this is where I want to be, forever.

My loved ones are all here. We're on holiday, I think, in a place I don't recognise. Having said that, maybe my brain, with all the overtime it's been working the last few days, has uncovered a deeply-buried memory of this idyllic place, that I don't seem to know anything about. Maybe I'll make the connection when I wake up. God, how I don't want to wake up.

Whether it's real or a figment of my imagination, where we are is beautiful. The sun is shining brightly, the sky is unfathomably blue, and the palm trees are so perfectly-formed that they could have been hand-carved by the most gifted sculptor in the world.

There are voices all around me, and to my ears they sound like sweet music.

My parents are there, my sisters, Gemma and Anna, and my brother, Max.

Max is playing keepie-up with a football, occasionally flicking little waves of sand in my direction. If I were awake, and this were really happening, perhaps I would have a little sisterly moan at him, ask him to move a little further away in order to avoid ingesting the grains of sand or catching them in my eyes. But this is not really happening. This is a dream, and in the dream, I let my little brother flick as much sand at me as he likes, because the only thing that matters to me in this moment is being close to my family.

I recline on my sun lounger, reviewing the scene. My eyes are sensibly shielded from the brilliant sun by a pair of shades, and my head is protected by a straw hat. This is perfection, I think to myself, allowing a smile to spread across my face. *This* is my life. All that matters to me is right here, and it's perfect.

Suddenly the sky starts to cloud over, and I know that means that I'm about to wake up. I can feel this fragile link to everything that I hold dear slipping away, and I have no way to grab hold of it. I beg – someone, anyone – to leave me here, to let me stay in this moment, but I can feel myself being pulled away, back to reality. All the faces that I love begin to blur, until they're vague, featureless, and suddenly the voices are gone, and an eerie silence descends as the sky continues to darken. I try to make out the slightest sound, but there is nothing around me now other than generic, hovering shapes, and I can't distinguish one person from another.

'Please,' I say out loud, and it's the sound of my own pitiful voice that finally rouses me awake. I open my eyes, but I don't move. I don't have to, to know that, once again, I have woken up in my own personal hell.

I can hear light snoring coming from my right, and it prompts a tear to roll down my face and land on my pillow. The only way that I can think to describe how I feel right now is that I think my heart is literally broken.

I feel as though I'm in mourning, for the life I used to have, the life that I am beginning to fear I will never get back. What if I don't? What if I never get to see my family, my friends, my house again? What will become of the car that I bought only five months ago, the one that I worked so hard to afford?

I could miss all the momentous occasions in my family and friends' lives. Maybe I'll be conspicuously absent from Gemma and Mark's wedding. Maybe I'll never meet their kids. Maybe I will never again be able to debate with Anna whether *Die Hard* is a Christmas movie. Perhaps I won't be around when Max turns thirty.

There are so many things about my life that I miss already. Even aside from the earth-shattering stuff, perhaps I won't ever know how *Game of Thrones* ends. Or whether they ever find out what caused all the devastation in *The Walking Dead*.

I need to stop assuming the worst. But it's not easy. It's been almost twenty-four hours since I called the police, and yet I'm still here. Why haven't they come for me yet? Or perhaps they did come, but they haven't been able to trace me yet. I have literally no idea how big this island is. I was so sure they would be able to track the phone though.

I really did dare to think that I was going to be saved. I had my hopes built up so high, that now that they've come crashing down, it feels like the weight of them falling on me has literally crushed my spirit. And, of course, my poor heart.

I had to try to act normal – as normal as possible – for the rest of the day yesterday, all the while thinking that at any moment, my cavalry could burst through the door and scoop me up and carry me off to safety. I had to spend a whole day doing normal, boring things, like pretending to read a book. It wasn't even one I'd ever normally read – it was Jamie's suggestion, since there is nothing else to do in this place. I was cajoled into making bland, perfunctory conversation, and above all, to do my best to convince Jamie that the unfortunate *episode* that I suffered from has passed, and that I am, in fact, Jen again.

That I'm Jennifer Mayhew, fluent speaker of Spanish and lover of this man, whom, in reality, I wouldn't touch with a barge pole.

I've had hours of lying awake, listening for sounds of help, to think about what to try next, and the fact that today is Monday is the one thing that's helping me to stay afloat. Bessie's shop will be open, hopefully. Perhaps she will even be expecting a delivery from the mainland. Even on the Isle of Carn, Monday must be a massive step up from Sunday.

Birds are singing, cheerfully, just outside the bedroom window. I focus on their song, relying on it to help lift my spirits. Can birdsong ever be anything but cheerful? I decide not, as what I hear makes me giggle a little, in spite of my low mood.

One bird is making the same sound, in little patterns of four or five repetitions, then pausing, as though waiting for a reply. Sure enough, a few seconds later a different bird then makes a noise, as though directly responding to the first. This one is a lower, less enthusiastic sound, and his pattern only consists of two sounds, then he stops. The birds' little conversation carries on for at least a couple of minutes, until only the first one's little pattern can still be heard. I can't help smiling to myself as I wonder if the second bird has simply decided he doesn't want to talk any more, or whether he became so uninterested – or offended, perhaps – that he felt compelled to fly away, in a huff.

It makes me smile to think of these birds having human-like conversations, and I'm thankful for their presence and their entertainment. It occurs to me that I've never really taken the time to really listen to birdsong before. It's always just been something that was there, something I've taken for granted, like having my freedom, and feeling safe.

The birdsong has lifted my mood ever so slightly, but if their little performance is going to be the only thing I have to look forward to for the rest of my life, well, then that doesn't bear thinking about.

45

'Who's next?' DI Jackson enquires. He is standing facing out onto the office floor in Natalie's place of work. So far, he and Nixon have interviewed three of her colleagues, and none of them have offered anything of use to the investigation.

All of the meeting rooms on this section of the office floor have glass walls, meaning that although staff aren't able to hear what's being said in the room, they can certainly see everything that's going on. And Jackson can see the whole east side of the floor from where he's standing.

There are people chatting, and typing, and talking on the phone, and Jackson wonders – not for the first time in his life – what it must be like to do a civilian job. Those people on the phone right now are probably talking about printers that need fixing, or resource plans that need jiggling. Perhaps some of them are even making sneaky personal calls.

Those people undoubtedly have their professional rough days, he thinks to himself, but he's quite sure they don't deal in the despair that he comes face to face with every day, not to mention the death.

'That's us,' Nixon answers. 'Natalie's team is small – we've spoken to them all. Unless we start looking outside the team and across the department as a whole, there's no-one else to interview.'

Jackson sits back down, resting his elbow on the solid wooden table that takes up most of the space in the relatively small room, and then allowing his head to rest on his hand for a moment.

'There's about a hundred people in total, across the department,' Nixon adds, keen to avoid going down the route of looking for the proverbial needle in a haystack.

'Is it just me, or is this case going nowhere?' Jackson asks.

Nixon tries not to let himself think in terms of lost causes, but even he has to admit that this case is throwing up dead ends every which way they turn.

'We certainly don't have much to go on,' he acknowledges gravely.

'You can say that again.' Jackson seems a little defeated, but the spikiness that radiated from him only moments ago is no longer evident. 'Tell me, Nixon, do you think she took off?'

Nixon looks around the room, wondering whether they should keep this kind of conversation for in the car, or back at the station, rather than the goldfish-bowl that is the third-floor conference room in Natalie's place of work. He gives out a sigh.

'I'm just not sure, Boss. It doesn't seem to make sense, but then the abduction theory doesn't really pan out either. I don't like Lowell for it, he just doesn't seem like the type. Maybe we should go over everything back at the station, try and get our heads around everything.'

Jackson takes the hint and gets to his feet without saying anything. He doesn't wholeheartedly agree with Nixon's assertion regarding Lowell. He knows only too well that people are adept at deceit. Lowell might look every bit the hapless, clueless nobody, but there's something about him that Jackson can't put his finger on, and he's a long way from being discounted as prime suspect.

Whether it be Lowell or not, Jackson hopes that when they get back to the station and triple check all the facts, they will realise that they've missed something, and an answer to this seemingly unanswerable question will just come to them, out of nowhere.

Missing something earth-shattering will, of course, mean

a fuck-up, which Jackson can't stand on his watch, but it's preferable to the alternative.

A young woman is missing, and no-one has the slightest fucking clue what's happened to her.

*

Kevin slumps down onto the couch that the police officers occupied yesterday, when they had dropped the bombshell about Natalie. Then, he had felt nervous, anxious, scared for his own freedom. Today, he feels all of those things and more. He saw the look that the older one flashed him as he left – they'll be back with more questions, Kevin is sure of it. And today, on top of the dread he feels for himself, he has a new feeling to contend with: hopelessness. He thought he could do something, he really did. He even pictured himself being the hero, the one who solved the mystery and delivered her home, receiving resounding praise from her nearest and dearest and a subtle apology from those cops who had made him feel as though he had something to hide. But good intentions and all the hope in the world weren't adequate tools to conjure up someone who simply wasn't there, he had found out the hard way. When you didn't have a badge, people were reluctant to answer your questions, and anyway, he had seen Natalie leave those pubs with his own eyes – he had walked her to the train station, for goodness sake. But what else could he do, other than go back over that evening, in his head and on foot, accosting people who had no more reason to know where Natalie had gone than he did.

Unsurprisingly, his one-man mission failed, and now he's back home, defeated. He has no more ideas for today. He knows where Natalie lives on account of having been there a few times, but not only is she not there, the place will be taped off right now, probably being pored over by more

183

cops, intent on finding something to crack the case.

He checks his phone once again, because it's the only thing he can think of doing, and loses his temper at the sight of the blank notifications menu. He hurls the phone across the room, hearing it land with a crack over by the kitchen door, and concedes that he is not going to be the one to find her, after all.

46

Today is Monday. Please God, let there be a ferry today. Or a small boat, captained by a friendly, helpful rescuer who will whisk me back to the mainland. Any vessel will do, I'm not fussy. And just one, that's all I need. If I thought for one moment that it wouldn't result in my certain death, I'd bloody swim across.

I'll try calling the police again, obviously, but the more I think about it, the more I think that might be a bit of a lost cause. Now that I've had more time to run over everything in my mind, I've decided that Jamie must have tampered with the mobile, somehow, to make it untraceable. Did he tamper with the phone in the phone box too?

He must have predicted that I would go snooping when he was asleep, and he made no attempt to keep me away from the contents of those drawers when he found me yesterday morning. It was no problem for him that I would come across the phone, and to latch onto the hope that it gave me, because he knew fine well that it would be of no use to me at all. He probably even wanted me to find it, and to try to use it, all to no avail. He really is a sick, twisted individual.

Without the option to track the mobile, the police would be reliant on my scant, unverified details about where I am, and for all I know, I could have sent them on a wild goose chase when I asked them to come to the Isle of Carn.

What assurances do I have that anything Jamie has told me about this place has been true? None. In fact, it would be far more surprising if he had told the truth than if he had simply plucked the name of the island and some vague details out of thin air.

185

So, I've concluded that I am, to all intents and purposes, stuck here. Unless there is a ferry service, and I can manage to get myself on one. There has to be some kind of service, right? I mean, unless it's a private island ...

Oh God. What if that's it? What if this is just some private island that some rich person just decided to buy – maybe Jamie – that is not accessible without permission? What if Jamie and Bessie and Davie are all from the same warped, creepy family, and this island is where they bring their victims because they know they'll never be traced? *Bloody hell.*

I need to know what I'm dealing with here. I need to have a proper, unaccompanied look around this island, and I need to figure out what I can possibly do to get away. If there is a ferry port, it will be pretty recognisable, I should think. I've been on ferries before, as a child, when my family and I used to take day trips to places like Dunoon, and Bute, and from memory I think a port would be pretty damned hard to miss. In saying that, Dunoon and Bute are well-known, much-visited places. Where the hell am I?

If there is a port, then there would have to be a timetable available for perusal, and a ticket office.

The key problem remains the lack of means to buy a ticket, as I don't have any money of my own. Since Jamie appears to have thought of everything else, I suddenly wonder what he's come up with in terms of finances for me. Is he going to produce a debit card with the name *Jennifer Mayhew* emblazoned on it, and allow me access to funds? If not, how would he explain away the fact that I have no bank account of my own? As absurd as it is, I really hope that he has gone to the trouble of fabricating this one additional thing, so that I can at least have a fighting chance of getting to the mainland.

It occurs to me that, even if I could get to the mainland with Jamie, my chances of escape would be dramatically

186

enhanced (as compared to not getting to the mainland at all). As soon as my feet hit solid ground, I would run, as fast as I could, and scream as loud as I could, for help. Jamie may have his merry little band of helpers, willing to do his bidding and maintain his warped pretence here on the island, but there is no chance his evil little scheme will hold up anywhere else.

So, either I need to ask for *my* bank card, in a nonchalant, 'I just forgot where I put it,' kind of way, or I need to convince Jamie to accompany me 'home.' I could tell him that I'm just really missing my mum, especially after the little meltdown over the phone that I'm still recovering from, and harass him to take me to see her. So far, he hasn't refused anything I've asked of him, so would he do this for me? Granted, he always seems to have an angle worked out for whenever I ask him for anything, but I think this might be my best shot.

I have to be a lot cleverer than I have been up until now, perhaps smarter than I've ever been in my life. I certainly have to be a lot more cynical and anticipate that he will try to shut down any avenue that I try to exploit. I must be mindful of the fact that, even if Jamie does furnish me with a bank card, there may not actually be any funds available to draw on. And how feasible is it that there will be a place to actually draw funds out! Similarly, I have to assume that his corrupting reach may extend to anyone working in the ferry ticket office, and that if I try to buy a ticket, they might inform him.

I try to determine how I should make the absolute best use of this day. Trying to access the Internet one more time would be worth a try, but with my sceptical hat on, I must again assume that somehow Jamie will have managed to rig that, too. I suppose it can't hurt though. Maybe that should be goal number one for the day.

Depending on what I can achieve with Internet access, my other goals might have to be altered slightly, but for now

I refuse to get my hopes up. Goal number two should be to just go exploring, scouting for any clues I can find as to how anyone ever reaches or leaves this island, and if I find a ferry port, I'll note down whatever details I can find.

I won't tell Jamie what I'm doing, obviously. I'll say I'm going for a run. Yes, that's a good idea. A run will actually probably do me some good, anyway. At least I have my trusty trainers here, courtesy of Jamie's raid on my wardrobe.

Goal number three will be to convince Jamie to let me go home to see my family – with or without him. The chances of him allowing me to just leave, just disappear off the island as though nothing has happened, are zero, as far as I'm concerned, but when he insists that he must come with me, I'll accept his suggestion. Getting off this island is the key, and although I've scheduled it as goal number three for today, it remains firmly priority number one, and is the only thing that gives me any chance of reclaiming my life again.

I get up from the bed in one swift movement, not caring whether I wake Jamie or not. I'll kill two – or maybe it's actually three – birds with one stone: I'll go for a run, check out the Internet access, and do a reconnaissance mission on the ferry situation.

I'm extracting my running gear from the drawer when Jamie stirs. 'Hey, hun, what are you doing?' he asks, still half asleep. He's forgotten my embargo on pet names, obviously. 'What time is it?'

'I'm not sure,' I reply flatly, answering his second question first. 'Early. I'm going for a run.' I don't wait for a reply, I simply make my way into the bathroom, and thankfully Jamie doesn't follow me. Me going for a run must be acceptable to him, which makes me worry that goals one and two are unlikely to produce much of a return. I'm still going anyway. If I know one thing for sure, it's that I'm only going to get home if I make it happen myself.

I quickly wash up and dress in my jogging trousers and a

long-sleeved sports top (it's dry outside, but it looks a little chilly), and search the kitchen for a sports bottle, or similar receptacle that I can take with me. I still have the coins that I took to the phone box, and I doubt the cost of using the Internet will be more than the amount I have. I can broach the subject of my own personal finances later, if it comes to that.

I find a water bottle that looks like it's probably meant for use when camping, but it's a bottle with a lid, and that's all I need. I fill it to the top, and head out. I'm almost at the front door when I remember that there is a small music library on the phone I found. I retrieve the phone from the living room and set about trying to find earphones. I think I remember seeing some in one of the desk drawers, and sure enough after some rifling around I find some white bud earphones. I don't really like these ones – I always find that the 'buds' feel too big to fit properly inside my ears, but since I can't see any others, for example the sports kind that I normally use, which also loop over the top of your ears, I'll just have to use these ones. *Ew.* I give them a quick clean first, in the kitchen, making them as sanitary as possible without actually washing them, and completely ridding them of function.

I browse through the playlists on the phone as I make my way out of the house, all the while listening for movement from the bedroom and not hearing any. It strikes me that the events of the last few moments are so ordinary, so mundane, that if a fly on the wall were to witness them, for all intents and purposes, Jamie and I could be just like any other couple. Girl gets up to go for a run, boy stays in bed. Except that in this case, boy has girl effectively imprisoned, and girl is clutching at straws, trying her damnedest to escape.

47

These shitty earphones keep trying to make their own escape as I run, and I must have replaced them about four times, into each ear, so far.

The music – when I can actually hear it – is helping me take a break from my thoughts, and as Chris Martin belts out *You're a sky full of stars*, my body responds to the song's cheeriness, and my feet try to keep pace with the beat.

I haven't found what I'm looking for yet. I've managed to get further than I have on my previous outings, and in the twenty minutes or so that I've been on the move, I'm glad to say that I haven't been accosted by any undesirables, so that's a plus. The downside to there being no people around – even if all the people here are quite possibly psychotic people – is that I really have no idea where I'm going. I should say, I really have no idea if there is anywhere else worth going to.

What I'm looking for is a port, and although I've deliberately stuck to the coastal route rather than heading for the parts I'm familiar with, I've seen no evidence of any boats of any kind so far.

I keep jogging, willing myself not to give up, both physically and mentally. It's been a while since I've been able to run for this long without stopping, so I assume that, as well as the training I've been doing at home, an extra surge of adrenalin must be powering me forward.

That toxin-free air probably has something do with it too. It certainly makes a change from inhaling car fumes and goodness knows what else pumps around a heavily-populated city.

It's less breezy today than it was yesterday, and, in actual fact, it's really nowhere near as cold as I expected it to be. I'm sweating from the exertion, of course, but I think I would probably have been fine with a t-shirt rather than the long-sleeved top I chose.

I set the playlist to shuffle when I came out, and a song comes on that I think I recognise from the radio, although I haven't heard it often enough to know all the words by heart.

The beat of this song is perfect for me to run in time with, and I start to hum along to the tune. After a few seconds, I begin to register the words, and instead of buoying me up, the song starts to drain the energy out of my body.

Where are you now? the singer asks. *Was it all in my fantasy; were you only imaginary?*

'No!' I yell, 'they weren't imaginary!'

I swore I'd never doubt myself again. I know that my family, my friends, my job and my home aren't imaginary. In fact, I can now see them all, flashing before my eyes, as if to prove that they're real. I even see Kevin: his smile, his eyes, that made me all but swoon only a few days ago. None of those things are merely a fantasy.

The images float past my eyes, as though I'm looking through a kaleidoscope, and I start to feel dizzy. I feel like I have to stop moving, so I do. I'm having another anxiety attack – only this time I know what is happening to me, and I have the tools to deal with it.

I'm sobbing, and breathing hard at the same time, which is not a good combination, and makes me feel light-headed. My throat is burning, and my eyes are having trouble trying to maintain focus, but I tell myself that the feelings are temporary; that I can ride this out; that I'm not in any real danger.

I manage to get my breathing under control, and I sit down on the grass, knowing I've made it through the worst of the attack. My eyes can see more clearly now, as well, and

I look around me, trying to comprehend where I might be.

I'm still hugging the coast, and I think I can make out mainland of some description, but it could be light years away, in real terms, since I have no means to get there.

After a few more minutes of rest, I feel confident enough to get back up on my feet again, and this time I'll stick to walking, at least for a while. I wipe my eyes and blink a few times to clear the mist. I do a double-take when I think I spot something, out of the side of my eye. I focus my gaze firmly on what I think I saw, and unless this is some kind of mirage that I'm seeing, there is a boat on the water, and it is heading here, for this island! It's far too small to be a ferry, but nonetheless, it is a vessel that can travel through water, and it's coming this way!

Is it the police? I can't tell much about the boat, since it's still a significant distance away, but this could be it! This could be the police responding to my mayday call, coming to get me! They're a whole day late, and they put me through hell, making me think I was stuck here without a hope, but I can forgive all that.

I'm standing as still as I can, and it reminds me of that game that we used to play at parties when I was a child, the one where you had to stand as still as a statue when the music stopped. I'm really seeing the boat – it's not a trick of the mind – but I'm going to stand here, and watch it, unflinching, until it gets here. I don't want to take my eyes off it, even for a second.

My breathing quickens again, and I can feel tears coming, but this time it's excitement and relief instead of hopelessness that are provoking these reactions, not fear.

This boat is my lifeline. My ticket back to my life.

48

'Who *is* that?' Gary asks out loud, even though he is alone in the control room.

The boss hasn't materialised yet, which is odd, and so is the fact that someone is arriving on the island without his knowledge.

Gary only came back on shift an hour or so ago, after having had a few hours' respite when the puppet master took over the reins himself, and should probably feel refreshed, but he didn't sleep well, and he attributes that to the constant unease he feels, working on this *project*. And the utter shame he feels at being so foolish as to walk right into the trap that was set for him with not the merest suspicion that he was about to be done up like a kipper.

He had long considered Jason a good friend, but after his part in what had turned out to be the job from hell, he feels bound to re-evaluate that. Jason's 'introduction' had been more than welcome at the time, with Gary's previous temporary contract having ended only three weeks previously, and the money was decent, on a par with the best day rate he'd ever signed up for. The job description was sketchy at best, now he came to think about it with the benefit of hindsight and hours of thinking things over, but he was qualified, available, and eager to get back into the saddle after weeks of lazily browsing job sites and applying for a total of zero positions, holding out for something that would interest him more than the usual, run of the mill posts that were ten a penny.

So, Jason had 'put in a good word', and before he knew it everything had come together. A few weeks' work with the possibility of an extension, working with pretty high-tech gear, all expenses covered, and a little bit of travel to boot. Not anywhere exotic, but it would be a change of scenery, and if someone else was picking up the tab to get him there, then he had no issue with it whatsoever.

He hadn't even interviewed, not really. He simply showed up, met the man who called himself 'Mr Smith' (a red herring that Gary judges himself for not calling *bullshit* on more so than any other part of this whole charade) and signed the contract. And then the weirdness began. In truth, there had been a flicker of something when he had first met him. Nothing tangible that he could explain if he were asked, but the man gave him the creeps. The length of the contract was 'as yet undefined, due to the rather unpredictable nature of the project,' which was not necessarily out of the ordinary in his line of work, but the need for 'absolute discretion', to which he had to agree in writing, did strike him as relatively out of kilter. But to be headhunted for a role that would set him up for a very comfortable few months afterwards was an ego boost on top of a welcome injection to his finances. The travel didn't bother him at all, and, as for the 'project', he hadn't bothered to ask many questions. Installing hardware, being on hand for monitoring and maintenance – what was there to ask? The boss was smart, Gary realised as he thought back to the conversation. He had immediately followed up the confirmation of the monetary compensation with, 'Are you okay with all of that?' Gary had been distracted by the figures, jumping ahead to thoughts of how to spend all that lovely dough. What he could and would do with the cash was definitely a factor in making him answer in the affirmative. But there was something else that made him say, 'Yeah, absolutely.' If he were honest, it was the reluctance to say no to the man that made him agree. He had never felt intimidated in the way that he did standing in front of 'Mr Smith'. But Jason *was* a good friend, he had consoled himself. He wouldn't put him forward for a job that would land him in any trouble. And the contract would be over in a few weeks, and Gary could simply walk away with whatever information was to be kept discreet and a nice few extra grand in his bank account.

Technically speaking, the job is indeed easy, like taking candy from a baby. But now Gary knows why the man gave him the creeps. He is clearly a psychopath. Or maybe a sociopath, Gary doesn't quite understand the distinction, but he's damn sure he's in the company of one of them. As far as he's concerned, this guy should be the subject of a study somewhere, potentially in a true crime documentary.

Gary does what he is told because he has no choice. But that doesn't mean he has to be okay with it. The nausea that threatens to derail his task has been ever-present for the last day or so, and now he can't bring himself to sleep.

What the hell is the man going to do to this woman? But then, of course, the psycho is not the only one involved in this ghoulish spectacle, even if he is undoubtedly the architect of it. Alex, Bessie, Davie, and now Gary himself, are all culpable, whether they were fully aware of what they were letting themselves in for or not. Gary suspects that Alex is a second unwitting victim, or should that be a third? But as for the others, why are they playing along? Did the man get under their skin too? Kidnapping a woman and subjecting her to unrelenting mental cruelty were things that were definitely not mentioned to Gary, and he can't stomach the thought of these other people knowing what was in store and going along with it anyway. There has to be something innocent behind their motivation, something radical, or else they're just as bad as the guy who is pulling all their strings. And dealing with three or four psychopaths is not a scenario that Gary wants his mind to entertain.

But what can he do now? What can any of them do? He gets the impression that Alex is feeling the pressure, too, but of course, he is in even more of a vice than Gary. When he's alone, Alex looks almost ill with guilt, or regret, or perhaps a combination of both. He doesn't look like a man who is *au fait* with the sheer cruelty that's been inflicted on her – Natalie.

Gary calls her that now; he can't help himself. Just like he can't help himself calling the scary man 'The Psycho'. He feels truly sorry for her. He wishes there was something he could do. He wishes he could rush in there, and tell her that she's right, that she's the victim of something he would never have believed if he hadn't seen it with his own eyes. He wants to tell her that she was taken from her own home, right when she thought she was perfectly safe, and that enough remnants of her own life were transported here with her to make her doubt her sense of reality. If he could, he'd call the police himself, and have them come here, and throw the book at the guy who put it all together for what he's done.

But what about what Gary has done already? And Alex? And the others?

None of them are completely innocent in this. They all came here of their own accord, for all he knows they were lured by money and blinded enough not to suspect what the man was planning. They've all signed contracts, presumably, and Gary doesn't think the other guys will have gone through theirs with a fine-tooth comb – he certainly didn't – so who knows what they agreed to in the small print? Besides, the lengths that The Psycho will go to don't give Gary any comfort that he wouldn't just doctor the contracts to make it look like it was all their idea, at the merest hint of rebellion.

Gary is stuck. His situation is nowhere near as desperate as the one that Natalie finds herself in, and he feels slightly guilty at making any kind of comparison, but if Natalie is going through a nightmare, he is certainly in the midst of a bad dream.

Perhaps even if he knew it wouldn't get any worse, that

might make a difference. As it is, he has no idea how far the man is going to push Natalie, and that makes him fearful. Tearing her away from her family and trying to make her believe that they don't exist is bad enough, but Gary gets the feeling that the end game is not going to be to jump out from a concealed position and yell, 'Surprise! We kidnapped you, but you can go home now!'

No, Gary knows that he is working for a sinister man. Someone who oozes darkness from every pore, and Gary is sadly resigned to the fact that things will only get worse – for Natalie, for Alex, for Gary.

Gary leans forward to try and get a better look at the mysterious visitor arriving ashore, but he can't tell who it is. The compact drone that's being used to follow Natalie around is hovering far enough from her that she won't suspect anything of it – it's cunningly disguised as a bee, anyway – and Gary doesn't want to shift its viewpoint away from Natalie to investigate the boat more closely, in case he misses something that he shouldn't. One thing he does know for sure, however: it won't be the police.

49

It's not the police. It's Davie. Fucking Davie, and some woman I've never seen before – not Bessie. They're docking a few hundred feet ahead of me, but now that I know it's them, and not someone who can actually help me, I wish I was invisible. On the contrary, I could probably be quite easily spotted from space, with the right equipment, since the top I chose to wear for my run is a very noticeable, luminous pink.

What are the chances that Davie has had an unexpected change of heart, and decided he's actually on my side in this stupid game, and has hatched a plan to return me to safety? That was the question I asked myself in the seconds after I recognised his face and realised there was another person with him. Call me a hardened cynic, but after days of disappointment, I quickly deduced that the chances of that being the case are slim to non-existent.

I start to walk away from where they are, wanting to move faster, but the lead has returned to weigh down my legs, and they are unable to achieve any pace.

'Jen!' I hear Davie's booming voice, cutting through the air. He's spotted me. He knows it's me. Well, who else would it be? I let out a little ironic laugh at the thought of me possibly being mistaken for someone else, like Bessie or maybe a third or fourth female inhabitant of the island. I'm feeling heavy with disappointment and dread, but the mental image of Bessie kitted out in the outfit I'm wearing makes me giggle. If I don't laugh, I'll cry, again, and I'm so sick of crying I'd gladly donate my tear ducts to anyone who may be in need of some.

I don't turn around. I'm not heading back towards the house, towards Jamie – at least I don't think I am – but I won't stop or slow down for them. I've had enough of all these wretched people, and I have one goal – to find a means to get home.

Some power is returning to my legs, probably as a result of the adrenalin that has kicked in, born out of the anger I'm feeling at being thwarted yet again.

I'm uttering clichés that might spur me on, whispering them to myself, at first, then saying them out loud, since there is no-one close enough to hear me, and even if they were, who cares if they hear?

What doesn't kill you makes you stronger.

If at first you don't succeed, try, try and try again.

Pick yourself up, dust yourself off, and start all over again.

I'm clenching my fists, and unclenching them as I walk, gathering some speed now that I've recovered from yet another knock.

'Jen!' The woman's voice calls for me this time, and alarmingly, it sounds like she's not too far behind me. Is she running? I don't want to turn around, to even acknowledge that they're referring to me. I don't want to talk to this woman, whoever she is, whatever fabrications she's bound to want to subject me to. She must be running, because the next time she yells, I can tell that she's gaining on me.

I make the split-second decision to run, even though I don't really know where I'm going to end up. I set off as fast as I can, feeling even angrier now that I'm being forced into some ridiculous cat-and-mouse style chase. I try to head in a direction that hopefully will not lead me back to the village.

Curiosity makes me steal a glance behind me, and it's a huge mistake, since I see that both Davie and the woman are trying to catch up with me, and turning my upper body back round to face the front so swiftly makes me lose a little of my balance. I try to correct myself, but just as I think I'm back on track my foot makes contact with a large boulder hidden in the long grass. My ankle folds underneath me in a horribly unnatural way, and I tumble to the ground, the fall seeming to happen in slow motion, but also too quickly for me to do anything about it.

'Ow!' I yell, grabbing hold of my right ankle, which is smarting from the sickening contortion it was just forced into. My left wrist has also been subjected to some trauma, and there is pain searing all the way up my arm. I remember when I broke my wrist, about five years ago, and the intensity of pain feels similar to that time. I test it out, to make sure I still have full range of movement, and thankfully I do. It might just be sprained. I use my other arm to help me get back to standing, but when I try to put weight on my injured ankle, a violent jolt of pain tells me that I'm not ready to walk freely again yet. I lower myself carefully onto the ground, hoping the pain will subside in a few minutes.

The woman and Davie have caught up with me, now, and the woman is standing over me, fussing and asking me if I'm alright. Davie crouches down beside me, puts his hand on my shoulder, and asks the same thing.

'Fuuuuuck!' I scream, taking them both by surprise. In truth, I've probably taken myself a little by surprise too. All my anger, and frustration, and now utter helplessness has come to a head, and I just need to let it out. 'What the fuck is wrong with you people?' I demand, shouting at Davie then looking up at the woman. 'Why were you chasing me?' I glare at her, my nostrils flaring, like a rage-filled bull.

'We weren't chasing you, love,' the woman says, with a soft, understanding voice. 'I was sure you must have seen us, but then you started walking away, and I knew that something must be wrong.' She has crouched down to meet my eye level now, too, and has started stroking my hair. 'After the way you were on the phone the other day, and

200

what Jamie said, about you having one of your turns …'

I knew I'd heard her voice before. Of course. The woman on the phone. 'Wait a minute,' I say, holding up my hand and stopping her mid-sentence. 'Who are you supposed to be, again?' I know that I should still be pretending that I've recovered from my *turn*, but that ship has sailed now. I was *never* going to play nice with some stranger who has the audacity to pretend to be my mum.

The woman and Davie exchange confused glances – beautifully rehearsed, I think to myself; they really are quite skilled in the art of deception.

'Jen, it's me,' she says, right on cue, and I know exactly what her next word will be. 'Mum.'

I give them a sarcastic smile, shake my head, and say, 'Oh, fuck off.'

50

'What is he playing at?' Gary aims his question and his anger at the screen, but the electrical equipment offers him no answers. He is seething. His boss hasn't appeared yet. In fact, Gary hasn't seen him since yesterday, when he came in only briefly, to check that all was proceeding smoothly. He didn't mention anything about this little pantomime that's playing out in front of them now, and Gary can't contain his frustration. How is he supposed to keep Alex on his toes if even he doesn't know what's going on?

He stops to think for a second, wondering if there's any chance that Davie could have taken it upon himself to bring Angela to the island, of his own accord. No, he concludes. Davie would have no means of contacting Angela, and vice versa (Gary doesn't know if Davie and Angela are their real names; probably not), and, besides, the actors simply do whatever they're told to do. So why has the man organised this curveball without telling him? Does Alex know about it? Gary wasn't even aware that The Psycho had any direct link with the actors, other than through the control room, through Gary, but clearly, he does.

Gary checks on Alex, and sees that he's milling around the house, doing nothing much at all. If he is aware of developments, it certainly hasn't changed his behaviour or routine. But then, Gary thinks, what would he change? Presumably all he has to do is be there, and act like he was fully aware that Angela would come over. That doesn't require much preparation.

Gary wonders whether he should ask Alex if he does, indeed, know what's about to befall him, but he doesn't know whether that's a good idea. Whenever there's been any significant information to impart, or specific action to direct before, the boss has always been at the helm, controlling all his puppets from his self-made pedestal. So where is he now?

Gary notes that the two actors are helping Natalie back to the house now. She's hobbling on her bad ankle and going along with it because she has no choice, and they will probably get to Alex in about fifteen minutes. If the boss doesn't show before then, and Alex is unaware of the plan, will Alex put his foot in it? Will it be Gary who gets it in the neck, for not warning Alex?

Gary needs to play it safe. 'Boss, come in, will you?' he asks over the radio. Under his breath, he adds, 'I need to know what the fuck is going on.'

51

I'm back at the house. Jamie, Davie and Angela (my fake mother) are all fussing over me, feigning concern over my possibly sprained, perhaps even broken, ankle. 'Take me to a hospital, then,' I suggested. In other words, *'Get me off this island, onto the mainland, amongst people who are actually, genuinely interested in helping me!'*

'Of course,' came the reply. Davie would be more than happy to take me to the nearest hospital, just as soon as they'd let Jamie know what had happened. With no mobile reception where I was, or back at the house, they couldn't possibly whisk me off to safety without at least telling him what was going on. He would be going out of his mind with worry, they said. Who knew how long it would take for me to be seen at the hospital, after the hour and a half journey there, and then, what if my ankle had to be put in plaster? How could we possibly leave Jamie fretting for that length of time, without any news?

Sensibly, I thought, I suggested that we could find Bessie, and that she could go around to the house to tell Jamie. That way, by the time Jamie was up to speed with events, Davie, Angela and I would be on the boat, on the way to hospital.

That suggestion was shot down in flames. If we were going to do that, we may as well go straight to Jamie, and even let him accompany me to the hospital. Why wouldn't I want him to know as soon as possible, and to help, and to come with me?

'Because, like all the rest of you, he's a fucking psychopath!' is what I wanted to say. Longed to say. I was close to it, but something held me back. I still don't want to

push them too far. They're all in this together. This sick, evil, twisted game that they're all playing. What can I do? I'm one against God knows how many? I mean, what if this madness extends beyond this island? What if this little collective of nutters is able to poison the minds of others, and make them believe that it's actually *me* who needs to be certified?

I'm not sure what's worse: the pain radiating from my ankle, or the feeling of tightness inside my head, that is making me feel like my skull is in danger of exploding.

I feel like a trapped animal, backed into a cage, but with no sharp teeth or advantageous bulk to at least give me a fighting chance. I really can't think of a way that I can escape from this, especially now that I'm effectively lame.

I refuse to let any of them touch me. They all seem to think that because they're playing their little parts so well, that they can take liberties like hugging me, or tending to my ankle, or worst of all, stroking my hair in a motherly fashion. They can't. They don't have the right to touch me, and now they know that.

They're in the middle of a little pow-wow right now, in the kitchen. They must be wondering what to do with me, now that I've apparently found the backbone I had temporarily taken leave of and am becoming more of a problem for them. From what I can hear, so far, they're all still maintaining their impeccable façades, and the primary topic is how they can help with my injury, if I won't let them near it, or near me in general. I actually don't think my ankle is broken, probably just sprained. Nonetheless, I'll keep pushing for them to take me to a hospital. Just being off this island has got to be miles better than being here, hasn't it? I need to know that a real, proper world still exists outside of this tiny, remote area that I'm imprisoned in (or is it *on*?)

Will they agree? I don't know. Will they come up with some crooked way to make sure I don't actually get free? I'd put money on it. But I have to try. I can't just give up now, it's not in my nature. What would that look like, anyway? Me making my peace with the fact that this is my life now, here with Jamie? Not seeing my family again, or my friends. Knowing that nothing about this is right but having everyone around me constantly tell me that I'm mentally ill. Living a lonely, depressed, torturous existence, with no hope; no joy; no love. Is that what's to become of me?

It does happen – I know, I've read of cases of it happening. People have disappeared before; been presumed dead, then they've turned up years later, telling their story of how they were locked up by a deranged person and almost forgot who they really were. Will that be me? Will I *ever* be found?

'Jen?' Jamie approaches me gingerly, as though he knows he needs to tread carefully.

'What?' I ask, bluntly.

'Why don't we get you to a hospital,' he suggests. 'You should get your ankle checked over. Best be on the safe side.'

'Better still, why don't you just take me home,' I counter. 'You know, to the home I left behind, to come and be here with you, to support you. I assume the place is still standing? You haven't burnt it down, or taken a wrecking ball to it, or anything?'

He looks at me blankly.

'You know, my house?' I raise my voice. 'Come on, Jamie, at least try to keep up with your own bullshit story! We're only here until your contract runs out remember? Two years? And we've been here for five months. Why would I sell my place for the sake of two years?'

'You don't own a house,' he says, his voice barely audible. He's like a frightened child right now.

'Ha.' I make a sound and smile, and under normal circumstances that gesture might even be interpreted as a laugh, but it's not. 'Of course not,' I say drily. 'Alright then, take me to hospital in Glasgow, and then once I've been checked over, I'll go and visit the house that I *think* I

206

own, and you can explain to me why there is a nameplate on the door that says *N. Byron*, why the house contains all my stuff, and how I can tell you exactly what it looks like, where everything is, the names of my neighbours …'

'Jen, why would we go to all the way to Glasgow to get you to hospital? Do you know how long that would take?' He has found his big-boy voice again. 'It takes over an hour just to get across the water, then you'd be talking about over five hours on the train. Why would you want to wait that long? What if your ankle really is broken? We need to get you seen as soon as possible. Besides, we couldn't possibly expect Davie to hang around, and it's not fair for him to have to keep going back and forth. We'd have to stay the night, and it might not be convenient for him to come back and collect us tomorrow …'

'Good!' I yell loudly, and unexpectedly, and he visibly recoils. 'I don't care if he can't come and collect us tomorrow, that's the whole point! I don't want to fucking come back here, to this place, ever! What part of that don't you understand? I want to go home. To *my* home! To my family's home would be even better, because they could save me from all you fucking nutters!'

Davie and Angela emerge from the kitchen, with suitably shocked expressions on their faces.

'Yes, *you* nutters!' I shout, wishing I was more mobile, so that I could move towards them and scream my frustration out into their faces. I'm on a roll now. I don't even care what the consequences are, or how Angela's face crumples in disgust every time I utter the F-word. I've had my fill of these monsters treating me like I'm a crazy person, when I know without a shadow of a doubt that I'm the sanest one amongst them.

'I really think we should get you to hospital,' Angela says, her face now soured with pity, like she too recognises that I resemble a trapped, hopeless animal, in its final moments, clinging pathetically on to life. 'Davie, would you mind? I'm really sorry. I hate to ask you, but ...' She gestures towards me, signifying that I am the problem she is apologising for, the burden that now weighs heavy on them all.

'Of course, hen,' Davie assures her, placing a comforting hand on her shoulder. 'It's no trouble at all. Anything to help.'

She gives him a crumpled smile of gratitude and turns back to me. 'Shall we go now, love? It's not swollen, so that's a good sign, but I'm sure they'll do an X-Ray anyway, just to check. That was quite a nasty tumble you took.'

'I know. I was there, remember?' I sneer at her. 'I took a *tumble*, as you so quaintly describe it, because you were chasing after me. Why couldn't you just leave me alone? Why did you have to run after me like that? Who *does* that?' My voice is raised again, because now that the floodgates have opened, all my distress is flooding out, and it will take a mighty dramatic force to stop it.

'There's no need to shout at me, Jen,' she snaps, her veneer of calm slipping for the first time. There is anger in her pale green eyes. 'I came after you because I'm your mother. Jamie told me that you've not been yourself the last few days, and I was worried about you. Davie was kind enough to come and pick me up, and bring me here, thinking it might help you to have me around, but when I got here, you ran away from me! What kind of mother would I be if I didn't come after you, to make sure you're alright?'

'You are not my mother!' I scream at her, so violently that the force of my breath blows some of her auburn hair away from her face. 'Don't you *dare* try to tell me that you're my mum! And your *concern* worked out brilliantly, didn't it? Look at me! I'm sitting here with a crocked ankle, and you wouldn't even sanction taking me to the hospital without first running it past *him*!' I point towards Jamie, who looks ashamed. 'You want to know what kind of mother you would be? Well, let me tell you: a shit one. If you'd put concern for your not-even son-in-law above concern for your own daughter's wellbeing, then you'd be an absolutely deplorable mother!'

'That's enough, Jen!' Davie intervenes now. Jamie stands in the middle of the room, stationary, as though he can't decide what to do. Angela theatrically raises her hand to her face, which I assume is supposed to signify that she's tearful about what I've just said to her.

'We're all just trying to help you,' Davie scolds, his voice angry. 'You're obviously going through something here, so we're accommodating your behaviour as best we can, but there's absolutely no need to speak to your mother like that.' He is admonishing me. This absolute stranger is scolding me, for being rude to another absolute stranger, who is lying through her teeth to me.

'And who are you supposed to be, all of a sudden, Davie? My father?'

This comment, and the venom so obviously contained in it, draws a loud gasp from Angela, and a slightly more understated one from Jamie.

'That's uncalled for.' Angela whispers, her mannerisms becoming more and more dramatic with every word. If anything, now, if I was a movie critic I would definitely say she was over-acting.

'Don't start with the fake emotion,' I warn her. 'Before you think about launching into your tall tale about what's-his-name Mayhew no longer being with us, and how I should respect his memory as well as my fake mother, blah, blah, blah – have I pre-empted that correctly? Before you do that, let me tell you, unequivocally, that *my* dad is still very much alive. He's Iain Byron, and my mum is Gillian Byron, and neither of you are fit to lick their boots. And, while we're at it, there's also Anna, Gemma and Max, my sisters and my wee brother, all of whom live in Glasgow, like me, far away from you fucks, and your warped delusion!'

I literally feel like I could go on ranting until the sun goes down. I've been biting my tongue for days, trying to work out what might be the smartest way to play this – back when I thought of it as something of a strategy game – refraining from letting rip in case it brought me some harm. Now, the only fear I have is succumbing to the madness that this dangerous group are trying to encase me in. My need to escape from them has never been greater, but now I know that feigning compliance is not going to achieve anything. Playing their game is only going to leave me open to what they ultimately want – me accepting their lies. Perhaps even believing them. No, that can never happen. That *will* never happen.

I've paused to take a breath, a temporary interlude in my rant, and Davie has taken advantage.

'I think I'll leave you for now,' he says to Angela, in a manner that shows he is trying hard to keep a lid on his temper. 'If you need me, you know where I am.'

Angela looks at him a little despairingly, but all she can do is nod, and say, 'Okay, Davie. Thank you. And I'm *so* sorry.'

Davie pats her arm. 'It's okay, love.' He steals a glance at me, and I think he shakes his head a little, although I turned away too quickly to be sure. He leaves, and now it's just me versus Jamie and Angela. Jamie still looks overwhelmed, while Angela is doing her best to look hurt, and shocked by my outrageous behaviour.

'Now what?' I ask. 'Poor Davie's feelings are hurt, so I don't get to the hospital, is that it? How does anyone get on and off this God-forsaken island, if not for Saint Davie?'

'Jen, I really think you should calm down, hun,' Jamie interjects, as though someone has suddenly inserted some fresh batteries in him. 'All this bickering is getting us nowhere, and Angela came here to see you because she was worried about you. You shouldn't be yelling at her like that.'

I struggle to my feet, wincing with pain when I put weight on my ankle, but it's not so bad that I can't walk, albeit gingerly.

'Where are you going?' Jamie asks.

'To the hospital,' I reply, matter-of-factly. 'If you bastards won't take me, I'll find a way to get there myself.'

'Jen, don't be ridiculous,' Jamie derides, following me as I hobble out of the living room. Angela doesn't move from the couch she's seated on. I must have well and truly pissed her off. Good.

I stop in the hallway, and turn to look at Jamie, who, in spite of everything, still doesn't really look as though he's angry with me. He actually looks concerned, and I find myself holding back from being as nasty to him as I've been to the others, or even as I was to him a little earlier. I try a different tack.

'Look, Jamie,' I appeal, my voice as calm as I can force it to be, 'I really want to get to a hospital, okay? I'm in a lot of pain, I feel like no-one is listening to me, and I'm very pissed off that Angela deemed it more important that you be kept in the loop about my whereabouts than I get treatment. Now, I'm obviously at a bit of a loss here,' I gesture towards my ankle, 'but if no-one around here is able or willing to help me, I'm going to get to the hospital somehow, or I'm going to die trying.'

'Don't say that,' he says, grabbing hold of my arms. 'Of course, I'll help you.' He looks down at the ground as he says it, like he's just admitted to something awful, and is ashamed. 'Please, don't wander off by yourself again,' he pleads, his eyes apologetic. 'I do worry about you, you know.'

I rest my head against the wall, and then bang it gently off the surface a couple of times. I am literally, as well as metaphorically, banging my head against a brick wall here.

I probably would die trying to make it off this island on my own. I don't want to die. But I also don't want to stay here, against my will. Which is worse?

'I'll talk to Davie,' Jamie offers. He let go of my arms almost instantly, when he noticed my expression, and now he stands with his hands in his pockets, looking like he has been drained of energy again. 'I'm sure he'll still take us over. He's a good guy, honestly. I really think he just thought it would be best if he gave you and Angela some space.'

I take a long look at him, and a strange sensation comes over me. Is it sympathy? Pity?

'I meant it, you know, about wanting to go and see my place, my parents,' I say. I'm in a calmer mood now, but I'm not going to go back to playing dumb.

'O-Okay, we can do that,' Jamie stutters, and I want so much to believe him.

I'm not on the mainland yet – I'm not even on the boat – but maybe, just maybe, I can find a way to get out of this. My only option now, as I see it, is to latch onto the first person I see that isn't Jamie, Angela, or Davie (or Bessie, for that matter), and tell them everything. Even if they suspect that I'm a little unhinged, surely a decent person wouldn't just completely ignore such a cry for help, would they? Are there people in this world who could see someone in the state that I'm in, and just walk away, and forget all about me, because it's none of their business? Please, no.

I need to choose my stranger wisely, I realise. *Don't just blurt it all out to the first person you see*, I coach myself inwardly. *Wait, and look for someone you think will definitely help you. Look for a hero.*

Yes, that's what I need. I need a hero.

52

'Right. Let's walk through this.' DI Jackson sits on the edge of DC Nixon's desk, facing the incident board. He takes a swig of his coffee and waits expectantly for Nixon to summarise the facts of the case so far. Slater and McClure look on. 'Nixon, go,' Jackson commands.

Nixon takes his place at the side of the incident board, somewhat surprised at being given the order to lead the briefing. The sleeves of his white cotton shirt are rolled up to the elbow, as is his preference when he's in the office. He wears a maroon tie, slightly loose at the neck, grey trousers and black leather shoes, and to an outsider he could be mistaken for a school teacher about to commence a lesson.

'Right.' He points to a photo of Natalie, a simple headshot measuring seven inches by five inches. In it she is smiling, facing the camera straight on. The photo was found in an album during the search of her home and was deemed to be the most suitable for their purposes.

'Natalie Byron, thirty-two years old. Last seen disembarking from a train at Dalmuir station at 23:12 on Thursday the ninth of November. Reported missing by her parents on the morning of Saturday, the eleventh of November, owing to no contact since early evening on Thursday the ninth. Her father, Iain Byron, let himself into Natalie's house on the Saturday morning, and found the house to be empty. Natalie's phone, purse, house and car keys were found in the house, and her car was parked in the driveway.

'There were several items missing from the property, according to Iain Byron, including clothing, shoes and toiletries. No valuables appear to have been taken – we found a laptop, a tablet, and a PC which was still plugged in but switched off.

'There were no signs of struggle anywhere throughout the house; no blood, no breakages.' Nixon takes a breath, scanning the faces that are focused on him. In the absence of any questions, he carries on.

'We've checked with all hospitals in the Greater Glasgow area – none have reported any admissions or are treating any females fitting Natalie's description since she was last seen. Likewise, her photo has been shared with all ports and police stations in the UK, and Natalie hasn't been flagged anywhere. Her passport was found in the house, so we can be pretty confident that she hasn't left the country.'

'In terms of last known movements, what we know is that Natalie met with Kevin Lowell,' he points to a photograph of the man on the board, 'on the evening of the ninth, but parted company with him at around 22:40, and boarded the train to Dalmuir. Lowell then made his way to Queen Street, and caught his train home, getting off at Lenzie station. The last we see of Natalie on CCTV is at Dalmuir station – after that, we have nothing. We've checked with local businesses that were open at the time – a Chinese and two Indian takeaway joints, but none of them recalled seeing her.

'The distance from the station to her home is less than a mile, so we're assuming she walked. We talked to the local taxi firms and none of their drivers recognised her. We were able to confirm that the message sent to Kevin Lowell stating that Natalie had arrived home was, in fact, sent while the phone was at her property, and, of course, her mobile phone was found there, plugged in. All but one of the residents of her street have been interviewed – we've tried several times to speak to the next-door neighbour but have been unsuccessful – and there are no witnesses to her entering the property that night, although we are working on the assumption that she did.'

Nixon takes a long breath, gathering his thoughts. 'Kyle, do you want to walk us through what you've found on her phone?'

'Sure, Graeme,' Kyle McClure answers, somewhat patronisingly, glad that his moment in the spotlight has come around. He clears his throat. 'I've gone through her texts, calls, WhatsApp, and Instagram,' Kyle confirms, pacing around the room as he speaks. 'I didn't find anything particularly unusual; all recent contact was with the people we've spoken to: family, friends, and, of course, Lowell. Her contacts list didn't throw up anything new, either. We've gone through all of them and followed up, but the list is not exhaustive. Most are female, some old friends that she hasn't seen or spoken to for a while. There's a couple of tradesmen in there, her doctor's surgery, her boss. Nothing seemingly untoward.

'She's not a prolific user of social media. She doesn't go on Facebook or Twitter much – the only one she tends to use regularly is Instagram. The last photo that she uploaded was on Wednesday the eighth, a screenshot of a scam email that she got purporting to be from Apple – she was warning folk to look out for it. There are a few messages on there between her and her friends, sharing links to other pages, and so on. No-one we haven't come across already. The same goes for WhatsApp. There's a family group chat, some messages between her and her girl-friends, and Lowell. Basically, we've tracked down and spoken to everyone she's had contact with in the last month, and it's looking like the phone is a dead end.'

'Okay, thanks, Kyle,' Jackson utters with a sigh. 'Slater, talk to me about the financials.'

'Okay. As you know, we found Natalie's purse in the house, and there were two debit cards and two credit cards in there. The last time any of the accounts were accessed was

Thursday at 17:09, when she withdrew fifty pounds from what appears to be her primary bank account. I assume this was to cover her date with Lowell: dinner, drinks, etc. We're monitoring the accounts, obviously, but without the cards and her phone the only way she would be able to get any cash out would be in person, with ID, and both her driving licence and her passport were found in the house.

'Nothing much to report about the accounts themselves, to be honest. Her salary is paid into her RBS account, and there are all the usual direct debits on there: mortgage, utilities, gym membership. Debit card usage is minimal. She seems to prefer cash, and usually makes a withdrawal on a Saturday that seems to last her through the week. One savings account with RBS, and another one with Bank of Scotland. She makes transfers to both every month, for the same amount or thereabouts. No significant deposits or withdrawals since May, when she received a credit of three grand from Arnold Clark. Her parents confirmed she traded in her old car and took the cash instead of putting it towards the new vehicle.

'Two credit cards, both with Bank of Scotland, one with a balance of a couple of grand that she's been paying off at a hundred a month for about a year, and the other with an in-credit balance of three pounds twenty. Nothing irregular – she doesn't seem to spend on either any more, and the last transaction was October last year. Nothing unaccounted for here, Boss. She's a creature of habit.'

Jackson gives a wry smile. 'Yes, I've heard it mentioned,' he answers. There remains a nagging sensation in his mind that Natalie's tendency towards habitual behaviour makes it even less likely that she would disappear of her own accord, for no apparent reason.

'So where does that leave us?' Jackson asks of his team, standing up and moving to stand beside Nixon at the incident board. He continues without waiting for a response. 'She gets off the train at Dalmuir, returns home, texts Lowell, sticks her phone on charge, sets an alarm for the following morning, and goes to bed. Yes?'

A collective murmur makes its way across the room, as the other detectives signal their agreement.

'Right. So, sometime between half-eleven on Thursday and eight o'clock the following morning, when she doesn't show up for work, what happens?'

Nixon, Slater and McClure exchange glances. Kyle McClure is first to offer a hypothesis. 'She takes off, sir.'

'Why?' Jackson challenges. 'Where to? And why not take her phone, her car or her passport? Plus, what is she doing for money?'

'She doesn't want to be found, sir,' McClure responds with conviction. 'She knows her phone and her cards are traceable, so she leaves them behind deliberately. Maybe she had some cash planked away in the house that she's using.'

'But why?' Jackson asks again. 'Slater, is it possible that she's been stashing some cash at home?'

Slater shakes her head. 'I don't think so, sir. Assuming her CRB salary is her only income, the amounts she takes out each week would not be conducive to her building up a honey pot in the house. She saves regularly, so if she needed a lump sum she'd just take it from one of her accounts, I reckon. There are no debit or credit card transactions pointing to any booked travel, so if she is a runaway, she had to have bought her bus or train ticket on the hop.'

'Everyone we've spoken to has been adamant that she wouldn't take off like that, Boss,' Nixon adds.

'It just doesn't feel like an abduction, sir,' DC Slater opines. 'No forced entry, no evidence of struggle, the neighbours didn't see or hear anything ...'

Kyle McClure nods in concurrence.

'And what abductor goes to the trouble of taking the clothes and other stuff? For all we know, she's met up with someone, and they're financing whatever she's doing.'

'Makes sense,' Kyle McClure offers in support of his colleague's assertion. 'Otherwise, what are we saying? That someone waited for her to come home, managed to get in without making any fuss, had enough time to swipe her, and bags of clothes and shoes, and take off without anyone noticing a thing?'

'So, what's her reason for wanting to go off the radar?' Nixon asks, his tone accusatory. 'If she has done a runner, she's made an effort to avoid being tracked down. Not only that, she's planted the seed that something might have happened to her, by leaving her keys and phone in the house. Why? Everyone she's been in contact with, that we know of, over the last few months, is still on the scene, and they're all insisting that everything was fine, that she was fine. There's no history of mental illness, not so much as a day off sick in two years, so what would she be running from?'

'That we know of,' Jackson repeats, latching onto Nixon's mention of the people Natalie has been in contact with.

'You're thinking she could be involved with someone we don't know about, sir?' Slater asks.

Jackson pauses for a second before answering. 'We have to consider it,' he replies. 'It's not the first time we've seen someone take off with a partner that nobody else had any clue about.' He mulls over what he's just said, and the officers seem to do the same. The room remains silent for over a minute. 'OK,' Jackson says, feeling in desperate need of some progress, 'so if we park the idea that she's done a runner, just for a minute, what could we be dealing with?'

'Someone could have been waiting for her, in the house,' Nixon volunteers. 'Someone was already there when she got home. They hid, waited long enough for her to go to bed before they acted. Maybe even waited for her to fall asleep, to cut down on any struggle.'

Jackson looks pensive. 'But we've got no foreign prints

or DNA to work with, right?'

'That's right. We've got Iain Byron's prints everywhere, but no foreign DNA at this stage.'

'So, someone's waiting for her,' Jackson repeats, running with the theory. 'How did they get in the house, and back out again with Natalie and bags of stuff, without anyone in the street noticing a damn thing?'

'They could have parked in the lane beside the house,' Nixon answers. 'At that time of night, it would have been pitch black and pretty deserted. And it's far enough from the house on the other side that the neighbours wouldn't necessarily have heard the engine starting.'

'Okay,' Jackson replies, but it's non-committal. 'So, who? Why? No-one's mentioned any unwanted attention?'

'Nope, nothing. Lowell's the only guy who's been on the scene lately, and he looks clean. He went home on Thursday night, worked all day Friday and was out again with pals on Saturday.'

'And we've got nothing on him?' Jackson asks. 'You said yourself, Nixon, he was hiding something. What is it?'

Nixon shakes his head. 'He's clean as a whistle, Boss, not even a parking ticket.'

Jackson sighs frustratedly. 'So, it's random? He restrains her while she's asleep, possibly drugs her? Bags up her things and puts her in the car. Takes the tunnel instead of heading back along the street, where there's a chance his car will be noticed. Where's the nearest camera on the main road?'

'Heading west, the closest one is at the junction at the bottom of Duntocher Road,' Slater confirms. 'If he headed east, there's one just before the Town Hall.'

'Check them,' Jackson orders. 'From quarter past eleven onwards.'

'What are we looking for, sir?' Slater asks.

'A needle in a haystack,' DC McClure quips sarcastically.

'Jesus Christ!' Jackson yells, making everyone else jump. 'Has it escaped your attention, Kyle, that we've got nothing? Absolutely nothing. What about the appeals? Has no-one come forward with any information?'

'Only the cranks,' DC McClure answers, a little sheepishly in the face of Jackson's admonishment. 'An old woman in Carlisle was certain she'd seen her in Sainsbury's, but it turned out to be a local woman who, to be honest, looks nothing like Natalie. Loads of shares on Facebook, so it's getting out there, but nothing that helps us. I think it's worth talking to the friends again. Especially Julie Coulter. I just got the feeling that there's something she's not telling us.' He looks to DC Slater for corroboration of his suspicions, and she thinks for a moment before nodding her head in concurrence.

'Agreed,' she answers. 'I haven't managed to get hold of Natalie's uni records yet, but Coulter said they've known each other for years, since they were at school. We should ask her if she knows anything about why she left so abruptly without finishing her course.'

Jackson nods. 'Follow it up,' he says.

53

It's all arranged.

Davie, having been sweet-talked by Jamie into getting over the strop that he threw an hour or so ago, has agreed to transport me – and Jamie, and Angela, of course – to Mallaig. From there, we'll have to make our own way to the nearest hospital with an accident and emergency department, and we then won't have handy means to get back to the island, but obviously that is of no concern to me. I don't care about making it to the hospital. I don't even care if my ankle really is broken – the only part of this scenario which is relevant to me is the chance to escape from the clutches of my captors.

Once I get to Mallaig, and can find a suitable person to help me, Davie, Jamie and Angela will be nothing more than blots on the landscape of my memory that I can't wait to scrub off.

We're just waiting for Davie to let us know when he's ready to go. It wouldn't surprise me if he's sitting comfortably in his drab, depressing living room, watching the antique clock tick down, enjoying the idea of keeping me waiting, out of spite for the way that I yelled at him earlier. I was totally justified in doing it, of course, and I can't stand the man, but at this precise moment he holds all the cards, and the key to my freedom. As much as it pains me, I'm going to have to act contrite for the next couple of hours, until I've broken free from their shackles. It means grovelling to Davie, and no doubt having to make some concessions where Angela is concerned, but it's worth it if it gets me home.

I'm sitting on the couch with my poorly ankle elevated. The pain isn't even that bad any more, now that I've had some painkillers, that Jamie gave me. I was reluctant to take them at first, but when I insisted that he show me the packet that the pills came from, he duly produced an opened box of supermarket own-brand paracetamol, and the foil that had been emptied to the tune of two tablets. I scrutinised the pills themselves, checking for the tell-tale 'P', and the strength of the medication. I even took a little test bite, to verify that it tasted how I would expect. The bitter, chalky taste was unmistakable, and I concluded that they were the real thing. I washed the two painkillers down with a glass of water about ten minutes ago, and thankfully they now seem to be doing their job. I'm still not looking forward to trying to support my weight on this ankle, but at least the gnawing pain has subsided to more of a dull ache.

Angela hasn't uttered a word to me, since my outburst. She's in the kitchen, staying out of my way, until such time as we're forced to share a boat over to Mallaig. She's behaving as though she is very much the injured party in this scenario, complaining to Jamie of the toll this whole thing is taking on 'her nerves', and Jamie is playing along like a loyal little lapdog, indulging her with tea and sympathy. He left the two of us alone together while he went to plead with Davie, but thankfully she is maintaining the illusion of being just as upset with me as I am with her (if not more!) and has left me in relative peace.

I'm propped up against several cushions, courtesy of Jamie's fussing, and he made me a cup of tea when he returned from Davie's negotiating table, so I'm about as comfortable as I can be, given the circumstances.

I can hear Jamie moving around in the bedroom. He's packing *things*, just in case we are required to stay on the mainland overnight. In his mind, not returning to this island would be a temporary, worst-case scenario. In my mind, it's a burning ambition.

I glance at the clock on the mantelpiece, which looks like

it could do with a full-on assault with a duster to get rid of the layers of dust that have been allowed to settle on it and see that it is now twelve minutes past eleven. Assuming that the clock is, in fact, showing the correct time. I feel like I've fallen down the proverbial rabbit hole here, so who knows? Time is getting on, anyway, and I'm itching to leave.

'Jamie?'

He appears in a matter of seconds, wearing his stock eager-to-please expression. 'What do you need?' he asks, but not in a belligerent way.

'Do you know how long Davie is going to be? My ankle is starting to feel really sore again.' It isn't, not really, but if he believes I'm suffering he might be moved to try and speed things up a little.

He frowns, and his facial muscles tighten as though he's trying to solve a puzzle. 'Damn, I thought the paracetamol would have given you some relief for a while,' he says, coming to sit on the couch beside me. 'I'd go and chase him up, but to be perfectly honest he took a fair bit of convincing to even agree to take us over, so I don't want to take the chance of annoying him, just in case,' he explains.

I sigh. I don't want to take that chance either. If Davie is my only hope of salvation, then adhere to his schedule I must. 'Okay,' I say, grudgingly. 'Did he give you any idea, though, how long he might be?'

He presses his lips together and shakes his head. 'Sorry. You could probably take another paracetamol, though,' he suggests. 'You know you can take up to eight over twenty-four hours?'

'Yeah, but it hasn't even been one hour since I had those other two,' I remind him. 'It's okay, I'll hold off for a while.'

Jamie regards me with a look of sympathy. 'I wish there was something more I could do,' he says quietly. He gets up and leaves the room again, and I'm left feeling confused. How can he do that? How can he look at me like he really,

really cares? I've always been a subscriber to the school of thought that the eyes don't lie, but since I've been thrust into this brand-new world, I don't quite know how – or whether – to trust my instincts any more. I mean, ninety-nine percent of the time, every fibre of my being is telling me that Jamie is my enemy; he is the man who has made me his prisoner and has done his best to manipulate me into thinking that there is something wrong with my mind. How can it be, then, that when my eyes met his only a moment ago, for a split second I truly believed that he was concerned about me? Furthermore, how can it be that I'm sitting here, kidnapped and crocked, feeling sorry for *him*?

I don't have time to dwell on this unsettling sense of confusion, since Angela is standing in the doorway, demanding attention by her sheer presence.

She leans against the door jamb, her arms folded across her chest, projecting hostility. Her mouth is a straight line, and her eyes are stern, although there is a tinge of redness surrounding them, as if she has been crying. There is even a little smudge of mascara around them, for extra effect. As much as I despise her, I have to concede that she is actually playing the part of 'woman in distress' quite admirably.

Yet, of all the strange, deceitful people I've run into since I woke up here on Saturday morning, somehow Angela is the one I've developed the most hatred for. Probably because she is the only one who has tried to impersonate a member of my family, but there is something else about her that makes my flesh crawl whenever she's around. Her face, somehow, seems vaguely familiar to me, but how can that be? And her mask slipped earlier, I remember. Only for a brief second, but when she lost her temper and snapped at me, I could sense that she hadn't meant to rise to my persistent baiting. Her gaze hasn't strayed in the few minutes since I first noticed her standing there, and the passionate dislike I feel for her is only intensifying with every passing second. Technically, since it's not her boat and she won't be driving it, I don't necessarily have to be nice to her, the way I unfortunately have to be with Davie, in order to secure my trip. Having said that, since I'm already on a shaky peg with Davie, and he is unquestionably on Angela's side on the evidence of our little *tête-à-tête* earlier, it's probably best that I don't deliberately antagonise her.

I try to ignore her, resting my head back against the couch cushion, suddenly feeling exhausted. No wonder, I think to myself. It's not even midday yet, and already I've had to deal with more drama than I normally go through in an average month. In fact, in the past few days, I've probably burned through more nervous energy that I do in an average month, as well. If there is a positive to be found in any of this – and believe me, it has been hidden under layers of sheer awfulness – it's that I'm bound to return home a few pounds lighter than I was last week. That should aid my jogging performance.

I yawn loudly, and close my eyes, thinking back to Thursday night. I think about my date with Kevin – a real, official date, not just a catch-up – and how the most pressing worry I had to deal with when I got home that night was whether it was wise to start seeing him again, regularly. I'd give anything for that to be my number one problem right now. I'd give anything to be living the largely uncomplicated, stress-free life that I led before I fell asleep that night.

Why don't I remember anything from then until Saturday morning? What did Jamie do to me? And was it only Jamie? What if they were all part of it, the process of extracting me from my house?

I'm not a light sleeper, but neither do I fall into a coma when I doze off. They must have drugged me. And with something strong, considering I lost more than a whole day of my life.

All along, I've been assuming it was Jamie who kicked

the whole process off, and somehow roped in the others to help him maintain his charade. But what if that's wrong? Maybe it was Davie who did the heavy lifting, literally. He certainly has the build for carrying an unconscious adult out of a house and into a car. Jamie has an athletic build, but he is not brimming with bulging muscles. The more I think about it, the less sure I am that he is capable of doing what someone must have had the strength to do.

And then, once they got me to Mallaig, I guess they must have used Davie's boat to transfer me here. The thought of them man-handling me, manipulating my limbs into appropriate positions for transit, makes me feel violated. I've known for days that they're all taking advantage of my mind, but now it's really hitting home that they had free reign to do whatever they wanted with my body, as well, for however many hours they rendered me unconscious.

A shiver of horror makes me open my eyes, and Jamie is standing over me, looking worried again.

'Jeez!' I exclaim, 'you gave me a fright!'

'Sorry,' he says, 'I just wanted to check you were okay. Davie is here. We can go now.'

Davie is here? Yes, he is. I see him. He's standing by the door, chatting quietly to a stony-faced Angela. Why didn't I hear him come in?

'Great,' I say, the word sounding more sarcastic than I intended. I go to lift myself off the couch, and Jamie rushes to help me, crouching low and placing my arm around his shoulder so that I can lean on him.

I'm not in a position to reject his assistance, so I allow him to prop me up and we make a laboured journey out of the living room and into the hallway, following Davie and Angela, who remain deep in whispered conversation that I'm not quite close enough to make out.

I feel as though I've just awoken from a nap, even though I only closed my eyes for a couple of minutes, so it

226

feels good to be greeted with a firm blast of fresh air when I hobble outside, still aided by Jamie. We begin the slow, but thankfully not too painful, trek to the boat, allowing Davie and Angela to forge ahead at their own pace. Davie, like Angela, appears to have been rendered mute whilst I am in the immediate vicinity, which I can't say is a major inconvenience – all that matters is that he is fulfilling his promise.

Jamie doesn't seem much in the mood for talking either, so we simply trundle along, like a half-hearted, possibly drunk three-legged race team, each lost in our thoughts.

I have no idea what Jamie is thinking. Maybe he's regretting offering me help? I wouldn't blame him.

What I'm thinking is, that this is it. This time, it has to be. I really am going to get off this island.

*

Nothing. Nada. Zero. Zip.

That's the sum total of what they have in relation to this case. There have been no genuine sightings. CCTV up and down the country has produced no hits. No money has been withdrawn from her bank accounts; no transactions have been made.

There has been no contact, not from Natalie, nor from anyone holding Natalie. She has vanished. Jackson has seen it before – it does happen. The woman has quite simply disappeared.

'Boss?'

It's Graeme Nixon who comes bounding towards him, looking pumped up. 'Boss, we've got something.' He leans on Jackson's desk. 'The next-door neighbour, the one we couldn't get a hold of? She's been in hospital since last Wednesday, just got home. She saw the appeal; says she looked out of her upstairs window and saw a guy letting himself into Natalie's place with a key.'

'When?'

'Couple of weeks ago, in broad daylight. She said she kept meaning to ask Natalie about it, but she was stressed about her surgery coming up and totally forgot. She wasn't well enough to go and challenge the guy, but she saw him come back out about half an hour later.'

'Have we got a description?'

'Slater's calling in the sketch artist now.'

Jackson grabs his jacket from the back of his chair. 'Let's go.'

54

'No! No! No!'

I can't believe it. Or maybe I can, and that's what makes it worse, if it can get any worse. I don't know that it can.

I'm back on the island. I'm back in this eerie, clinical bedroom, in this lumpy, uncomfortable bed, looking out at those huge, foreboding mountains. I'm awake, but I'm groggy. They must have drugged me – again. How? With what? I think back to when I accepted the paracetamol that Jamie offered, wracking my brains for details. I checked. I double checked. These people will, it seems, stop at nothing to prevent me from leaving this island, but producing their own drugs, that look and taste exactly like regular painkillers? Isn't that a step too far? Am I living in the Twilight Zone? Then rational thought returns to me, like the comforting hug of an old friend. Oh, how I wish I had an actual old friend here to give me a hug.

The water.

Of course. I downed almost half a glass of water to wash away the bitter taste of the paracetamol. There could have been anything in there, and I wouldn't have noticed, because all I was focused on was whether I could trust my own judgement over what I was tasting, and seeing, and believing.

How could I have been so stupid? They were never going to let me get to the mainland! I can't believe I ever entertained the idea that they would.

My head hurts, as much from the emotional pain of what I have just come to terms with as the after-effects of whatever they used to knock me out. Rohypnol? I don't know much about that drug, but what I do know is that nothing good ever happens to anyone who falls victim to it. And it would appear that I have. If not that, then something similar.

Once again, my head feels like it is filled with cotton wool. Thoughts are whirling around inside, but they are stunted, incomplete. I vaguely remember the events of earlier. I realise I don't actually know how long has passed since I was last conscious. Outside it is dark, which means it could be any time between four in the evening and eight in the morning. The last thing I remember is walking – or rather hobbling – beside Jamie, my heart full of hope that I was finally going to make a viable break for freedom; my head full of the plans and tactics that I was going to use to get myself rescued once we reached the shore. I remember the sharpness of the breeze; the beauty of the coastline; the silence that hung between Jamie and I like a heavy curtain. And then I remember nothing. I must have begun to feel the effects even before we left the house, I realise. Didn't I only close my eyes for a few seconds, while I sat on the couch?

What I want to do is scream from the top of my lungs, but who would hear me? My incarceration here is complete, final. My spirit is so depleted, it is now no more than a wisp of smoke that lingers for a short time after a candle has been extinguished. In fact, that is how I feel: extinguished. If a fire ever burned inside me – the will to escape, the hope of being reunited with my family; the dream of returning to my normal life – these people have been devastatingly effective at putting it out.

My eyes have adjusted to the darkness now, and I see that Jamie is not in the bed beside me. All at once, I feel relieved, but also heartbreakingly lonely.

Presumably his absence signifies that it is only late afternoon, or early evening, not a time for anyone except a medicated, trapped, pathetic case like me to be in bed.

I look down at my injured ankle, and for the first time I

notice that it is heavily bandaged. Did they really take me to the hospital? I snuff out the question almost before I finish asking it inside my head. Of course, they didn't. How would they explain the fact that I was completely unconscious? They must have simply raided their little box of tricks and found what looks like a *Tubigrip* bandage, the kind that the doctor gives you when you suffer a sprain, or any kind of injury other than a true break. I wasn't convinced it was broken, anyway, if I'm being honest, but I still can't help feeling like this is just one more slap in the face, as if they haven't quite delivered enough blows already. Not content with dragging me here, for what I fear may be a lifetime of imprisonment and misery, they seem willing to forego the intervention of any kind of recognised medical professional in order to ensure that I get the care that I deserve.

I move my leg, and the pain quickly reminds me of just how pathetic my plight really is. I consider whether I should get up, and go and investigate, to find out who is still around and what the next phase of my nightmare may involve. I can't. I'm broken. Officially, perhaps irreparably, broken. I don't have the will to move. All I can do is sit here, in the dark, and mourn the life that I don't think I will ever get back.

55

Alex is chewing on his fingernails, a nervous habit he has long since tried to conquer without success. He's bitten down so hard that he's actually managed to break the skin on his left thumb, and a tiny trickle of blood escapes. He doesn't even realise until he tastes the metallic tang, so preoccupied is he with the dilemma he is faced with.

He's been pushing back on their instructions – no, demands – for two days now, and he senses that he is fast running out of options. How much longer will they tolerate his disobedience? The voice that speaks in his ear is no longer the same calm, measured voice that it was in the beginning. Only a mere couple of days ago, although it feels like so much longer, he would heed the man's advice, draw on his knowledge if necessary, and despite the discomfort of the earpiece it felt good to have someone backing him up, directing him. Now, the voice is like the proverbial devil on his shoulder. It is a different voice, he is certain. This new voice is … sinister. It hisses its evil intent into Alex's ear with an undeniable threat, leaving Alex in no doubt that his concerns on day one of this job were absolutely not unfounded. His instincts were right on the money, in fact – this is not a job. This is a living nightmare. And the man who has emerged as the one in charge of this nightmare is clearly not a man who appreciates being challenged.

But Alex won't do what he's been told to do. Not this time. What the hell is wrong with these people? They're sick in the head. So sick that they let their victim believe that her time had finally come, that she might actually get the chance to alert someone to her plight. They even let her get as far as the boat, knowing that the drugs would take effect at the right time, leaving them free to return her, listless and hopeless, to the house that even Alex now thinks of as a prison.

He didn't ask enough questions, at the start of all this. He barely asked any questions, in fact, and now he's embroiled in something that hurts his brain even to think about. And embroiled he is. He can't see a way out of this, no matter how hard he concentrates, or how viciously he attacks his fingernails or the tender skin around them. Almost certainly, what he's involved in is criminal already. So maybe he's fucked, no matter what. But even if he is, there's no way he's going to do what they're asking. Demanding. He will not force himself on that woman.

*

'Get that over to the friends, the work colleagues; I want to know who this guy is, got it?'

'Yes, Boss.'

'I'm going to see the family. With a bit of luck, someone will recognise this guy. Get Slater to check the CCTV again, starting with the footage from Central and Dalmuir from Thursday night. If this is the guy we've got to assume he's been following her, which means we might get lucky and spot him lurking around.'

'You got it, Boss.'

*

I'm sitting in the bath. My hair is wet. I'm shivering, so I suppose I must have let the water go cold, without even noticing.

There is a strange numbness that has descended upon

233

me, possibly some kind of defence mechanism deployed to reduce the effects of the horror associated with my plight. The anaesthetic must have cast its web to my skin, now, as well as my brain, my appetite, and my inherent thirst for life.

I stare ahead, looking into the taps but not daring to register the face that stares back at me in the reflective metal. I don't want to see what I look like. Whoever I used to be, I feel as though I am not that person any more. I feel like I'm hollow. Crushed. My resolve, my happiness, and my hopes and dreams are nothing more than powdered crumbs, like a biscuit that has been pulverised.

My ankle still hurts, but not as much as before. The last few days have been a blur of misery, pain and utter hopelessness, peppered with lies and insults to my intelligence by Jamie, who continues to impress upon me the reality and severity of my 'mental health' issues.

Something has changed in him, however. I may be delusional, but since I hurt my ankle, and had to live through the painful charade that was Angela playing the role of my mother, something in the back of my brain has been trying to grab my attention, where Jamie is concerned.

'I do worry about you, you know.'

There was something about the way he said it; the way he looked at me, using his eyes to reinforce his words. Did he really mean it, that he worries about me? But that would be ludicrous. He has kidnapped me, for God's sake. He has repeatedly told me that I am someone I'm not, and implied that I am mentally unstable. He keeps me here, shackled to this place that is too far away from anyone I know for me to be in with a chance in hell of breaking free. And yet I believed him. Just for that brief moment, I think I actually believed that he was on my side. Maybe what happened was that I latched onto Jamie's apparent concern because I was feeling so ganged up on by Angela and Davie. They were so against me, so ignorant of my feelings and quick to show their anger towards me. Me, a woman supposedly suffering from some kind of mental breakdown. Agonisingly, I wonder yet again whether I am; whether this is a psychological crisis of my own doing. It's become part of my daily routine now, like the way I would previously have checked my mail or made my bed.

'Does Natalie exist?'

'Am I Natalie?'

'Have I lost my mind?'

The answers are always the same: Yes, yes, and no. That much has not changed. I'm still me. I'm just not allowed to believe it.

56

'I know it can be difficult to try and identify someone from a sketch, folks, but please, take a good look. Have you got any idea whatsoever who this man might be?'

The Byron family is congregated in Iain and Gillian's living room, and Mark Houston is also present, with his arm wrapped supportively around his girlfriend, Gemma.

Gillian Byron shakes her head. 'No, I've never seen him before,' she says tearfully. 'Who is he?'

'One of Natalie's neighbours saw a man fitting this description entering her home with a key,' Jackson explains.

Gillian gasps in shock.

'Jesus Christ,' Iain exclaims. 'When?'

'The witness said it was a couple of weeks ago, but only reported it earlier today.'

'What? Why?' Max asks, wearing an angry expression.

'The witness has been unwell,' Jackson replies, 'they've been in hospital since before Natalie was last seen; they didn't realise the significance of it until now. Anna, Gemma, Max, do any of you have any idea who this could be? An old flame, maybe? Someone she works with, or used to work with?'

'Nope, I don't recognise him,' Gemma answers, staring intently at the page in the hope that some new clue may arise from it.

'We met a couple of the guys she works with at her thirtieth birthday party,' Max offers, 'but he wasn't one of them.'

'Are you certain?' Jackson asks. 'Do you know their names?'

'I could probably point them out,' Max replies. 'They're probably friends with her on Facebook. One of them is Jonathan, I know that. Can't remember the other one's name off the top of my head. But I'm certain – neither of them is this guy.'

'All the same, if you could identify them for us, that would be great,' Jackson says, going over the interviews he carried out at Natalie's office and not remembering a Jonathan.

'Sure,' Max says, taking his phone from his pocket and navigating to Natalie's friends list.

'Also, we believe that Natalie had a run-in of sorts with a man at university, and subsequently dropped from her course. Is there any chance that there could be a connection?'

Iain and Gillian exchange puzzled looks. 'What are you talking about?' Iain asks.

'She left university because she failed her first year,' Gillian tells him. 'She took it quite badly, and she decided it just wasn't for her in the end. What's this about a run-in with a man?'

'Apparently, Natalie made an accusation of inappropriate behaviour which resulted in the male student being investigated. She later withdrew her complaint, but the insinuation is that Natalie then left because of the fallout. She never mentioned any of this to you?'

Iain and Gillian shake their heads, visibly shocked at the revelation. 'Callum Connell, does that name sound familiar at all?'

'No.'

'And she never mentioned anything recently, to any of you, about being followed, or hassled? A flyaway comment, something that might not have made sense at the time. No?'

'We would have told her to call you,' Iain answers solemnly, and Jackson recognises his expression as that of a man who has the wind knocked out of him.

'You should know we're doing all we can to try and track

237

down this man, Mr and Mrs Byron,' he assures them.

'Find him,' Iain urges. *Before I do*, he thinks to himself.

part three

57

Gary has no influence now. He wasn't naïve enough to truly believe that he ever did, but now there is no question. He is a minion. He was brought here under false pretences, to participate in a sick game that he would never in a million years have signed up to be a part of, had he known what would happen. If he'd had the slightest inkling about what would go on here, the first thing he would have done would be to go the police and spill the beans on The Psycho and his twisted operation. As it is, he is up to his neck in something highly illegal, and he is now intrinsically linked with a real-life monster who will seemingly stop at nothing to achieve his warped goals. And since he has Gary under his thumb like an ant that he could squish at any moment if he chose to, he has decided that Gary should serve a new, different purpose. And as much as it shames him to admit, Gary has neither the courage nor the appetite to refuse him.

He stares at his hands, hovering over the equipment, cursing them for the damage they've helped him to inflict.

*

The man's threats are explicit now. They are no longer for Alex to infer via his tone. They are real.

'Do you really think you're in a position to protect her, Alex?' the voice taunts, with an evil-sounding laugh. 'Big Bad Alex,' he sniggers cruelly. 'How about this,' he whispers, 'if it's not you, it'll have to be someone else. How do you feel about that, Al? Hmm?'

Sick to his stomach is how Alex feels. Terrified. For himself, for the woman. What choice does he have?

He stands up suddenly, needing to move, needing to do something with the nerves that are eating away at him. He goes to the kitchen window and stares out, but sees only his own anxious reflection.

'Tick, tock, tick, tock,' the man goads. 'Whenever you're ready, Alex. Time is running out, my friend.'

*

I'm lying down. Again. It's pretty much all I do now. What else is there to do? Trying to escape is a fruitless pursuit, and every time I fail it only serves to knock me down even further into the depths of despair.

My hair is still wet, but like so many other incidental things, my appearance, and the risk of catching cold are things that no longer concern me.

I hear Jamie coming into the room, and before I can decide whether to acknowledge him or not, he takes up position beside me on the bed, leaning on his left elbow as he faces me. I can hear that he is breathing heavily, more heavily than usual, although it is not clear to me why. Curiosity prompts me to turn my head and look at him, interested to know what could be making him short of breath.

'How are you feeling, hun?' he asks, sliding his hand across my abdomen and leaving it to rest there, the warmth of his skin creating goose-bumps when it makes contact with my shivering body.

I lie still for a few seconds, glaring at him but not moving my body beyond the instinctive flinch that I made when he put his hand on me. He's never done anything like this before. I look carefully at his face, my own breathing starting to intensify as I read an expression that I'm not familiar with.

'What are you doing?' I ask tentatively, not feeling good about the distinctive change in Jamie's demeanour. He wears a painted-on smile, and his eyes are dancing around, like the eyes of someone under the influence of drugs. For the first time since I came into contact with him, I feel genuinely under physical threat from this man.

'What do you mean, hun?' he asks, shuffling his body closer to mine, lifting his hand in the process but replacing it on my stomach when he's moved as close as he wants to. 'I'm just asking how you are. Are you feeling any better? I hate to see you like this.' His voice seems different, though I can't pinpoint what's changed. As he says the last sentence, he moves again, laying his head on my chest, so that the stubble on his head scratches my chin.

I jerk away from him, managing to get to a seated position, forcing him to also sit up and back away. 'Don't touch me,' I say, trying to sound authoritative.

He laughs, but there is no humour in the sound. He moves up onto his knees and shimmies towards me again. 'Come on, Jen, I'm just trying to show a little affection,' he urges. 'This isn't a walk in the park for me either, you know. How do you think it feels to have you recoil from me every time I touch you?'

He gets close enough to touch me, and I almost jump off the bed, hoping that the old, familiar Jamie will return soon. The Jamie that *worries* about me. Didn't he say that? The Jamie in front of me is a different man from the one I've known for the last few days, and the one who seemed so sympathetic towards me when I was up against the wrath of Davie and Angela. This Jamie stares at me with menace in his eyes. He's lowered his backside onto his legs now, so that he's still on his knees, but his weight has shifted backwards. He looks genuinely angry.

'Jamie, please don't …' I say, putting my hands out in front of me in a protective gesture, trying to keep him at bay.

'Don't what, Jen?' he lunges forward, taking me by surprise, and grabs at my wrists before I have a chance to get away. 'Don't expect any attention, or fucking affection, from my *girlfriend*?' As he yells the words, he pulls me down forcibly onto the bed, and within seconds I'm pinned under him, no match for his larger size and superior strength.

'Get off me!' I cry, using all the power I can muster. In spite of the adrenalin that is coursing through my veins, and my fighting instinct being brought to the fore, Jamie is able to overpower me with frightening ease.

'What's wrong with you, Jen?' he practically spits at me. 'I'm your boyfriend, for God's sake! Why am I not allowed to touch you?'

He holds my wrists above my head, and even though I wriggle and flex my arms every which way I can, I am unable to break free. Jamie is straddling me now, effectively holding my whole body down. Although I can move my legs from the knees down, there is nothing I can do to displace him. His eyes are vicious-looking, as if he has been possessed by some devilish creature who is hell-bent on hurting me.

'Stop struggling!' he yells, and I'm so frightened of him that I do. I stop moving altogether, and just look at him. Tears escaped from my eyes during the struggle, I realise as I feel the wetness on my face. Jamie stares right at me, looking almost surprised that his command worked. He looks at me without saying anything, and the silence is awkward and suffocating. He's still holding my wrists tightly, but he appears conflicted, as though he doesn't know what to do next.

After a few more seconds of our heaving breaths being the only sound in the room, I take a chance and speak. 'Jamie, you're hurting me,' I say quietly, calmly, hoping to appeal to the side of him that I've seen up until today. Up until two minutes ago.

He looks away, screwing his eyes closed but keeping

the pressure on my wrists. I try again. 'Jamie, please.' I'm tearful again, but my eyes don't waver from his face. If I can pressurise him into looking at me, maybe I can make a connection.

'I can't do this,' he says, releasing his grip and moving himself to sit on his knees again.

Although my brain doesn't quite comprehend what's happening, my body reacts instantly, and I shoot off of the bed, almost falling as I do. Pain from my ankle hits me like a dart, but it doesn't stop me from making a beeline for the bedroom door, only for Jamie to fly off the bed and follow me.

'Jen, wait,' he urges, grabbing hold of my waist just as I reach the door. 'Look, I'm sorry, okay? I'm sorry.' He twists me round to face him again, and I see that his eyes are red, and right now, he looks more worried than dangerous. 'I'm so sorry, Jen, I didn't want to do any of it, I swear. Please believe me, please.'

I can't keep up with his changes in demeanour. The man in front of me now seems like a completely different person to the one who was on the verge of assaulting me only a few moments ago, but he's now got a hold of my elbows, and is shaking me as he pleads with me to forgive him.

'Okay,' I say, stalling for time as I try to devise a plan to get away from this obvious danger. I want to know what has come over him, to make him behave so differently, but my first priority is to diffuse the situation so that I can escape from his grip. 'Really, it's okay,' I say, trying to sound soothing. He gives me a pained smile, like gratitude. 'You're hurting my arms, though.'

He takes a nervous look around him, and then back to me, still holding onto me. 'Jen, listen to me,' he urges, his voice barely audible. 'You're in danger, okay? I know you have no reason to trust me, but …'

We both hear the noise at the same time, and while it

makes me jump, it prompts Jamie to lift his hands off me, and place them on top of his head as he steps backwards, yelling 'Shit!' over and over.

'What?' I ask, totally bewildered. 'What is it?'

Before Jamie can answer, I'm thrown forward by a force from behind, as the bedroom door is swung open.

'Police!' I hear a man yell, and my fear turns to relief, and then joy, when I realise that finally, the cavalry has arrived. I am being rescued.

I flop down on the bed, frozen in shock, as a man barges into the room. He grapples with Jamie and manages to get him into a position where he can place handcuffs on his wrists. 'No!' he screams, struggling with the larger man who tells him he is under arrest for my kidnap.

'Natalie, don't believe what they tell you,' Jamie yells, 'it's not true, any of it.' The man starts to lead Jamie out of the room, and Jamie continues to rant, but I'm too startled and confused to take anything in. My mind is overwhelmed with questions and emotions, and I'm glad I'm sitting down already, because it feels like the room is spinning around me.

Why is Jamie suddenly calling me Natalie? Who should I not believe, the police? I called them, and told them what Jamie had done, and now they've come for me. At least, one has come for me. Why would I not believe him?

In a few seconds the policeman is back, squatting down beside me, asking if I'm alright; if I'm hurt in any way. He tentatively puts a hand on my shoulder, probably thinking that some physical contact will snap me out of my daze. I turn to look at him, and a flood of tears is unleashed, as I come to terms with the fact that my ordeal is over. I cover my face with my hands, and the young officer pats me on the back to comfort me, asking if I'd like a glass of water. 'Yes, please,' I say, between sobs, and he rises to his feet to oblige.

'Don't worry,' he urges, giving me a final pat on the shoulder. 'You're safe now.'

Upon hearing those words, I unleash another outpouring, and the officer looks glad to be leaving the room to get some respite from this hysterical woman.

'I'm safe,' I whisper to myself. I never thought I'd say those words again.

58

I didn't even realise at first. It took several minutes for the events I had witnessed to really sink in, and all I could do was lie back and breathe and try to make sense of everything that's happened to me since I was last at home. It was only when I took a sharp breath, steeling myself to deal with the next part of this rotten adventure – the good part – that I realised how dry my throat was, and remembered that the police officer had gone to get me a glass of water, and had not yet returned.

I have no real concept of time here, but I realised he had been gone for a disproportionate amount of time, considering the kitchen is only metres away. I thought perhaps he had taken Jamie somewhere, to make sure he couldn't run, but where? And why wouldn't he have come back by now? And isn't is quite strange that only one man came to rescue me? Wouldn't they send a team of two, three, even four? Jamie's words still niggled at my mind, although they faded into relative insignificance in light of the fact that my wishes had been granted. My call had been answered.

I got up off the bed, feeling stronger than I had for any of the days that I've been here, and went to investigate. I pulled the door handle, and almost lost my balance as it resisted my attempt. I tried again, twisting the handle this time, even though I couldn't remember ever having to before. 'No,' I whispered, as once again the door didn't budge a centimetre. I felt all my newfound strength drain from my body, and sank to the floor, trembling.

That was a while ago. I'm not sure how long. I don't even know how I could have failed to spot the keyhole in the door, although since it's situated quite far above my eye level, I suppose I just never registered that it was there. It might have been disguised, for all I know. I can't remember.

It doesn't matter now. I feel like nothing matters now.

59

'Jonathan Davis, thirty-nine, worked in the same department as Natalie until eighteen months ago, when he was moved to a different team, on a different floor. Neighbour told us he's on a skiing trip with his fiancée, and there's photos all over Facebook to prove it.' Nixon turns his screen around to let his boss see for himself.

'Okay,' Jackson sighs. 'He looks nothing like our guy, anyway. What about the other one?'

'Stephen Gardiner, thirty. Worked at CRB until May of this year, now working in a call centre over in Kilmarnock. He was on night shift all last week – quarter to midnight to quarter past seven; he turned up every night. I'd put money on him not being our guy either – he's about five feet five if he's lucky, and his hair is longer than Slater's. Unless they're extensions, which I very much doubt, he'd have to have grown about six inches of hair and shrunk about six inches in height in the last few weeks to be the man we're looking for, Boss.'

'Shit. OK, how many more to look into?'

'Forty-two male friends in total, four without profile photos. The family were able to identify seventeen of them. Most are old school friends or guys she worked with or still does. I'm working through the list.'

'Slater, what have you got on the guy from uni?'

'Not a lot unfortunately, sir. Callum Richard Connell, completed his degree in computer science in 2004 and set up his own software development company. The company was dissolved three years ago, and we don't have much on him since then. No social media accounts that we've been able to find, so there's nothing linking him to Natalie that way.'

'Okay, keep looking. I want everything we can get on him. Anything more from the CCTV in the area?'

'No cameras on her street doesn't help us, and no sign of anyone fitting the description tailing her at the station when she got off at Dalmuir on Thursday night. Obviously Central was much busier, so still checking but nothing so far. I'm checking the traffic cams, but without a license plate, it's a stab in the dark. I'll keep looking.'

'Keep me posted. Kyle, I want that appeal out again – I went her photo fresh in people's minds.'

'Yes, Boss.'

*

'Couldn't resist trying to be a hero, could you, Alex?'

Of course, the voice with the cold, sinister edge belongs to the man who lured him into this in the first place. This is the voice that has been hissing horrifically unreasonable orders in his ear for the past day or so.

He doesn't recognise the room they're in, but it is definitely not in the house where Alex has spent every waking hour carrying out this man's instructions and hating himself more with every passing minute. He doesn't know how he got from the bedroom, where he finally found his backbone and tried to help Natalie, to this room, but the dull ache at the base of his skull goes some way to explaining why he appears to have experienced a blackout.

This room has to be the creepiest place he's ever seen in his life.

He raises his eyes to see a massive screen dead ahead, which is broadcasting what he assumes are live images from the house. He can see Natalie, sitting on the floor with her back resting against the end of the bed and her elbows resting

251

on her knees. He can tell that she's sobbing, and he wonders what lies in store for her now that a cat has been thrown amongst the pigeons. He feels a stab of guilt, the sorest one yet, as he remembers that she thinks the guy who stormed in to the house to 'rescue' her is a policeman. He wonders if she's sobbing with relief, or if she knows the truth yet. That whoever that guy is, he's not on the side of the law that will be of any help to her at all.

'I'm sorry, am I interrupting your viewing?' the man asks, stepping directly in front of Alex, obscuring his view of the screen. He folds his arms across his chest and leans back slightly, observing Alex like he's an animal in a viewing cage. 'You really have become quite taken with her, haven't you?' he goads, smiling his sinister smile. He laughs, throwing his head back in an over-exaggerated gesture. 'That, my friend, is one of the reasons I chose you, believe it or not. I picked up on your pathetic weakness of character pretty much the moment I met you.'

'What is all this about?' Alex asks bluntly, frustrated by his tormentor's performance.

The man pauses for a second, seeming to give the question some thought. He pulls a chair over, making a point of dragging the legs noisily along the ground. He sits himself down, slightly to Alex's right, and leans forward, placing a hand on his own thigh to support his weight.

'I'm glad you ask, Alex,' he breathes, in a tone that Alex deciphers as threatening. 'Just for fun, though, why don't you tell me what you think this is all about?' He leans back again, not lifting his gaze from Alex's face. Alex doesn't respond, other than to intensify his own stare. 'No? No clue at all? I'm surprised at you, Alex. I mean, I knew straight away that you were soft, but I didn't peg you for an idiot as well!'

Alex still says nothing. He wants the truth, and if he offers up his own hypothesis, this crazy man might just go along with it, leaving Alex none the wiser.

'Well, I hope you're sitting comfortably,' the man laughs, crossing one leg over the other. 'I'm not in a hurry to go anywhere, are you?'

'Come on, you're not going to tell me you haven't been enjoying yourself. Not even a teeny, tiny little bit?' He draws his thumb and forefinger together beside Alex's face to illustrate his words. 'Come on, mate, let's face it, that in there, earlier, that was more action than you've had in ages!'

He laughs, like the sick bully he is, like all the bullies did when they were making fun of Alex, all through his childhood. He's been putting up with it his whole life, but this is new. He's never been cable-tied to a chair before.

'You're sick,' Alex tells him, his face smeared with disgust.

He sees the other man's eyes flash with fury, and it looks like he has to check himself for a second to reign in his temper. He clears his throat noisily and rises to his feet, hovering over Alex.

'Sick?'

'That's right,' Alex replies, struggling to mask the fear in his voice. 'How did you even dream up something like this? And for what?'

The man shrugs, showing no emotion at all. 'It was too easy, my friend,' he says, nonchalantly. 'And as for your second question, that's easy too. She fucked me over. No-one does that and gets away with it.'

Alex swallows, his mouth dangerously dry from the nerves he is suffering from. He also feels like he has to try to swallow his disgust at what the man in front of him has done.

'Whatever she did, she can't possibly deserve this,' he insists, staring at the ground because he can no longer bear to look at the monster standing before him. 'And what about her family, have you thought about them? Jesus Christ, the

253

police will have been searching for her for days now, what if they find us here?'

The man bursts into uproarious laughter, making Alex flinch in surprise. It lasts for a long, uncomfortable minute.

'Wow, you really don't have a fucking clue, do you, Alex? Just how do you think they're going to find us here, eh? Who's going to tell them, you? Bessie? That halfwit of a technician who passed himself off as a cop?' He laughs again, a sickening noise to Alex's ears.

So, that's who the other guy is. Just how many people does he have doing his bidding? 'How did you get her to go along with it?' Alex asks, desperate to know the answer to a question that has been bugging him for days now. 'Who is she, and why is she here?'

'For God's sake, pay attention, will you?' He gives a theatrical sigh.

'Look, let me spell it out for you,' he says, sitting down again, repositioning his chair so that this time he is facing Alex. 'When you have money, Alex, you can get what you want. Not all the time, but most of the time. And when you approach people who don't have money and offer them some, well, let's just say it makes it easier to get what you want. Like when I got you to sign up to my little project here. Do you follow?'

Alex looks at him disbelievingly. 'So, Bessie and Davie and the other woman, Angela, they're all going along with all this because you *paid* them?'

'In a way. In the beginning, anyway. A little bit of ingenuity and a little bit of creativity go a long way in this life, Alex, you should be mindful of that. And if you want to get ahead the best way can sometimes be to literally be one step ahead. So, I did my homework. I found out that this island is owned by this family, the Bains. And what do you know, they're quite a close-knit bunch, truth be told. Didn't take too much convincing to dance to my tune once I'd let

254

on that I had uncovered some ... information that they might not necessarily want made public.'

He looks to Alex for some kind of response, but Alex's face is neutral. *What kind of information?* he wants to ask. *What did you threaten them with?* But he doesn't think he wants to know the answer.

The man sighs, as though he's bored, but carries on nonetheless. 'Bessie didn't think she could do it, in the beginning. Kept saying she couldn't keep up the pretence under pressure. I managed to persuade her she could play her part, seeing as it was only small.'

Alex swallows again, feeling nauseous now.

'She even loaned me her boat. Good old Bessie.'

Alex shakes his head. 'It's still a risk,' he says, voicing his thoughts out loud. 'What if one of them has changed their mind about keeping quiet about it. What if they've phoned the police?'

The man's smile takes an age to spread across his lips, but when it makes it, it's the smile of someone with nothing to fear.

'You really think this is amateur hour, don't you, Alex? Honestly, if I gave a shit about your opinion of me, I could be really offended by some of the stuff you've come out with. Luckily, I don't.' He grins. 'What, do you think I just left everything up to chance? Do you really think I would pull off something like this and run the risk of old Bessie blowing the lid on it? She *can't* call the police, you muppet. She can't phone anyone. Well, that's not strictly true – she can phone anyone she wants, but ultimately she'll get me on the other end of the line.'

'But ...Davie left the island, the other day,' Alex reminds him. 'What if he ...?'

'Uh-uh.' The sound is like an electronic buzzer. 'Wrong again, buddy,' he says delightedly. 'Davie does what I tell him to do,' he states. 'I'm "the director", remember? I told

255

him to take a little jaunt out with his wife, just far enough that he could make it look as though they were coming back from the mainland. They were gone half an hour, tops.'

Alex sighs, defeated. Half an hour is nowhere near long enough for Davie to have made it to the mainland, or anywhere else where he might have been able to raise the alarm if he has been having concerns. Alex remembers the treacherous journey from Mallaig less than a week ago, when he felt as though he might be sick as a dog for two reasons: the choppy, terrifying tide and the fact that the fairly innocent ruse he had signed up for had turned into something far more sinister, and he couldn't see a way to back out of it.

Are Bessie and Davie and Angela – is she Davie's wife? – really going to let this crazy guy get away with this? Yes, they are, he tells himself. He knows first-hand how persuasive and intimidating the crazy guy can be – he's living proof of it.

'You've gone awfully quiet there, Alex. Everything okay?'

'You really think she deserves all this, and all those other people too?' The expression on Alex's face is the same as hers was, all those years ago.

The man's smile is gone, temporarily, and his lips purse, as though he's sucking on something sour.

'She tried to ruin me!' he yells, spitting out the words with unveiled contempt. 'But she didn't know, did she?' He smiles conspiratorially. 'She didn't do her homework on me, did she, Alex?'

60

2002

He knew she would show up. Her playing-hard-to-get routine had been part of the fun, just her little game. But he enjoyed a challenge – it made a change. She was different in a lot of ways, and that was why he was drawn to her. She was cool towards him, practically ice cold, and on the face of it she was indifferent to him and his charms. But he could see right through her. And he had been proven right – she had shown her face after all.

The fact that she had brought along her skanky little pal (who apparently needed no invitation to either the party or to attack his booze) irked him. But it was something he was willing to overlook, reminding himself of the bigger picture.

There were plenty of other freeloaders who showed up whenever there was a free party at the mansion, but he didn't mind as long as they showed him the respect he deserved.

He let her take it all in for a while before he made his move. She wasn't quite so indifferent now that she was seeing it for herself. The best thing about having wildly successful and wealthy parents was the fact that they liked to reward themselves for their achievements by enjoying ridiculously expensive and excessively frequent trips away. And while the cats were away, the mouse most certainly had to play.

Once the pal had gone off with some loser from the rugby team he made his move.

'Here you go,' he said sliding up beside her as she studied one of the framed degrees on the wall and handing her a bottled beer.

'Thanks,' she murmured, her eyes barely shifting focus from the frame.

'I'm glad you could make it.'

She seemed to take an eternity to turn her head, to acknowledge him, and when she did her smile was tepid. She said nothing. He could feel irritation beginning to burn.

'What's say we go somewhere a little more private?' he asked her, leaning forward and whispering in her ear. In actual fact they probably could have remained undiscovered in the study for quite some time, but his father's workspace didn't suit for what he had in mind.

She wasted no time in turning now, her face twisted in an ugly expression. 'I don't think so,' she said blankly, placing her unfinished beer on the sideboard and making to walk away.

'Hey, where do you think you're going?' he asked angrily, his temper ignited by the disdain written across her features. How dare she. He grabbed her arm.

'Hey, get off me!'

'Just what is your game, huh? You lead me on for weeks, giving me the run-around, playing hard to get, then when I finally get you here you treat me like a fucking mug? Who do you think you are?'

'Callum, get off me!' she cried, trying to pull her arm away, but he gripped it tightly. 'What are you talking about?' she asked, bewildered. 'How have I been leading you on?'

He stared at her intensely, enjoying the power, the feel of her squirming under his grip. No-one had batted an eyelid at the commotion. Aside from the deafening music and the hum of conversation that made her squawking redundant, this was his house, and not a single soul was about to get involved in something that didn't concern them. 'You know fine well how,' he told her. 'And you don't get to mess me around.'

She squirmed again, and he couldn't stop himself

laughing. 'Let's just quit the playing, shall we?' he said menacingly, grabbing her other wrist and forcing her backwards until she was pinned against the wall. He trapped her hands under his and leaned in, his excitement increased by her attempts to struggle.

He hadn't even made meaningful contact when he was compelled to release his hold and attend to his injured groin, where she had sucker-punched him with an angrily driven knee.

'Bitch!' he shouted, making after her once the initial shock of the pain had subsided. But she was too fast, and there were too many bodies in the way for him to catch up with her, especially since he wasn't moving freely. 'Bitch!' he yelled again, louder this time, as he saw her reach the front door and run outside.

61

'So, you did all this because she kneed you in the balls?'

Callum narrows his eyes. 'I did "*all this*" because she tried to ruin me, Alex, which you would have remembered if you were paying attention. She complained about me, tried to get me kicked out of the uni. Tried to stitch me up for "assault".' He makes the quotes in the air with his fingers. 'Mud sticks, Alex, and there aren't many who'll take the side of the "suspect" over the "victim", believe you me. But like I said, she didn't know who she was dealing with. She didn't know you do not cross the Connells. My dad is one of the best lawyers in the whole fucking country, and by the time he was through, she didn't have a leg to stand on. I don't know where the cow ended up – I never saw her again after that. Maybe she was scared, I don't know. Just as well; she would have got what was coming to her if I'd caught up with her, I tell you that.'

Alex shakes his head. 'And then what? You just spent the rest of your life plotting to get even with her?'

'I never even thought about her again after that, Alex,' Callum hisses, bringing his face so close to Alex's that he can feel the warmth of his breath on his skin. 'I am a millionaire, Alex, did you know that? And do you know why I am a millionaire? Because I work harder than most, and I'm smarter than most, but most of all, because I don't take any shit from anyone. Not in business, not in life. If someone so much as tries to take the piss, then they get what they deserve – sometimes from me, sometimes from my old man. But they get what's coming to them.' He pauses as though he is expecting another question, but Alex remains silent.

'But then I saw her one day, out of the blue. In fact, it was her voice I recognised. I was in Starbucks, and I heard her laugh – it went right through me like the sound of nails on a chalkboard. I would know that laugh anywhere. I would have knocked that laugh right out of her, along with her teeth, if I'd had the chance back in the day. And you will never guess who she was with! Only that little skank of a pal that she hung out with back then, her little partner in crime who was complicit in the whole plan to screw up my life. You should have seen the two of them, laughing and joking, probably at some poor bugger's expense, knowing those two. I thought the other one clocked me for a second, and I turned away, but when I looked back she seemed none the wiser. But that Natalie, she looked right at me at one point. No, scratch that, she looked right *through* me. That's the arrogance of the bitch, Alex! She didn't even fucking recognise me!'

Alex winces as Callum yells loudly. 'It was a long time ago,' he offers, feeling under pressure to say something, anything. 'I guess everyone does stupid things when they're young, things they regret.'

'Not to me, they don't,' Callum growls. Alex nods submissively.

'I followed her,' Callum explains, getting up and pacing in front of Alex. 'I was so tempted to confront her there and then, in the middle of the coffee shop, humiliate her like she humiliated me, but something stopped me. That's the thing about me, Alex, I learn from my mistakes. I went to my father, back then, and asked him to help me. And he did, don't get me wrong, but he could only do things by the book. I wanted revenge that she would remember, that would make her remember me. Having a go at her in a coffee shop wasn't going to cut it.'

'So, you followed her? Where?'

Callum's smile returns. 'Everywhere,' he says.

'She's not the brightest,' Callum tells Alex, still moving around while he revels in his victory. 'You wouldn't believe how close I got, without her suspecting a thing. She wears these massive earphones wherever she goes, and if she hasn't checked her phone in all of thirty seconds she has a mini panic-attack. She leaves her jacket – with her keys inside – unattended when she goes to the loo on her little solo coffee and laptop sessions in Costa, and if I hadn't been such a charitable person, I might not have handed them in once I'd made a copy, after she accidentally "dropped" them.'

'So, that's how you got into the house.'

'Bingo. Young women really should be more careful you know, Alex, there are a lot of unsavoury people around these days, you know?'

'And what about all the stuff? Her clothes, the photos. What was all that about?'

Callum shrugs, his shoulders lingering at his ears for a second. 'I wanted to mess with her mind,' he says nonchalantly, as if the notion of inflicting psychological trauma on another human being is no big deal. 'It worked, didn't it?'

'Of course it didn't work,' Alex answers forcefully, finding courage from somewhere to answer back. 'Do you honestly think you've got her believing she's someone else? You saw what happened the other day. She went nuts.'

'Mission accomplished,' Callum replies. 'Of course I didn't think she'd buy it, you moron. I mean, I guessed she'd probably doubt herself at first, especially when she saw the photos and everything, but the goal wasn't to get her to believe it, idiot. It was to mess with her head. She knows it's not real, of course she does. But that doesn't help her, does it? All she knows is she's stuck here, with you and Bessie and Davie, and that all of you keep telling her she's mental. That works for me.'

'So, what happens now?' Alex asks, feeling like his brain

is about to shut down from the exertion of processing what the man has told him. The pain from the site of his injury, where he must have been struck by a blunt object of some kind, is bringing tears to his eyes.

'For you? Or for her?'

'Both,' Alex replies, feeling a little selfish but at the same time, desperate to know his own fate.

Callum gives another shrug of indifference. 'Well, since it seems like I've gotten everything out of you that I'm likely to get, truth is, you're free to go.'

Alex jerks his head up in surprise. 'What do you mean?' he asks suspiciously.

'What part of "You're free to go" are you struggling with?'

'But … you just told me everything. Why would you let me go? What if I go straight to the police and turn you in?'

Alex instantly regrets digging a hole for himself, but he doesn't believe for a second that this man hasn't considered the possibility of Alex going to the police. He is an out-and-out psychopath, but he clearly possesses a startling amount of cunning.

Callum laughs yet again, clearly unperturbed. 'Turn *me* in?' he asks, incredulously. 'What exactly have *I* done? Correct me if I'm wrong, old chap, but you're the one who's been holding a woman against her will for the last few days. You're the one who was on the verge of assaulting her, not even an hour ago!'

Alex gulps down the nausea that begins to rise from his stomach.

'Say you did go to the police, and they turned up here, asking questions. What's Natalie going to tell them, Alex? Not forgetting about all this lovely footage I've got just lying around, waiting for someone to find …' He points towards a pile of technology in the corner, and Alex winces as he catches sight of Natalie on the screen again. 'I mean, the bird might be mental, an unreliable witness, but the camera never lies, does it?'

Alex closes his eyes, knowing he is truly defeated. The man is right. Alex has no leverage at all. If he tries to take the organ grinder down, he will almost certainly condemn himself for the part he has played in Natalie's ordeal. He will go to prison, for certain. This man who boasts of his high-flying lawyer father, will probably never see the inside of a police cell, never mind a jail. And what did he say about people who fuck him over? If this debacle is what he considered the appropriate response to whatever Natalie did, the details of which are still unclear, what would he dole out to Alex for ratting him out?'

'So, you're willing to let me go?' Alex seeks confirmation, sorting the pieces into place in his head as he speaks. 'You know I can never tell anyone anything about this without implicating myself, without going to prison. I don't even know your real name.'

Callum claps his hands slowly and loudly, giving Alex a mock applause. 'You're a smart boy,' he teases, patting Alex on the back. 'I knew you had a brain in there somewhere. It just takes a while to find it. I did consider the possibility that you might think sacrificing most of the best years of your life is worth it, for the sake of a woman you only laid eyes on for the first time not even a week ago, because I've seen the way you've been looking at her. Plus, you seem like an honourable guy to me.' Callum is revelling in his taunting, lapping up the fear and resentment that oozes from Alex like perspiration. 'But honour is for fools, Alex, that's a lesson you should learn. I don't think even a big softie like you would be willing to put your neck on the line for some random you got paid to screw with. Would you?'

His real question is not whether Alex is willing to put his own neck on the line in the pursuit of justice for Natalie, but whether he is willing to take on the man who got him into this mess, and see who comes off worst. Hearing the harsh truth of the part that he has played in punishing her for something that happened years ago makes Alex feel close to vomiting. A single tear escapes from his eyes as he tries to think of a way to get himself and Natalie out of this and fails, miserably.

He can't go to prison, he just can't. He would die in there. And this guy is telling him he is free to go, but how? He will never be free. This guy, he knows, is not about to hand over all the evidence that points to Alex being a kidnapper and an attempted rapist, which means that even if he does walk away now, the threat will always be there, he will never be free.

The man who did all this is clearly insane. He orchestrated the abduction of a woman from her own home, transported her hundreds of miles away to an island that barely passes for an inhabited part of the world, and all just to satisfy some sick, petty revenge.

Alex knows he will never be able to turn a corner without wondering whether the man will be there. Alex will never again feel safe in his own home, knowing that *he* is most likely spying on him, like he stalked and spied on Natalie, just waiting for Alex to so much as look like he might make a wrong move. The man is a dangerous control freak, and now he has ultimate control over Alex.

'What about Natalie?' he asks quietly, fearful of what the answer might be.

The man sits back down again, an arrogant smirk adorning his face.

'Well,' he begins, switching to statesman mode again, 'she, for the moment, is not free to go.' He winks at Alex and gives out a long sigh. 'There are still a few things we need to, shall we say, iron out,' he says, speaking casually, as though he were discussing plans for a day trip or something equally as insignificant. 'Nothing for you to bother your pretty little head about, Alex.' No-one would ever guess from his tone that he was talking about his plans to torment another human being.

'You've punished her now, she's had enough. I'm sure she'll be more than happy to apologise for what she did, and then you can call it quits. You should give it up now, let her go home. She won't tell anyone, I'm sure of it. Just like I won't tell anyone.'

Callum smirks again, his arrogance shimmering around him like an aura. 'We'll see,' is all he says, and Alex feels a chill as he once again wonders how far the man will go to achieve what he wants to achieve. And what his ultimate goal is.

'Anyway, I think it's time you left, Alex,' Callum tells him, walking away. He picks up a large pair of scissors and releases Alex's bonds.

'But how?' Alex asks him, rubbing his hands to soothe the pain from where the cable ties were digging into his skin. 'How am I supposed to get home?'

Callum looks to a spot above his head, as though he is thinking. 'Not my problem, mate,' he tells Alex with a smirk.

62

It's getting dark, and I can hear a fierce wind whipping up a frenzy outside the bedroom. Another day, drawing to a close. How many is that now? I've lost count.

Only a short while ago, I thought this was going to be the day that I would remember forever as the day that I was liberated. Now, I can't see that I'll ever get free.

I don't know what's happened to Jamie, but my intuition tells me he's not sitting comfortably in the living room, enjoying a late afternoon cuppa and one of his ginger crunch biscuits. He tried to warn me, you see. 'You're in danger,' he said, and suddenly all those times that I'd found myself confused about his motives, puzzled by the glimpses of genuine feeling that I thought I saw in him, made sense. There have been times when, defying all logic, I have found myself wanting to believe that he actually cares about me, that when he said he was worried about me, he meant it. And now it seems like he might actually have been on my side.

And now he's gone. And now I am not so convinced that it was Jamie who was behind all of this. Whoever did this to me has Jamie now, and God knows what they've got in store for me next.

Suddenly I hear a key in the lock, and I jump in fright and surprise. Instinctively I make a dart for the corner of the room, furthest from the door, but I've got nothing to arm myself with.

'Hey, Nat, how are you doing? It's been a while, hasn't it?'

It's not Jamie, nor is it the fake policeman from earlier, the one who bustled Jamie out of the room. The one who told me he was the police, but wasn't. This is a new man, and I've lost count of how many people are involved in ruining my life.

'Sorry, Nat, you're looking a little perplexed,' he says, moving towards me in slow, careful steps. I regret backing myself into a corner, literally. 'Is it because you're trying to place the face, or because I called you by your real name?'

'You,' I growl, as the recognition dawns on me, like the clouds parting to reveal the sun.

'Still got it,' he says, making a clicking sound with his tongue and pretending to brush imaginary lint from both his shoulders. 'How long has it been, thirteen, fourteen years? The beard's a relatively recent thing.' He rubs his chin and cheeks, and the bristles produce a soft noise. 'I wasn't sure about it at first; wasn't sure it suited me. But then, you've got to keep up with the trends, don't you? Every bugger has got one these days. And do you know what? I think it quite suits me.'

He looks at me as though he expects me to comment, but my lips are sewn together.

'You'd know all about that, eh, Nat? Keeping up with the trends, I mean. Look at your lovely hair. What is it they call this, then, a "dip-dye"?' He reaches out to touch my hair, and I pull away from him. 'Yep, you've still got it, too, you know,' he says, seemingly unperturbed by my withdrawal from his advance. 'Still a good-looking girl, if you don't mind me saying so. Still able to pull the blokes, anyway, am I right? I mean, that Kevin that you were out with last week, he wasn't exactly beaten with the ugly stick, was he?'

He registers the shock on my face at the mention of Kevin's name, and laughs. 'I mean, he's not *my* type, obviously, but I can appreciate a handsome face when I see one.'

'What do you want from me?' I ask, feeling more terrified than I ever felt with Jamie. Even when I think back to that first morning when I woke up to find myself here, and Jamie waltzed in to the room like it was just any other, regular day, I don't remember feeling such abject fear as I'm feeling in this moment. I didn't know Jamie. I knew he was a stranger, that he was taller and stronger than me, but somehow there was a limit to how much he could intimidate me, physically. This man is not Jamie. He's probably about the same height as him, perhaps an inch or two shorter, but up close I can see that he's changed a lot since I knew him as a student. These days he's built like something out of the fake wrestling federation that my little brother used to be obsessed with when he was a kid. And unlike with Jamie, I know all too well what this man is capable of.

He laughs again, revelling in my obvious terror.

'Well, you see, Nat, I'm not really sure, to be honest. I haven't quite decided what comes next. I'm flying by the seat of my pants at this point, if you must know. I have to hand it to you, though, it has been thoroughly entertaining, watching you flit from one disastrous plan to another, getting more and more antsy with every passing day. But, believe it or not, this is the most exciting bit so far. The thing is, I'm not like you, Nat. You see, you're a planner, aren't you? You love to have structure in your life. Same routine, day in, day out. Work, gym. See your pals this day, visit your family that day. You're really quite predictable, you know. Predictable, but just a little bit ditzy – no offence. Not that I'm complaining; don't get me wrong. No, your routine and your rather lackadaisical approach to life made it so much easier for me to keep up with you.'

'You've been following me,' I whisper, my veins pulsing with rage as well as repulsion. It explains so much of what has gone on here, but it makes me feel more violated than ever before. My stomach lurches at the thought of him stalking me, watching me, keeping tabs on my life. I feel a cold sweat break out on the back of my neck.

'Do you know, Nat, I'd almost started to think that you might be as thick as that wet lettuce you just spent the week with, but actually, you've got a lot more going on up here than he does.' He points a finger at his temple.

'Jamie,' I say, wishing with all my heart that I could be reunited with the man I've spent the last week trying to escape from.

'Er … yeah, Jamie,' he says, with a sinister smile.

'Where is he? What have you done with him?'

He frowns in mock confusion. 'What have I *done* with him?' he asks. 'What are you talking about?'

'Well, someone pulled him off me, one of your hired goons presumably, and now he's gone, and you're here. So, where is he?'

He shrugs and pulls at a non-existent thread from the sleeve of his designer sweater. 'Couldn't tell you, Nat. I'm not the guy's babysitter.'

'And what about Bessie and Davie?' I prod further, the ratio of fear to anger beginning to skew in favour of me challenging him. 'Will they be joining us again, any time soon?'

He smiles again, and his eyes are cold. 'Bessie and Davie. Well, they're, um … otherwise engaged for a bit. But don't worry, Nat. We don't need the others. We'll be fine, just you and me, together. It'll be like old times, eh? We can catch up. You can fill me in on all the bits I don't know, and I'll give you a little run-down of what I've been getting up to for the last fourteen years. How does that sound?'

'Why are doing this to me?' I demand, and maddeningly I hear my voice cracking with emotion. I mustn't let my panic, and the pain that has caught up with me from my ankle, take over. I mustn't give him any more satisfaction than he's getting already.

He shakes his head disapprovingly. 'What was I saying about you being intelligent?' He takes a step towards me,

270

his bulk even more foreboding up close. 'Why do you think I'm doing this to you, Nat? Any guesses? Go on, have a go.'

His voice is more serious now, his expression cold and unamused. He no longer looks like he's finding this funny. He stares at me, his breathing starting to quicken, waiting for me to offer a response. I flinch as I remember the last time he was this close to me. I can still feel the pressure of his hand around my throat as though it were happening right here, right now.

'Because of what I did to you,' I concede, lowering my head, trying to steal a glance around the room in search of a weapon that I might be able to use. But there is nothing. I am helpless. I look up again and see that he is glaring at me with hatred in his eyes. He doesn't speak, he just stands there, detesting me.

'I'm sorry, okay? I'm really, really sorry.' There are tears falling now, tears of trepidation. 'I shouldn't have done it. I was a stupid kid, and I never meant for it to go as far as it did. Please, Callum. I've said I'm sorry. What more can I do?'

He takes a step back, his face blank, as though he is processing an apology that he hadn't expected to hear. He turns and starts to walk away.

'Please, Callum,' I carry on, following him as he heads for the door, 'you wanted to pay me back, teach me a lesson. I get that. And believe me, I've learned my lesson. What I did was so wrong. But please, can we put an end to all this now? I just want to go home. I won't tell a soul about any of this, I promise you. I just want to go home, that's all.'

He turns to face me. 'Soon,' he says, and turns away again.

'No, no, please don't lock me in again!' I try to make a lunge through the door, but he shoves me back and I stumble halfway across the room from the force of his push. I hear the door slam, and the key turn in the lock. 'No,' I whisper.

63

'Davie!' Alex shouts, thumping loudly on the door. 'Davie, are you in there? It's me, Alex! I mean, Jamie! Open up if you're in there, will you?'

It's unlikely, given that the door is locked and there are no lights on indoors, but Alex is desperate.

'Shit!' he exclaims. Where the hell is he? It's almost pitch-black now, even though it's only just gone four o'clock, and the tiny sphere of light from the torch on his phone is close to useless in a place where there are several square miles of absolute nothingness.

'Davie, please,' he yells again, launching himself against the door. He's been poring over the details of what he's been told, searching through a mire of dead-ends for a through road that will lead him in the right direction. He can't get off the island on his own, and he knows now that the phones are rigged so that all attempted calls are diverted, but Davie has his boat, and surely, he must be willing to help. Just what has Davie and his family been threatened with? The man obviously thinks he's got everything sussed out, but there must be something he hasn't thought of. Something that Alex can work to his advantage and maybe, just maybe, have a chance at doing the right thing.

His end goal chops and changes like a windscreen wiper flitting from side to side, from saving himself, and leaving Natalie to fend for herself, to saving Natalie, and taking whatever may be thrown at him; from being a coward to setting himself up as a hero. Currently, his conscience is throwing jabs at him like a professional boxer, and he's leaning towards making himself a hero. But at this rate, unless he can track down Davie or even Bessie, he has more chance of dying a cold, painful death in the darkness than saving someone else's life.

He doesn't want to think about how much further the man might go in his quest for his own brand of justice, but there is no question that the man must be stopped. If he can go as far as he did by proxy, what is he capable of when he is there in person, and there is no-one around to stop him?

Almost as soon as he started running, Alex regretted making a break for it and leaving Natalie behind, but he knows he's no match for the other man physically. Alex could never take him on and win, and he has been knocked out once already – he doesn't have time to waste being rendered unconscious again. And neither does Natalie. He needs to try a different tack – a non-physical one.

'No!' he cries loudly, the heels of his hands smarting from banging on the door so hard. 'Where are you, Davie?'

64

Bessie lifts her hand with the intention of using it to lift the receiver, but for the fourth time she doesn't make contact with the phone, and instead brings her hand to her mouth, nervously chewing on her fingernails. He's gone now, at least she's almost certain he is, but his voice is still ringing in her ears. His instructions, that she had to write down for fear of forgetting. His threats, that she will need no such reminder of.

She has to go through with it. She can't believe she was stupid enough to think that it wouldn't be this difficult, but she can't afford to be crazy enough to defy him. It's her and her family, or the girl. It may be the most selfish thing she will ever do in her life, but she is not about to throw herself or her loved ones under the bus for the sake of a complete stranger. That's not to say she will do what he has asked of her lightly. She's been sitting by the phone for twenty minutes, reciting over and over what she is going to say – what she has been told to say. It won't be hard to sound anxious and terrified – she genuinely is both of those things – but it will be hard to convince them she is telling the truth, unless she really concentrates.

Bessie is a woman who detests lies and has always prided herself on being incapable of disguising the truth. But today she does not have a choice. And the lie she has to tell is to the police, for goodness' sake! She whispers, 'God, forgive me,' before finally picking up the phone and dialling 999.

65

It's an unfortunate fact that all his expensive equipment will be ruined, but it's the price that has to be paid, and so Callum will pay it. Just like the cash he handed over to Gary for completion of a fine job done. A few grand is a drop in the ocean, hardly worth losing sleep over, and with gullible Gary's fate now sealed by his little foray in front of the camera, disguised as the would-be hero cop, he feels no need to worry about what his little assistant might get up to, now that he's on his way back to wherever he came from on that excuse for a boat that Bessie tried so hard to keep under wraps. The memory sticks are the only pieces of this elaborate jigsaw that matter. One for him to hold onto, and one for the police to find, and put all the pieces together to come up with one big, fake picture of what went on here. Everything else is collateral damage.

He takes a last look around, making sure he hasn't missed anything. 'Nope,' he whispers. 'All good.'

He pulls his dust mask down over his face and switches on the pressure sprayer which is filled with sodium hypochlorite. 'Bye bye, evidence,' he says in a sing-song fashion, commencing work on the technical equipment first.

*

'Bessie! Oh, thank God!' Alex exclaims, as the woman opens the door tentatively.

'What is it?' she asks, her face barely visible as she uses the door as a shield. Alex notices that there is a chain in place, preventing it from being opened any wider.

'Bessie, I need your help,' he pants, out of breath from an arduous hike from the shore to the only other property he has come across so far on the north side of the island. 'Can I come in?'

'No,' she replies quickly. 'What is it you want?'

Alex regulates his breathing. 'Okay, Bessie, I need you to listen to me. You know the man who threatened you, made you pretend that Natalie is really Jen? He's out of control, okay? I don't know how much he told you, but Natalie was kidnapped. That other man, he made me help, but I didn't know any of this was going to happen. And I need your help, to help her, do you understand?'

Bessie looks at him suspiciously for a moment, then starts to close the door. 'I don't want any part in this, anymore,' she says, uncertainly.

'No, Bessie, please!' Alex insists, jamming his arm in the small space just in time before Bessie can retreat back into the house. 'Did you not hear what I said? She's been kidnapped, Bessie. That man brought her here for … well you don't need to know all that. But she's in danger, and I need you to help me. You must have a way to contact the police, or a friend, or anyone that can come here and help us. Please.'

'I can't,' she says, and Alex realises that she's scared. 'I'm sorry, I can't help you.'

Alex shakes his head in disbelief. 'Look, whatever he's said to you, whatever threats he's made, if you help me, we can make sure he gets held to account for what he's done, and then you'll have nothing to worry about.' He raises his voice. 'Come on, Bessie, you're not seriously going to let him get away with this, are you? She's a sitting duck, in that house. God knows what he's planning to do.'

'Look, I've said I'm sorry; you need to leave now.' She tries to be assertive but her voice quivers.

276

'What about Davie, do you know where he is? And the boat – tell me where to find it and I'll go and get help. The police will come, and you'll be fine. He won't be able to get to you, I promise.'

Bessie blinks hard, and Alex sees a tear run down her face. 'He's got the boat,' she tells him.

He leans back and directs a curse towards the sky, and Bessie takes the opportunity to slam the door hard. Alex hears the key turn in the lock.

'No!' He yells, battering on the door. But what's the point? Bessie can't help him. Or she won't. And Davie and Angela are nowhere to be seen. So, unless there is someone else on this island, someone whom the man hasn't yet managed to get his poisonous claws into, he is out of ideas. Knowing the man as he now does, he doesn't feel good about his prospects.

He starts to walk, trying desperately to think of a plan, but the pain from the back of his skull announces itself every few seconds, thwarting every train of thought.

Regret hits with the same force as the pain in his head, and he curses himself for not doing something before now. He could have tried to take the man down, he thinks. He could have tried to catch him by surprise and disable him and get hold of the boat keys that he must now have on him. It might have worked, if he had doubled back instead of trying to source help. Who knows where the man is now, what he's doing. Alex knows he will need something significantly more fool-proof than the element of surprise to take him down.

He wishes he had a weapon of some kind, something to give him an edge. In the darkness he can barely see where he is going – he switched off his phone to preserve the three percent battery power it was clinging onto, in the hope that he will be able to call upon the device for its intended purpose at some point, once he has rescued Natalie. Sheer hope propels him forward, and he imagines how it would feel to be the one who brings an end to the man's vile game and delivers Natalie to her home. He stumbles on a rock and puts his hands out in front to steady himself, only just managing to stay upright. He realises his hands are shaking – he will need to try and get that under control if he is to play the part of a hero. He will need all his wits about him to succeed, as well as a weapon. He rummages around for the rock which impeded his progress, and picks it up, testing the weight of it.

66

'Sir, you're not going to believe this,' DC Slater exclaims, holding the phone away from her ear as she beckons Jackson to her desk. 'We've had a call from a woman who says she knows where Natalie Byron is being held: on the Isle of Carn.'

'Where the hell is that?' Jackson asks.

'The Inner Hebrides. H and I division are on their way there now, sir.'

'And she's alive?'

'So the caller believes, sir. Apparently she hasn't seen her for a few days but she's one hundred percent certain it's her, it's Natalie.'

Jackson lets out a cautious sigh of relief. 'Let's hope so.'

67

It's a bump from next door that wakes me, and my heart leaps into my mouth when I sit up. I don't remember falling asleep, but my brain must have experienced a short circuit and shut down for a while. I step out of bed as I would normally, forgetting again that my ankle still hasn't returned to full fitness, and whisper an expletive as once again I'm rocked by the nasty sensation that fizzes through my nervous system.

I hold my ear to the door, trying to determine what could have made the noise. Is it him? What does he have in store for me now? At least, before, I had the freedom to move around. The freedom to roam, even if it was only within the confines of the island, which is admittedly quite a significant area to move freely around. The freedom to brush my teeth, and take a bath, and even use the damn toilet. How long will I be locked in here for?

My stomach rumbles loudly to remind me that I haven't had anything to eat for several hours, and straight away my mind goes to the worst outcome imaginable: he is planning to starve me to death. Actually, dehydration will kill me first, and that will not be a pleasant way to go.

'Help!' I scream, banging on the door with all the energy I've still got in reserve. 'Please, Callum, let me out!' It may be pointless, but I grab the door handle, willing to apply all the strength in my body to the task of trying to fight my way out of here. To my surprise the door flies open, and I'm thrown backwards, stumbling across the room and landing awkwardly on my backside, giving me another area of pain to focus on aside from my ankle.

I'm jubilant and confused all at once. I haul my creaking body to a standing position and peer tentatively out of the door, reminding myself in the nick of time that it's Callum Connell I'm dealing with, and he would probably find nothing more hilarious than to wait for me to take a step out into the hallway only to slam the door in my face. But there is no-one there. The bumping sound startles me again as I tiptoe down the hall, glad that I dozed off fully clothed and with socks still on, as the floor is painfully cold as always. I peer into each room as I pass them, realising, as it happens for a third time, that the noise is being caused by the front door of the house slamming against the wall every time the wind picks up. If Callum is here, he is making himself very scarce, and I keep looking over my shoulder, terrified that he will jump out at me and haul me back into the bedroom.

I grab my jacket from the hook behind the door and step outside the house, confused and acting on auto-pilot. I feel like the guy who woke up in the hospital to a post-apocalyptic world in that movie, *28 Days Later*. It was eerie enough when I thought there was just me, Alex, Davie and Bessie here, but now that it seems like I'm the only one in the vicinity I feel like that guy must have felt: terrified.

I don't stray too far out of the house, because it is still very dark and I am not wearing shoes, owing to the thick bandage on my ankle. From what I can see, and hear, there is no-one else around. Not Jamie, not Bessie, not Davie, and not Callum Connell. What is going on?

I head back indoors, edging myself into the living room slowly, trying to psych myself for the possibility that he might be behind the door. But he is not. There is no-one in the room. Nor in the kitchen, nor the bathroom. I am here alone.

I don't know what to do. I have no idea where Callum has gone since he locked me in the bedroom, and God only knows what has become of Jamie. I don't know if I should get out of here, and run, or whether this house is the safest place to be.

I am so confused. For some reason, my mind keeps reminding me of all the post-apocalyptic movies and TV shows that I've seen, and that book that I hated from Standard Grade English about the *Triffids* or whatever they were called, because the creepiness of this empty house on this empty island reminds me of those post-disaster worlds. Nothing good happened to the people that ventured off in search of information, and of other people. I can't remember how the Cillian Murphy movie ended, but I'm pretty sure the common moral of the story in all of those stories was: stay put unless you want really bad things to happen to you. At least for a while. The differentiating factor for me is that there is a very finite number of places I can go to from here, and while, for the moment, I appear to be safe, if I go to any of the other places I know, or go looking in places I don't know, then I might put myself in danger.

My barren stomach makes another anguished cry and it helps me to make a decision. I have to eat, if I am to survive a journey into the unknown, so for the next few minutes, at least, I will take a breath, refuel my body and try to make sense of this new phase of my turmoil.

As I enter the kitchen, I notice for the first time that there is something odd about the room. There are pools of water at random points on the floor, and the cupboards and surfaces are all glistening with moisture. I check the kettle and it's cold, so I don't think the wetness I'm seeing could have come from its steam. Plus, it's every surface – the stream of hot air from the kettle wouldn't have created so much condensation as to make the entire room drip.

I reach out and test the liquid, touching the worktop recklessly without carrying out a risk assessment, but my fingers don't burn, or react in any other way. I edge my nose closer and try to pick up on any identifiable scent, but again there is nothing. It smells of nothing.

I stop short of tasting it, but in the absence of any contradictory evidence I assume it is just plain old water. The question of what it's doing all over the kitchen is one that can wait until I've had some toast, because maybe then my grey matter will work a bit more effectively and I can come up with an explanation.

*

Alex is almost back at the house, but the closer he gets, the less certain he is that he has what it takes to do what he needs to do. He's tried to plan it out in his head, picturing the scene. Everything depends on him being able to find the man, and catch him unaware, but even if he does, he then has to find the balls from somewhere to attack him. He can almost hear the crunching sound of the rock against bone, and the thought of it makes him feel ill. He envisages the blood and the chaos that would ensue if he were to strike the way he knows he will have to, and he is forced to stop walking to compose himself, taking in huge gulps of air to allay his growing anxiety.

When he stops it makes him want to turn around and head back to Bessie's, or to Davie's, or to the shore. It makes him want to hide himself away and hope that somehow this crazy dilemma he is stuck with will just go away. He has cried today, something that he hasn't done for many years, but the relief of the release did nothing to alleviate the shame of his weakness, his cowardice. Ten minutes ago, he was confident that he could rescue the situation, and Natalie along with it. Now, he's overcome with fear and paralysed by a panic attack.

He throws the rock away, hearing it land in the grass a few

feet from where he is standing. He can't use it. He won't. He needs his nemesis subdued, not bleeding uncontrollably. He might be able to throw a punch in anger, but a solid contact with a heavy, blunt object could make him a murderer, and that cannot happen.

He rubs his eyes, ridding them of the tears that are making his vision blurry, and tells himself that he has only one choice: to take action. He starts walking again, and the outline of the house becomes visible at the crest of the hill.

68

The living room has the same weird dampness going on as the kitchen, and in light of this oddness I have had a rethink and decided that I can't stay here, not knowing where all this water suddenly came from, and what is going on in the world outside this house. I have managed to hurriedly take on some emergency calories, and just need to add a few more layers of clothing so that I am prepared for whatever weather may come.

The sound of movement in the house disconcerts me and I crouch down, one arm still midway through negotiating the sleeve of my hoodie. There are footsteps; someone is doing what I did earlier: checking for presence in all of the rooms. And they are almost here; they have almost reached the bedroom.

I don't want to budge an inch. My hiding place between the chest of drawers and the wall is not likely to keep me suitably concealed when whoever it is in the house comes looking for me, but it's marginally better than being in plain sight.

Above the sound of my own hurried breathing I make out the sound of footsteps padding on the carpet, and a shadow falls over me as I'm found with ease.

I cower into the corner, making myself small, because I don't know what else to do.

'Hey, Natalie, it's okay,' he says, crouching down to meet my eye level. 'It's me, okay? It's me.'

I don't even have time to deliberate whether I am relieved to find that it's Jamie or whether I should still be scared of him, because suddenly there is the sound of multiple sets of footsteps inside the house, and Jamie's head does a one-hundred-and-eighty degree turn to the left with such speed that it looks like it must hurt.

'Alexander Beattie?' A man in a suit half-asks, half-states, as two uniformed police officers follow him into the room and seize Jamie by the arms. 'DS Andrew Blackie, Highlands and Islands police. I am arresting you on suspicion of the unlawful abduction of Natalie Byron.' He gestures towards the door with his head and says, 'Get him out of here.'

'No, wait, please,' Jamie says, as the two officers wearing what appear to be stab and bullet proof vests start to bustle him out of the room.

'Hold on,' I plead with them, rising to my feet, my right arm still not having completed its journey through my sleeve. 'That's not his name; he's Jamie.' The men pause uncertainly in the doorway, and the man in the suit looks at me in a way that I've become used to since I've been on this island, as though horns are sprouting out of my head. 'That's Jamie,' I repeat, confused and frustrated. 'Jamie ... what's his last name?' I tap on my forehead in the hope it might help push the information to the front of my mind. 'Baxter!' I yell, 'he's Jamie Baxter! Tell them, tell them you're Jamie!'

Everyone looks at Jamie expectantly, and he swallows hard, then shakes his head and lowers it towards the floor. 'I'm sorry, Natalie,' he says softly. 'I'm so sorry.'

'Take him,' the authoritative man instructs for a second time, and this time the officers do now remove Jamie from the room.

'What?' Who the hell is he then?' I demand, flummoxed.

'Natalie?' the suited man asks, ignoring my question. 'Natalie Byron? I'm Detective Sergeant Andrew Blackie; I'm with the Highlands and Islands division.' He opens up a black wallet and shows me a card with his name and photo

286

on it. 'Are you alright?' he asks, dipping his head to peer into my face for an answer.

'Are you really the police?' I ask him, doubting everything, even my own eyes.

The man offers me a kindly smile and nods his head. 'Yes, I am,' he says. 'We are.'

'Oh my God,' is all I can offer in return, as I collapse onto the bed and start to cry tears of relief.

*

'It's her,' DI Jackson relays to his team, gathered in the briefing room, prompting a round of celebratory smiles and a punch to the air from DC Nixon.

'They're sure?' Nixon asks cautiously.

Jackson nods. 'A hundred percent,' he confirms. 'H and I are arranging transport to Mallaig, and we'll meet her from there. Nixon, you and I will go. We'll need to leave now – it's a bit of a drive.'

'Okay, Boss.'

'Good work, everyone,' Jackson doles out somewhat subdued praise. He and his team did everything right, he firmly believes, but nonetheless there is a part of him that feels like a fraud for claiming this outcome as a victory. Regardless, the woman has been found, so whether he and his team have earned the right to claim kudos for a solved case or not, he is not going to decline it.

69

'Are you feeling better?' the policeman asks me. I've pinched myself several times in the last ten minutes to check that I'm not dreaming, and I'm not. They're here, finally. Real police, with real identity badges, and radios, and uniforms and everything. And they're milling around, doing God knows what, while I sit on a chair in the kitchen, wrapped in the duvet from the bedroom, sipping a cup of tea containing multiple sugars to try and calm my nerves.

'Yes,' I answer, and for the first time in days I am telling the truth in answer to a question. I am feeling a million times better than I was before they got here. 'I just want to go home,' I add, and the man nods his head.

'Of course, and we will get you home as soon as possible,' he assures me. 'I would like you to talk me through what's been happening, if you can. Do you feel up to doing that right now?'

'I'll try my best,' I answer with a cautious nod, not convinced that I really do feel up to recounting the worst few days of my entire life.

'Okay, let's start at the beginning,' he urges, taking a seat opposite me and readying his pen and paper for taking notes. 'First of all, what can you tell me about how you got here?'

'Nothing, because I don't know,' I tell him, and hearing it out loud makes me realise how ridiculous that sounds. 'I went to bed on Thursday night, and when I woke up again, I was here.'

'You went to bed at home, your own home?'

'Mm-hm.'

'And when you woke up here, that was Friday morning?'

'No, Saturday morning. Or at least, that's what he told me. When I woke up I had a banging headache and I felt like I had been asleep for about a week. I assumed they must have drugged me, to get me here. I literally don't remember a thing.'

'They?' the policeman asks, a mild frown creasing his brow.

'Callum and Jamie,' I answer. 'I mean, Alexander, or whatever that guy's name is, the one you arrested. He told me it was Jamie, and I found some paperwork in the drawers that was addressed to Jamie Baxter – I only know what he told me. I assume he and Callum must have brought me here together, but I don't know. I'm pretty sure it must have been Callum's idea, because it fits with the kind of person he is, but I don't know where Jamie comes into it. I mean, Alexander. I had never met him before.'

The man's eyes narrow slightly as he regards me, selecting his words.

'Ms. Byron, are you saying that there was another man involved in holding you here?'

'Yes, Callum Connell,' I explain. 'I knew him when I was at university. Except he said he doesn't go by that name any more; I don't know what he's calling himself now. I only saw him the one time, a couple of days ago, I think, or maybe yesterday – I can't remember now, which day was which. They've all rolled into one ...'

I rest my head on the heel of my hand and screw up my eyes, trying to coax my brain into producing sentences that make sense.

'It's okay, take your time,' DS Blackie says, stretching back in his chair.

I exhale loudly, trying hard not to start crying again. I'm not sure that I am cut out for raking over the facts of my 'unlawful abduction' right at this moment. I want to go home, and I want to see my family. I want to hold them all tight and never let go of them. But if I don't give my statement now, I will have to give it later, possibly when I get home. And I don't want any part of this nightmare, or this island to follow me home. I want to step off this cursed land and never speak of it, ever again. I want to purge it from my memory. I need to be brave and do this now.

'Okay, I'm okay,' I assure DS Blackie, taking another sip of my tea. 'I know I'm not explaining this very well. Let me start again.'

'Of course,' he says, and offers me a comforting smile. 'I appreciate this must be incredibly difficult for you. Take your time.'

'Okay.' I expel the air from my lungs again. 'The day I woke up here, it was only Jamie who was here. My head was … well it felt really foggy, and I couldn't make sense of what I was seeing when I looked around the room, and out of the window. He came into the room and started calling me Jen, and telling me that I was his girlfriend, that this was my home. I tried to run away but …' I scoff. 'Well, you know, there's not really anywhere to go.'

The Detective Sergeant nods.

'And then I found all my stuff here: my clothes, my towels, he even made fake photos of me with him in them. He … he must have hacked into my computer.'

'What kind of photos?' DS Blackie asks, his expression concerned.

'Just … photos of me, from holidays and stuff like that. He had photoshopped his face onto them.'

'Alexander Beattie?'

The name still sounds foreign to my ears, and my response is delayed. 'Yes, but he called himself Jamie.' I feel frustration starting to build. I feel like I've told him this already, a few times. Is he not listening to me? He nods.

'So, he told you that you came here voluntarily?'

'Yes, he told me I moved here because he was coming

and said I wanted to be with him. He said he worked here. He told me I must be having some kind of breakdown, and that's why I couldn't remember anything. He said it had happened before, a while back, and that I'd had to see a doctor the last time. I almost believed him, at one point.' I have to stop talking for a moment, because a lump becomes lodged in my throat and I have to swallow it down. It may have only been for the briefest moment, and it may never have gotten deep enough into my psyche for me to truly believe it, but he had me close. Close to believing that everything I know, everything I love, was a lie. 'But I didn't,' I say, as much for myself to hear as for the detective. 'I didn't believe him. I just kept trying to get away, but I couldn't; I had no way of getting off the island. And then I found this phone box, and I thought I'd managed to call you. The police, I mean. But they must have rigged it somehow, diverted the number or something. Because it was Callum on the end of that line. I didn't recognise his voice at the time, but I'm sure now. It was him. Taunting me. Playing with me.'

The detective's brows take a dive downwards again. 'Ms. Byron,' he begins, 'the member of the public who called us and told us you were here, they were only aware of one man being involved: Alexander Beattie.'

'Who called you?' I ask. 'Was it Bessie? But it couldn't have been, because Bessie knows his name is Jamie, not Alexander. And so does Davie, and Angela, they all call him Jamie. Does that mean there's been someone else here this whole time?'

The officer looks baffled again for a moment at the mention of the other names.

'The caller has told us that the man that we now have in custody introduced himself to them as Alexander Beattie and told them the same as he told you – that you were his girlfriend,' he says trying to get a handle on the events that have led to this point. 'It was only this morning, when they saw an appeal for information about your whereabouts, that they put two and two together and called us. They didn't mention another man. Do you know this other man, Callum, well?'

'That's not possible,' I answer, ignoring his question, trying to connect the dots and getting lost along the way. 'Was it a man or a woman who called?'

'A woman,' the DS replies, somewhat reluctantly it seems. 'A Beatrice Bain. Do you know her?'

'Bessie is the only other person who's been here,' I explain. 'There was Jamie, then there was Bessie, then there was Callum right at the end. But she called Jamie "Jamie". And her and her family were threatened by Callum, that's why they went along with all of this. How could she know that Jamie is not his real name? Why would she tell you he's Alexander when she thought he was Jamie?'

The detective looks as confused as I feel, and I wonder if the reason why I am not keeping up is because my head is so mashed. But what he's saying is not making sense. Bessie never once called Jamie 'Alexander'. And Callum told me he had spoken to Bessie, didn't he? He threatened her and the others into submission so that they would keep quiet about what he's done. So how did she know that Jamie isn't Jamie? And now that the police are here and can keep her safe, why hasn't she told the police that it was really Callum?

'Callum did this,' I tell DS Blackie, with every ounce of conviction I can dredge up from my depleted reserves. 'Callum Connell. I don't know who Alexander Beattie is, and I don't know who Bessie is, really, or why she didn't tell you about Callum, but I can guarantee you, one hundred percent, Callum did this.'

292

70

Alex should have seen it coming. *He* thought of everything, of course he did. He wasn't going to stick around and take the fall, was he? Alex spent enough time wondering what his next move was going to be, trying to second guess him, trying to understand what he was going to do now that he had been forced to reveal himself as the puppet master, pulling everyone's strings. What he was going to do to Natalie, now that she'd seen his face. Now that Alex has the answer, he can't believe that it was the one and only thing that didn't cross his mind. The one thing that was staring him in the face; the one thing that he was so stupid not to consider: *he* did nothing. He didn't have to – his fun had already been had. His trap had already been laid. And all that was left for him to do was to let Natalie know that he was the mastermind behind everything she's been through. And after that he just … left.

As much as Alex detests the man, he has to concede a grudging respect for the genius of it. Alex has no doubt that the plan will have been thought through to the letter; he will have obsessed over it. He will not have left any of his tracks uncovered; there will be no chink in his armour. Which leaves Alex quite royally screwed.

*

It's real now. I am actually going home. I could count on the fingers of one hand the number of times I have been on a boat of any description, and the only thing I can really remember about each of the occasions is feeling distinctly unwell. This time, though, even the rough seas are not affecting me. My stomach is full of butterflies; there is no more room in there for nausea.

Soon, I will be back on the mainland and, within a matter of hours, I will be home. I have never been so excited at the thought of spending time on the M8 in all my life.

Today is a beautiful winter's day. The sun is out, and the blanket provided by the police is doing a wonderful job of keeping the fresh wind at bay. I remind myself for the umpteenth time to release the tension in my shoulders and give myself license to relax. It does nothing to quell the butterflies, but I manage to close my eyes for a moment and just enjoy the feeling of the winter sun on my skin. I think back to the dream I had, the one where my family and I were all together, and I feel tears prick at the back of my eyes. There will be enough of those when I reach the shore, I know, so I take a deep breath and hold them inside.

I don't know how long I've had my eyes closed for, but when I reopen them I can make out the shore, and the butterflies flip out. This is it. I am so close now that I can taste the shoreline, and my heart flutters like one of the butterflies has escaped from my stomach and is trying to smash its way out through my chest.

As the boat edges closer it seems to slow down, and I have to fight the urge to yell at the man at the helm to keep this thing moving as fast as it can possibly go. I take deep breaths, letting the tears of relief come as they wish now, and through my sobs I can't stop smiling.

*

'I think this is them, now,' Max exclaims, and with perfect synchronicity the Byron family rises to their feet and rushes outdoors.

294

'Oh, my God,' Gillian explains, bringing her hands to her face.

It is. It's her. The distance between them is barely anything, but while the pilot of the police boat manoeuvres the vehicle into a position where his passengers can disembark, it feels as though they are still worlds apart. They are close enough now that they can see each other, and it will be mere minutes until they are able to hold one another, but those minutes are agonising.

She is smiling, and waving, and she looks the same as she always did. The family has formed a line at the shore, like a welcoming committee, and they are returning her smiles.

DI Gordon Jackson and DC Graeme Nixon exchange muted, pensive smiles, as they watch the woman they were tasked with finding step off the boat with assistance from their force colleagues and disappear into a huddle of bodies, an entire family entwined in a mass hug.

71

'Mum.' The restraint is gone, and the word isn't so much spoken as sobbed. There are several arms around me now, several hearts beating wildly and lots of tears spilling onto my shoulders. It seems like everyone is talking but I can't make anything out, but what they are saying doesn't matter. My head is on my mum's shoulder and I'm sobbing like a child, and her body is shaking as she cries too. She lifts my face so that she can see it, as though she is checking once more to make sure that it is genuinely me that has been delivered back to her, and her eyes flit around as though she doesn't quite trust them yet. She looks happy and tremendously sad all at the same time, and my heart aches for the trauma she has had to go through since I've been gone.

'I missed you so much,' I tell her, hoping that hearing my voice will convince her that her eyes are not deceiving her, that the police have truly brought back the right person.

'Oh, we missed you,' she says, and I realise that the other bodies have retreated now.

'Dad.' I turn to hug him, and he holds me in an iron grip.

'Thank God you're home,' he says with tears at the corners of his eyes, and in this moment I am prepared to rescind all my previous misgivings and do just that.

I move around the circle, tearfully reuniting with my sisters, my brother, telling them that I thought I was never going to see them again, and bursting into tears all over again as I see their faces for real, not just in my imagination. I hold onto them all because there is still the tiniest part of me that wonders if this is all just a vivid hallucination and they are about to disappear like they did when I dreamt about them. My joy is overwhelming, unquantifiable, but as I cling onto my family and tell them that I love them, the unbridled hatred that I feel for Callum is possibly even stronger than that.

72

'Since you have no actual evidence linking my client to any aspect of this case, Detective Inspector, I am going to call a halt to this fiasco, and you can count yourself lucky that I'm not coming after you and your colleagues for harassment.'

Alasdair Connell noisily snaps his briefcase closed and rises from his chair. 'This is over, let's go.'

Callum tries to hide his smirk, but it doesn't go unnoticed by the detectives.

When the lawyer and his son have left the room, DI Jackson slams his fist into the table, causing the full cup of water that Callum Connell requested, but never touched, to wobble and spill some of its contents.

'So, that's it?' Nixon asks, an unnecessary question. 'He just walks?'

'What do you want me to do, Nixon?' Jackson responds angrily. 'You bring me some evidence that trumps a corroborated alibi and is more than just 'she said', and I will put that cocky little bastard away. But in the meantime, yes, he gets to walk away, because an accusation from a woman who's just been mentally tortured for a week and testimony from us saying, "We know he did it", just won't stand up in court!'

Once they're in the car and far enough away from the ears of the authorities, Alasdair grabs his son by the collar.

'What is it this time?'

'Nothing, Dad,' Callum answers feebly, knowing better than to try and wriggle out of his father's grip. 'It was nothing, honestly. Nothing serious.'

Alasdair looks around him and notices a passerby expressing interest in the scene. Callum is not a small-made man but even he is diminutive in relation to his father's intimidating bulk, and Alasdair quickly releases his hold on his son's expensive shirt to avoid attracting any inquiry from the stranger as to what is transpiring. He neutralizes his expression and smooths down his own suit jacket, letting out an exasperated sigh. 'I swear to God, if this comes back to bite me …'

'I promise you, Dad, it won't,' Callum assures him, 'I took care of everything.'

Alasdair takes a long look at his son and shakes his head. 'When are you going to learn, you can't keep doing this shit? For fuck's sake, son, you're a grown man! The next time you get yourself mixed up in something, that's it, you're on your own. You need to fucking grow up.'

Callum nods submissively. 'I know, Dad,' he replies. 'I promise you, it won't happen again. It was just something I had to deal with. You know how it is.'

Alasdair takes a few steps back, and retrieves his briefcase from the spot where he laid it down.

He unlocks the car and both men get in.

'And you know how it is,' Alasdair reminds his son. He turns to him, his eyes steely with menace that Callum has seen a thousand times before. 'You know I can't turn a blind eye.'

You're going to suffer for this, are the words that Alasdair doesn't need to say out loud. Callum nods resignedly.

'Your mother wants you round for Sunday dinner,' Alasdair states, his eyes now fixed ahead, his point made and understood. 'Don't let her down.'

'Never, Dad,' Callum answers, and the two men continue their journey in silence.

73

I thought I would feel so glad to be home. Like when you've had a terrible day, and you missed your train and went for the bus instead, but it was raining so hard that every last centimetre of you is soaked through and miserable. And hungry. But then you finally get home and turn the heating up full, change into fluffy pyjamas and an even fluffier dressing gown, and settle down on the couch with a steaming hot cup of tea. That kind of glad. And I am thankful, of course, how could I not be? But it will take some time, I think, to re-adjust.

I didn't go straight home. I couldn't bear to be alone, especially somewhere that Callum himself has been. I spent the first few nights at my parents' house, grateful for the safety and company that they afforded me. But I had to face it some time, and today is the day.

It was no more than a week that I was gone, but those days felt like a lifetime. Those were days that sucked the life out of me and took me to my lowest ebb. My fear was that those days would turn into a whole lifetime, and that it would be one full of misery and loneliness, with not a single thing to look forward to.

Being home, and safe, from that terrifying prospect is wonderful. Being reunited with my family, my friends, even the thought of going back to work – obviously, I am gladder than I am able to express in words.

But as I turned the key in the newly-fitted lock and entered my home, ensconcing myself once more in reality, in normality, the environment felt, for want of a better word, weird.

My home feels different. It *is* different, and I don't know that it will ever be how it was before. This is no longer my safe haven, the one place I can retreat to and feel grounded, settled. The place where I would lock the door, toss my keys onto the table in the hallway, pop the kettle on and take a leisurely look at any mail that may have dropped through the letterbox. The place where I could flop gratefully into bed at the end of an evening and feel as though there's no place that I would rather be. This house is no longer that place. Because *he* has been here. *He* has been inside my home. And *he* took me from my own bed, to that awful place, where he made me think that I would never know what it felt like to step through these rooms ever again.

I have to find the courage to spend the night here, to sleep in my own bed again. I need to somehow get over the fear that what I am experiencing right now, in this moment, is a dream, and that at any second I might wake up and find myself still marooned on that island. Or the fear that every time I fall asleep, there is a chance that I will once again wake up in the throes of a real-life nightmare. I haven't lost hope that one day this crushing fear will leave me, and I will be able to return to the life and the person that I was before, but even taking temporary residence at my parents' house, and dozing off safe in the knowledge that my family were there, protecting me as if I were the most precious cargo in the world, hasn't settled my nerves. For now, the fear is not going anywhere. Because for now, and for all I know this will be the case forever, Callum Connell has not been held accountable for what he did. What he did to me, to Alexander Beattie, to those other people for whom I now feel a sliver of sympathy, knowing now that he forced them into going along with everything by threatening to ruin their lives.

'Not enough evidence to bring a conviction' are the words that echo around my head, punching me in the gut as I inspect my bedroom as if it were the first time. Hardly a surprise, since everyone except me was too terrified of Callum to actually tell the truth to the police.

I shouldn't have come here alone, I realise, but I decided this morning that I can't cling to my parents' coattails forever. I have to be brave, and I thought I was brave enough to come back here by myself. Maybe I was wrong.

I eye the bed as though it is a foreign object, an alien item that has no business being where it is. My feet feel as though they have been planted into the floor and I can't free them to take the steps needed to travel barely two metres. The room looks smaller than I remember, and suddenly I feel claustrophobic. I close my eyes and say out loud, 'It's okay,' but without a visual to concentrate on my thoughts return to the visit from the police, updating me on the progress of my case.

'But ... I was there,' I told them, taking no comfort from the fact that when they were delivering the difficult news to me, their faces were longer than the list of crimes that Callum Connell could and should have been charged with.

The older man, the one who had been leading the search for me from here in Glasgow, spoke first. 'I'm very sorry,' he told me, repeating the phrase that he had opened with. 'The fact is that we have been unable to collect any physical evidence linking him to any of the crime scenes. In light of this, the fact that he has a solid alibi, and the fact that Alexander Beattie is on film ...'

'But he was in my house!' I screamed in frustration, cutting him off. 'You said so yourself; you have a witness!'

He cleared his throat. 'We have a witness who saw a man entering your home whose physical description matches that of Alexander Beattie as much as it does Callum Connell. The witness's view was from a first-floor window; we can't rely on their testimony to prove beyond reasonable doubt that it was Callum they saw, not Alexander.'

I had accepted that what he was saying made sense, I

suppose, but I still couldn't bear to think that it could be *that* easy to fool the world. Cover your head with a beanie hat, pop on a pair of glasses, grow a bit of a beard and burrow your face inside your jacket and apparently you can pass yourself off as someone else and go around committing heinous crimes in their name.

I wasn't prepared to let it lie, even if they seemingly were. 'But Callum is far more built than Jam ... Alexander,' I insisted. 'Surely the witness would be able to testify that the man they saw going into my house was bigger, broader? Surely if you put them both in a line-up, the witness would be able to pick Callum out?'

The man gave a small shake of his head. His partner remained silent. 'The height difference between the two is negligible. The witness's account stated that the man they saw was wearing a "puffy" jacket, and that could easily account for any extra bulk. Add to that the fact that Beatrice Bain positively identified Alexander Beattie-'

'Because he threatened her!' I jump in again, interrupting him.

'Again, I'm sorry, Natalie,' he replied, holding up his hand as though to ward off any further objections, 'but Beatrice and the others are insistent that they only ever saw Alexander. And a decent defence lawyer would tear our witnesses' testimony to shreds in a matter of seconds. I really am very sorry.'

I lost count of the number of times he's said he is sorry. What he didn't say, but which I already know, is that Callum's father happens to be one of those 'decent' defence lawyers who would, as the policeman put it, tear to shreds anyone who dared to sling mud at his son. And finding any witness who would dare to go up against him would be a challenge in itself.

Alexander – the name still seems alien to me; I can only think of him as Jamie – has proven himself to be neither brave nor, ultimately, on my side, despite those brief flashes of concern that made me think he could care about me. The police haven't really told me all that much, other than the fact that he has pleaded guilty and has so far failed to indict Callum for any part of what went on during the days from hell that they conspired to inflict upon me. Reading between the lines it seems like he had very little choice other than to plead guilty. I was told that every minute, every hour, of my ordeal was filmed, and that the police have recovered the footage showing Jamie – Alexander – carrying out his campaign of falsehood. What they have not stumbled upon, conveniently for Callum, are any shots of him or any of the others involved, therefore my testimony plus Callum's alibi, black-and-white proof of Jamie – Alexander – doing his bidding, and the concept of plausible deniability equals Callum being spared any punishment for a crime that has turned my life upside down and left me in fear of sleeping in my own bed.

He knew that would happen, of course. He planned everything out to the very last, minute detail. He knew that the forensic officers who conducted their in-depth searches would find no trace of him anywhere. He knew that he had failed to create any link between himself and the island. He knew that he had terrified Bessie and Davie and Angela into maintaining their silence and feigning their ignorance, and that whatever he chose as his alibi would stand up to scrutiny. He knew that he didn't need to get close to me, to put his hands on me, to hurt me – not physically. He knew that messing with my mind the way he did would be enough.

The destroyed electrical equipment and 'sanitised' building which housed it were, as far as the prosecutors are concerned, an attempt on Alexander's part to wash away the evidence of his involvement, and it was only through his misfortune that a memory stick containing the damning video evidence was found in the grass not far away from where 'he' had tried to erase himself from the scene. I can tell from their tone and their body language that the detectives are not buying into the serendipitous nature of that discovery any more than I am, but without a fingerprint, or some DNA, or some other god-damned indication that Callum was anywhere other than his alibi says he was, their hands are tied.

And, as such, my nightmare has not really come to an end. I may be home, with all the assurances from my family and the police that Callum will never be able to harm me again, but hearing it doesn't make it true. Knowing that he is out there, laughing up his sleeve at me, and Alexander, all the others he took advantage of, and now the entire Scottish justice system, means that he *can* still harm me, even from afar. The very fact that he is free, at liberty to do whatever he likes whilst feeling confident that he will never be brought to task for it, chills me to the bone.

The man is dangerous. What if there is some other unsuspecting victim out there, whose path crossed his at some point and he took offence? Is he out there, plotting revenge against them? Does he have a list of people that he aims to get even with?

I have to stop thinking about it, about him. If the police can't do anything, then I certainly can't, and fear-mongering myself with unhealthy thoughts isn't going to get me back on track any time soon. In that vein, I make the bold move of sitting on the edge of my bed, and tears spring to my eyes. One day, perhaps, this house, this room, will feel like home again. But for right now, it feels ruined. The house is different, and there can be no question that I am different. All in all, I was doing pretty well before this. So, maybe I wasn't the best at 'adulting', but at least I was able to keep all the necessary plates spinning: job, house, car. I was never going to win any awards for being an upstanding, outstanding member of the community, but I was trundling along just fine. I'm struggling to remember how it must have felt, to live a relatively worry-free life. To wake up in the morning with a grumbling sense of injustice that I was being forced to vacate my lovely warm bed at an ungodly hour for something as tedious as work. To think nothing of walking home from the train station during the winter months, when the darkness would descend shortly before four o'clock in the afternoon and us commuters would have no choice but to brave the shadows cast under the black sky. To lie down on my own bed and not feel my skin crawl.

'If you change your mind,' the officer said, handing me a card with the contact details for a counsellor trained in dealing with 'victims' like me.

'Thanks,' I told her, accepting the card, all the while knowing that I wouldn't. I was fine, I told her. Totally fine. I don't need counselling. I don't need a support group. I don't need people fussing over me, making me talk about it, making me face up to what I've been through.

I keep the card in my pocket, though. I take it out and look at it, and wonder whether there is anything that can be done. I look down at my bed, and wonder again whether it will ever be my safe place once more. Can I rid my memory of those awful days? Can I find a way to put Callum behind bars? Will I ever get back the life I had before he filled it with fear?

I put the card away again because I don't think I can.

Acknowledgements

I owe a great deal of thanks to those who have supported and assisted me with this book, in particular those who read and re-read the drafts and provided me with the feedback that helped shape the story that Inference tells today.

To my amazing family, who have always encouraged me to be the best that I can be, and my dear friends who have been my cheerleaders, my biggest fans, I am eternally grateful, and could not have done it without you.

And thanks to Ringwood Publishing for affording me this wonderful opportunity and for guiding me so expertly along the way.

About the Author

Stephanie McDonald is the author behind *Inference*, a novel which has been several years in the making.

Born and raised on the outskirts of Glasgow, Stephanie discovered a passion for reading at a very early age and enjoyed creative writing as a child, harbouring dreams to one day become a published author. Fascinated and endeared by language, she gained an Honours Degree in Language Studies, specifically Spanish and French, and went on to forge a career in the Financial Services industry where she specialised in Risk intelligence.

Aside from reading (mostly crime fiction and historical fiction), her hobbies are sketching, jogging and hill-walking.

She got into writing initially by producing short stories and poetry, then, in 2016, she wrote and self-published her first full-length novel, *Learn to Let Go*. Her new novel, *Inference*, is a foray into the mystery genre, with a very strong homage to her Scottish roots.

Website:
slmcdonaldauthor.co.uk

Facebook:
@stephscribbles

Instagram and Twitter:
@stephmscribbles

Other Titles from Ringwood

All titles are available from the Ringwood website and from usual outlets. Also available on Kindle.

RINGWOOD PUBLISHING
www.ringwoodpublishing.com
mail@ringwoodpublishing.com

Where the Bridge Lies

Frank Woods

Where the Bridge Lies is a two-tiered novel with timelines changing between 1940s and 1980s Scotland. In 1941, the Clydebank Blitz robs Nessa Glover of her husband and five children. She then becomes a shipyard welder and one day visits Harmony, a commune built on notions of equality and unity. But not everything is quite as it seems. In 1980, Keir Connor's father dies, and he is left with a letter saying he wasn't his biological father. Keir leaves his home in Australia and travels to Clydebank to try and sort out his family history. His journey leads him on to Harmony, now Laggandarroch, a residential school for disadvantaged children. One thing is sure: Harmony is the key.

ISBN: 9781901514667
£9.99

Not the Life Imagined

Anne Pettigrew

A group of bright, ambitious teenagers embark on their medical degrees at Glasgow University, amid the social and sexual revolutions of the sixties. *Not the Life Imagined* is a dark comedy exploring gender discrimination, sexuality and the power of friendship.

'There have been many books written about the world of medicine, but Anne Pettigrew brings a fresh voice and moral authority to the subject. Well-written and lively...'
– Author Simon Brett, OBE, FRSL

ISBN: 9781901514704
£9.99

ISBN: 9781901514643
£9.99

Memoirs of Franz Schreiber

Charles P. Sharkey

Memoirs of Franz Schreiber gives a unique perspective on the trials and turmoil of life in Germany during the First World War and the lead-up to the Second World War. When Franz and his mother get the news that his beloved father would not be returning to their home in Berlin from battle-fields of the First World War, their lives changed in unimaginable ways. Following Franz as he grows into a man, the effects of war are endless, and the story of his life is littered with love, tragedy and danger.

ISBN: 9781901514254
£9.99

The Activist

Alec Connon

'*The Activist* is an entertaining and heartfelt antidote to sea tales penned by hunters and fishermen. In it Tom Durant joins a colourful crew of activists to turn the tables and hunt the hunters, chasing the whalers who ply their trade in defiance of an international ban. In telling Tom's story, Connon contrasts the best and worst of people as they face off across the mountainous seas of the Southern Ocean.'
- Callum Roberts, Professor of Marine Conservation at the University of York.

Memoirs of a Feminist Mother

Carol Fox

Carol Fox is a lawyer, best known in Scotland for successfully fighting mass equal pay cases for low paid women. Following serious fertility problems, Carol made the positive decision to become a single parent by choice, to have a child while she still could. Her story has attracted media coverage, sparking debates on motherhood and the right to be a single parent in the UK. This book is written as a memoir addressed to her only daughter.

ISBN: 9781901514131
£9.99

Millennial Munros
- A Postman's Round

Charlie Campbell

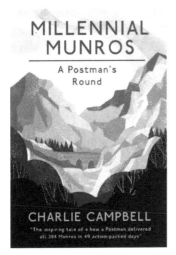

ISBN: 9781901514339
£9.99

Millenial Munros is the inspirational story of an ordinary bloke doing something extraordinary. Campbell completed an unprecedented endurance event, breaking the world record for a continuous self-propelled round of all Scotland's Munros, 284 mountains over 3000 feet in height. He averaged nearly six Munros every day. Charlie's entertaining account of his adventures is complete with maps, routes and other details to help inspire others to tackle these mountains.

The Gori's Daughter

Shazia Hobbs

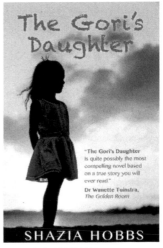

The Gori's Daugther is the fictional story of Aisha, a young mixed-race girl, daughter of a Kashmiri father and a Glaswegian mother, moved into the household as mistress alongside the Muslim wife and the children from both relationships. Her whole life is a constant struggle against the rejection and hostility which her background generates in both Glasgow's white and Asian communities. The book documents her fight to offer her own daughter a culture and traditions she can accept with pride.

ISBN: 9781901514124
£9.99